TAP

a love story

TRACY EWENS

TAP

a love story

For Cotter.
I love you, big guy.

Charm never made a rooster.

– DEAN ACHESON

Chapter One

Cade McNaughton was in the zone. A few hours into a dance he had envied since he'd first stepped behind a bar a few weeks after his eighteenth birthday. Back then, watching people with far more experience balance hard work, casual chatter, and craft was powerful.

Now here he was, behind his own slab of polished wood. It had been scary when he and his brothers first decided to go big or go home, but almost two years later, the Tap House ran as smoothly as every other part of Foghorn Brewery.

Cade had made that happen. He passed glasses amid the mix of beer, food, and perfume. Tina waited at the end of the bar for him to pour the last drink of her order and then she was gone.

Smiling for no damn reason, he wiped his hands on the towel he kept tucked in the back pocket of his jeans and continued listening to Brandon, the owner of Petaluma Body Shop on the outskirts of old town, share his most recent bad-date story.

"She brought her mom?" Cade asked as he brought up a new crate of glasses.

Brandon nodded, shoving a wad of Foghorn's loaded fries in his mouth. "Swear to Christ. Some shit about wanting to make sure I wasn't a murderer."

"So, how was the date after the mom checked you out and left?"

Brandon met his eyes and shoved more fries into his mouth.

"She... didn't leave?"

Pointing at him in a "bingo" move, the guy he barely knew in high school shook his head and washed down his fries with a gulp of Naked Neck. Bad choice—the garlic in the loaded fries called for a light beer, but Brandon never ordered anything else.

"Man, that's... You've got me. That's bad." Cade cashed out a couple who mentioned they were short on time before their movie and noticed the phone number scrawled at the bottom of the receipt as he cleared the spot next to Brandon. Call Me, it said above a San Francisco area code. The handwriting alone promised a good time. Tossing the dishes in the bin below the bar, Cade returned to get the receipt.

"Oh, come on." Brandon snatched the slip of paper. "Jade wants you to call her. Did you even talk to her?"

Cade shook his head and was gone taking orders before returning to Brandon while he poured beer. "She was sitting right next to you. Why didn't you get her number?"

"I tried."

Cade winced and gestured to the paper still on the bar. "Well, there it is. Give her a jingle. You could remind her that you were the quarterback in high school."

"Dude, we're over thirty. No one gives a shit about that anymore."

Cade wanted to tell him no one gave a shit about that an hour after they graduated, but Brandon was having a rough night, rough month. While Cade enjoyed playing around, he didn't kick people when they were down.

"How is it that you're wearing a T-shirt that says My Blood Type is IPA, and your hair is all jacked up, but women love you?"

Cade lifted a brow, sliding another glass of beer under the tap.

"Well, maybe not love, but they want you. Damn, I should have never messed things up with Kelly. Do you think she'll take me back?"

"Isn't she engaged?"

Brandon pushed his plate away. "True. Another one bites the dust. Well"—he brushed the front of his flannel shirt—"I need to do something. Maybe I'll get back to the gym and work on my ass." He huffed and took out his wallet to pay the bill.

"What does your ass have to do with going on a reasonable date?"

Brandon finished the last of his beer and stood. "You honestly don't have Instagram, do you?" He shook his head again as if Cade were some obscure freak of nature. He tossed a tip on the bar and was gone.

Several poured beers later, they had closed out happy hour, but the bar was still packed. With all orders in, the kitchen was slammed, so Cade did what he did best: he entertained.

"Give me a word, any word," he said, arms splayed wide.

"Gluteus Maximus."

"That's two words, and we all know what that means, ladies. I'm looking for a challenge here."

"The word of the night is definitely fine with a capital... F," another woman said, her gaze locked on Cade as if he should start running.

What the hell? Everyone normally loved this game. Cade glanced toward the kitchen. The crowd wasn't restless yet, but he must be slipping because they played Give Me a Word all the time. Someone shouted out a word, Cade gave the definition and used it in a sentence. Sort of like a spelling bee if the participants were buzzed and eating burgers.

"Oh no, fine is not the right word. How about delicious?" another woman purred and high-fived the woman next to her, who had long braided hair that reminded Cade of the movie *Avatar*.

"Ladies, you're losing me," he said as some of the food arrived and he lined up five drink order tickets. Practically every face at the bar was in his or her phone, and Cade once again cursed social media. What was wrong with old school socializing? He flipped glasses and started pouring.

"Is that my pale ale?" Tina asked.

Cade nodded.

"She wants a slice of orange." Tina rolled her eyes. She lost her patience when she was tired. Cade knew that about his favorite server now that they'd worked together for over a year.

"I'd offer you a break, but we haven't been this busy on a Thursday since, well, ever." He set four beers on her tray. "The crowd seems a little off tonight, and why the hell is everyone looking at their phones? Why come out, you know?"

"It's your body."

"Aw, Tina, are you checking me out? What's Pamela going to say when you get off work? She doesn't seem like she's up for sharing you."

"No." Her expression was unflinching as she added napkins and hoisted the tray. "I am not interested in your goods, but practically everyone else in the bar is. It's all over Instagram." Managing unbelievable balance, Tina pulled her phone from her back pocket without spilling a drop. After a few taps, she handed it to Cade and was gone. At the bell from the kitchen and Javier's growl, Cade set Tina's phone behind the bar and delivered orders. When he returned and flipped the phone over, Tina's screen saver was on.

"What's your password," he asked after setting three more beers and sending her off again. After typing in the numbers she called out, the image filled the screen.

A white bed in a room he recognized. A man lay on his stomach, arms overhead, holding a pillow in a tangle of duvet. The guy was naked save an edge of sheet barely covering his ass-ets. Soft light, definitely early morning, for an instant his tired mind ticked off the details as if it were an inventory order before finally screaming—
That's you, idiot.

Cade touched the screen to make the image bigger, but the bell dinged again, and he went back to work. By the time he returned, Tina was holding her hand out for her phone.

"Not the best time to have a Jack and the Beanstalk tattoo, eh?"

Cade glanced at his arm, strangely embarrassed, and handed back her phone. "Who posted that? Where? How does everyone know about it?"

"I'm assuming it's someone you know... intimately." She laughed and when Cade didn't, she stopped. "The poster tagged Foghorn. Most customers follow us, so now they've all—"

"Seen my ass."

"Well, most of your ass."

Cade set a pitcher of beer and three glasses on Tina's tray.

She patted him on the shoulder and picked up her order.

"Wait a minute. Tagged, meaning that picture is on—"

"Cade." Patrick's voice, pissed and familiar, rang out over the crowd.

"Shit."

Tina winced and was gone.

"Get it down," his brother and co-owner of Foghorn said, stepping behind the bar, phone in hand.

"Where did you even come from? I thought you were at home... nesting." Cade slid past his older brother to grab two rolled sets of silverware and set them in front of a couple absolutely on their first date. Cade normally enjoyed watching people get to know one another, but not tonight.

"I was at home and now I'm here. Get it down."

Heat that had nothing to do with the kitchen or the fact that he'd been going nonstop for the last five hours bloomed across Cade's chest. He dropped off two orders and would have given anything to avoid returning to the other end of the bar. God, he hated it when Trick was on a rant.

"Could you give me a minute? I found out about it ten minutes ago. I don't know who posted it. Maybe it's not even me."

Four women said at once, "It's you."

"Where would someone get a picture of my—"

"Lauren," Aspen said, waddling toward him.

"Wow, both of you. Do you two have a Cade-Fucked-Up alarm that goes off in your house?"

"You remember Crazy-Eyes-But-Who's-Looking-Above-the-Neck Lauren?"

"That's not nice." Cade wiped the bar in front of Aspen and pushed Trick toward his pregnant wife. Aspen, Foghorn's business manager, married Patrick last year. She wasn't always happy to work with Cade, but he knew deep down, way deep especially now, she loved him.

"I'm about to birth a human and your ex has tagged our business to screw with you because that seems to be what your exes like to do. I don't care what you do in your private life, but I don't have time to be nice. We are running a business here, Cade. You get that, right?"

Cade looked at his brother. There was no way he would ever tell his sister-in-law to back the hell up, but Trick had no intention of saving him.

"Right. I see how it is." He tossed another set of dirty dishes into the bin.

Did she just ask him if he got that? Of course he did. He got everything. Even though he didn't wear his stress on his sleeve, it didn't mean he wasn't a completely responsible third of their brewery. It was an unfortunate picture and he'd ask Lauren to take it down, or at least get rid of the tag, but it's not like he'd posted it himself. And what the hell did Aspen mean by "that seems to be what your exes do?"

What the hell? He'd been on top of everything less than an hour ago and now, after one picture, he was relegated to an irresponsible exhibitionist who dates crazies.

"I'll take care of it," Cade said.

Patrick stepped behind the bar and followed him. "No, that's not—"

Cade spun with anger he hadn't felt in years. They were chest to chest. "Back the hell up," he said softly without a hint of his usual jest. "I didn't post the picture. Someone else did and I'm embarrassed enough. If you were acting like my brother instead of my damn leader, you would understand that."

Patrick didn't back down, but he took in a breath and his expression softened.

"I will get it taken down."

"Tonight."

"I will text her once you get out of my face, and if that doesn't work, after working this ten-hour shift, I'll call her."

They stood for a beat, orders piling up, and then broke apart.

Patrick and Aspen left and once Cade caught up and pushed away the resentment, he texted Lauren.

Cade: Lauren, take it down.
Lauren: Hey, babe. Take what down?

Cade kneaded the back of his neck with one hand. There were so many reasons he and Lauren hadn't worked out.

Cade: You tagged the brewery. I need you to take it down or at least remove the tag.
Lauren: Why? I'll bet your buns are good for business.
Cade: We're not running that kind of business.
Lauren: Sure you are. I'll bet the bar is packed. You think those women, and I'll bet several men, are there for your beer?
Cade: I do.
Lauren: You always were too humble for your own good, babe.
Cade: Please.
Lauren: Fine.

Cade let out a steady breath and almost smiled before his phone vibrated again.

Lauren: If we can get together.

He should have known better than to think it would be that easy. Before he could ask where and when she'd replied.

My place. ASAP.

Cade slipped his phone into his pocket, and instantly, what used to be fun and flirty felt stupid and dirty. He knew what "get together" meant in Lauren's language. She'd ended their relationship a year ago, but he'd do what was needed to clean up this mess.

"Cadre," Tina said when she returned to the bar, the crowd finally easing up.

"What?"

"You asked for a word. I'm giving you one. Cadre."

"A unit of trained people. She had a cadre of servers at her disposal," he said, barely aware of his own voice.

"You're a smart guy, Cade."

"Yeah? Could you post that on Instagram?"

She laughed, and Max slid behind the bar and fastened his apron. They'd hired a relief bartender a few months ago. Cade could finally have some time off after a two-year stretch at full speed while they were bringing up the Tap House.

Following a fist bump and a quick bar rundown where Cade told Max who was drinking what, Cade was untying his apron and calling it a night. When he walked out into the early night air, the sky was dark and the stars were crisp as if he could reach up and touch them. The sky used to fascinate him as a kid. He could point out all the major constellations. He threw his leg over his bike and pulled on his helmet. Tina was right—he was smart. When had his body become more important than what was on his mind? The roar of his bike shook him free. Now was not the time for introspection. He needed his game face and at least three shots of espresso if he was going to deal with Lauren.

Pulling onto Main toward *Grind It*, the only coffee shop open after six, he tried to forget the look on Trick's face. Tried to forget how it screamed disappointment.

Sistine Branch hoped the lipstick she found toward the back of her bathroom drawer that morning hadn't smeared onto her front teeth. Sweet Lord, convincing four women that Knitterly was the best place for Stitches was exhausting. The annual knitting and crochet expo was based out of Los Angeles, but they held the event in a new city every year.

Sistine had gone once when it was in San Diego and it was incredibly well run. Now she knew why. These women were practically running a white glove over every inch of her place. And the smiling—someone save her from the smiling. But, if she landed this, sore cheeks would be more than worth it. Stitches meant national exposure and, more importantly, come July, over a thousand knitters would descend on Petaluma and her shop. This was big and since Sistine had barely scraped together her loan payment this month, she needed big.

"So, like I said," Deidra, the woman who smelled like gardenias and seemed to be the one in charge, poured more tea while the other three women continued to "meander." Great word, Sistine decided and remembered now was not the time for collecting words.

"The committee doesn't normally choose a shop your size, but this year, we are all about organic fibers and returning to the roots of our craft, you know?"

More smiling and nodding as Deidra stirred in some sugar.

"Historic downtown Petaluma seems like the perfect fit," Sistine said, trying not to sound schmaltzy.

Deidra tapped the spoon against her teacup and pointed it at Sistine. "Exactly what we were thinking. We want to highlight some of the smaller shops like yours, and this building is so lovely."

They both took in Knitterly's dark wood floors and crown molding, a huge chunk of which Sistine had hot glued to the wall moments before they arrived, and Sistine felt like she was watching the same scene replayed on a loop. How many times did they need to look around, review her policies, ask her about her insurance?

As many times as it takes. Can you pass up ten thousand dollars, Ms. Cup-a-Noodles-for-Most-Meals?

Ten thousand dollars. That was the holding deposit, and she would make so much more on top of that in shop sales. This one expo alone could save her shop, get her in the black and over the two-year hump that swallowed most small businesses.

"So if, and I'm feeling it's more of a *when*, but *if* we choose to hold the expo here, are you certain you can handle the capacity? Two years ago, we partnered with this great place in downtown Boulder. The shop was adorable, but the event was a mess. I'm sure you understand, I can't let that happen again."

"I completely understand." Sistine offered Deidra a cookie from the box she'd picked up at Sift that morning. Deidra smiled and indulged. Cookies were universal. "The fact that I own the building gives me flexibility I doubt other venues will have. The back patio expansion will be finished next month, and we're adding additional meeting spots out front."

"I love that idea. It will be gorgeous in July and that water, tea, lemonade station in front was a brilliant idea." She popped the last bit of cookie in her mouth and set her teacup on the work table.

"And, don't forget my connections with the town. One of my best friends runs the bakery. Another manages Foghorn Brewery."

"We had lunch there. I love that place."

"Right? It's fantastic. We could host a dinner or get-together in that space too."

"Could you get us a discount?"

"I could work something out."

Deidra clapped her hands together and Sistine wanted to join her. This was going better than she imagined, so she finished strong.

"And I know people in fire and medical. All of historic downtown will be ready for your expo."

"Fantastic. Can we get a look at those construction drawings of the back patio one more time?"

"Absolutely." Sistine opened her laptop and wiped her hand on her skirt, hoping to hide her nerves. She tapped the touch pad, but instead of her screen filling with the artist renderings of a remodel she was barely able to afford, there was a pop and the screen went black.

"Uh-oh. Looks like it's time for you to plug in. We've exhausted your poor laptop." Deidra giggled and reached for another cookie.

Sistine's laptop was plugged in. It wasn't her battery. Glancing toward the front of the store, she noticed the lights she hung around the front window were out.

"Hun, what's your Wi-Fi password again? It seems to have dropped me." The woman with the pink bow on her sweater approached them. Carrie? Candy? Damn it, Sistine couldn't remember.

Hoping her voice wasn't shaking, she gave out the password. It wasn't going to work, but it would buy some time. Looking to the branches that hung from the ceiling of her shop, Sistine now knew what was wrong. The sun had not started to set, so the four women who currently held her financial fate in their manicured hands had not figured it out yet, but something had blown the electricity in her entire shop.

Sistine leaned a hip on the counter and continued staring at the dark screen of her laptop hoping for an idea, something to explain why even though her beloved 1929 building had its creaks and quirks, it could handle the expo. She'd grown up surrounded by small business. She watched her parents struggle and knew more than anyone that perception was everything. Even though she knew she could handle this expo and that it would be a huge success, if these women didn't believe that was possible, it was over.

"Deidra, I think the electricity is off."

All four women looked to Sistine. "Huh, I don't know what happened. Maybe the guys doing the remodel hit something," she lied.

"Well, that's not good." The women glanced at one another.

"All of this will be finished well before the expo. That's good, right?"

Sistine smiled. Again. She guessed the lipstick was gone at this point.

After a moment of awkward where Sistine wasn't sure what else she could add, the committee grabbed their purses and moved toward the door. She wanted to grab Deidra by the front of her expensive blouse and say, "I can do this. I swear if you give me this chance, you will not be disappointed." But she'd majored in marketing with an emphasis on branding, and nowhere in her best practices did it say go batshit desperate if you want people to do business with you. So, hiding her desperation behind her last thread of pride, she walked them out and pretended not to notice Deidra avoided eye contact as she said, "We'll be in touch."

Cross-legged in one of the overstuffed chairs in her front room, Sistine tried to focus on the beauty of the sky as day began giving way to night. Cobalt, she thought. It was definitely a cobalt sky, but the remaining sunlight added flecks of bluebell.

Bluebell or lunar. Which one was lighter again? She glanced at what she'd termed her Wall of Yarn in her shop and confirmed the sky was flecked with bluebell. She left messages with both the contractor handling her back patio and an electrician Aspen recommended. Maybe it was nothing, a blown fuse. She hugged her legs tighter into her chest. Who was she kidding? She was raised in an old home in Bodega Bay. She knew all about fuses. This wasn't a fuse. She didn't know how to explain it, but she'd spent practically every moment over the past two years in this old building. Something was wrong.

Darkness settled on her shop and she tried not to take it as an omen. Instead, she made her way to her apartment in the back of the shop and grabbed her wallet and her laptop. The coffee shop near the river was open until ten on Thursdays. She needed to pull up her spreadsheets, look at her numbers. Somehow, she would come up with a plan if the expo fell through, if the entire building needed to be rewired.

"Have a plan B, C, and D," her dad told her from the time she was little.

Sistine had forty dollars cash in her wallet. There was no sense sweating over something unknown, a bill she didn't yet have. She'd get some tea and one of those microwaved sandwiches. Maybe she'd splurge for a tea latte.

Maybe she'd call Melissa back and—No. She needed to stay in the present. She wasn't that desperate. Not yet.

Chapter Two

Cade was struck by the similarities between bars and coffee shops. Music tiptoeing over conversation, people meeting, dating, or working alone. The only real difference was the zip sound of the frother. He sucked at making his own espresso, but he knew the lingo after dating a barista for a few weeks. Image and no substance. Again.

Damn it, why was his head all screwed up over one picture? He woke up that morning feeling great. A seven-mile run, followed by an hour at the gym, his bar had been packed, and then bam! As if being embarrassed had not been enough, he'd been scolded by his brother, the king of uptight and substance.

Moving with the line, Cade noticed Sistine sitting at a corner table by the window. She was chewing on a pencil, eyes scanning her laptop screen as she tucked her chin-length hair behind an ear and leaned in as if she were looking into a crystal ball. Taking the pencil from her mouth, she drew her oversized orange cardigan tighter around her small frame.

He liked Sistine. She was quiet and seemingly more reserved than the rest of the book club that met at the Tap House once a month. His mom was part of the club, as was practically every other woman in Cade's life. Well, every woman who admitted to reading.

He'd started spending time with Sistine, outside of bumping into her book club, when he volunteered to teach her how to play backgammon. Instead of giving things up for a New Year's resolution, Sistine said she preferred learning something new. She'd been telling the women of the club back in February that she'd yet to find a backgammon teacher, so Cade stepped up.

At their first lesson, he'd taught her the basics and explained that the key to any game was practice. Now, they played on Wednesdays around one o'clock during her lunch break from her shop. He would call Sistine his friend. Whether or not she felt the same, he didn't know, but at that moment the connection of having a friend like Sistine Branch was an anchor he needed.

"What can I get you, sir?"

Startled by the high-pitched voice of the young girl behind the register, he stepped forward and ordered. After slipping a couple of dollars into the plastic jar marked *Fun Fund*, he moved aside to wait for his caffeine. There were several people ahead of him, all on their phones, and hopefully not on Foghorn's Instagram.

Sistine was still concentrating on her laptop screen, and now that he was closer, he noticed she was wearing earphones. He waved a hand near her table, hoping to get her attention without scaring the crap out of her. Meeting his eyes, she blinked a few times as if struggling to place him in a coffee shop and tugged the cord from her ears.

"Hey, Cade." She lowered the screen of her laptop.

"You looked intent."

A smile teased her lips that appeared to come more from politeness than joy.

"Oh, I'm just... working on some things. Work, you know, reports and stuff."

He wondered why being with her outside of the Tap House suddenly seemed awkward. He wasn't nearly as confident in his witty banter skills without the wooden barrier and the flow of beer.

"Anyway," they both said at once. And then laughed, genuine this time.

"Sorry. I was in my own little world. You're obviously off work. Here for your caffeine fix?"

"I am. Did you know this place used to be a bank?"

She closed her laptop and her eyes widened. "Really?"

He nodded. "My parents banked here until they built the big freestanding one on the corner."

"Huh? I keep forgetting you all grew up here. Have you noticed lots of changes?"

"I have. One of the oldest buildings in downtown used to be a drugstore but now it's this incredible knitting store." Nice. Maybe his charm did work after all.

"Is that so?" She leaned on her elbow on the table.

"Americano and a doppio espresso for Cade," a male voice called out.

Cade grabbed his order and returned to the table. "You look like you're busy, so I'll—"

"Don't be silly." She put her laptop in her bag and kicked the chair opposite her.

"Can I get you a refill?" he asked, setting his drinks down and acknowledging an unexpected comfort in being invited to stay.

"I can get it," she said.

"I know, but I'd like to buy you a drink."

She shook her head. "Can't turn off the charm, can you?"

Shit. First rule of impressing a woman, never be transparent.

Whoa, are we trying to impress Sistine?

Ignoring the voice in his head, Cade held out his hand for her cup.

"It's an Earl Grey tea latte, but if you don't want to pay the extra two dollars, which I totally understand, I'll have plain tea."

He was about to tease her about his ability to spring for the extra two dollars, but she wasn't joking. Confusion must have registered in his expression because she settled her hands on the table and let out a breath. That's when he noticed the tension at the edges of her eyes and the way her breath appeared to get stuck in her chest.

"Be right back."

She was checking her phone when he returned with the tea latte and two cookies. "Peanut butter or chocolate chip?" he asked.

"Sorry?" She plugged in her phone and set it on the window ledge.

"Cookies." He patted the bags. "Peanut butter or chocolate chip?"

Sistine took the lid off her drink. "Peanut butter. I don't like chocolate."

"Seriously? I don't think I've ever met anyone who doesn't like chocolate."

"Guess I'm your first," she said, sipping her drink, foam on her upper lip and completely oblivious to the sexual connotation.

Cade spent so much time flirting or performing for women, he'd forgotten what it was like to have a simple conversation with the opposite sex. While their friendship was fairly new, they'd only had two or three backgammon lessons and she barely said a word to him during the book club meetings, he found that he needed her. That was a ridiculous thought. He didn't need her specifically, but more the simplicity of being with a woman late at night in a coffee shop.

"Do you ever"—she broke off a piece of cookie and put it in her mouth—"hmm, this is good." Pausing, she wiped her hand on the napkin as if she couldn't quite get her thought out without the use of her hands. "Do you ever feel like you're in too deep? You know, like you're giving it everything you have but you're still like buck naked in a room full of people who seem to know exactly how to dress?"

Cade stopped eating. What the hell was he doing thinking cookies and coffee would somehow undo his crappy night? She'd entertained him for a while, but she'd seen the picture.

"What? You don't have those feelings?" she asked. "Okay, maybe that was a bad analogy, or maybe I'm a complete freak." She looked down into her cup and closed her eyes. "Sorry. I've had a rough day." Glancing up when he still said nothing, Sistine scrunched her face. "What? Quit looking at me like I punched you."

"You could have told me you saw the picture. It's not like it's a big secret. Who told you? Aspen? I'm actually fine with it. You didn't need to pretend."

She rolled her eyes to the ceiling like she was searching for an answer. "I... don't know what you're talking about. What picture?"

"Oh, come on. It's okay. It's not a big deal. You've seen me naked now too. So what?"

She rubbed her eyes and leaned on both elbows. "Cade. I honestly have no idea what you're talking about. But now I'm intrigued. Why has everyone seen you naked? Did your pants split or something?"

Laughter and relief bubbled in his chest. Not only had she clearly not seen the Instagram post, but the way she asked about his pants was genuine and adorable. If that had happened, she'd likely offer to sew them right up for him. He smiled.

"You have a great smile." No agenda or innuendo in her expression.

"Thank you."

"You're a bit... intimidating when you're not smiling and then your face sort of comes off the page. You know?" She took another bite of cookie. "Is that a bizarre observation? Jeez, I'm on a roll tonight. Aren't you glad you stopped by? Anyway, back to your bod." She sipped her tea latte and licked the foam off her upper lip.

He stared at her, at her lips. It was her turn to wave a hand in front of his face.

"Cade."

"Right. Sorry." Breaking his cookie in half, he folded one piece into his mouth. After washing it down with strong caffeine, he told Sistine about the Instagram post, complete with all the crap that followed. He left out the part about Lauren and then realized he'd forgotten all about her.

He checked his watch. It was a little after nine. He'd lost track of time, which was surprisingly easy to do with Sistine. Her facial expressions alone were distracting. Maybe it was that she was rarely this talkative because when she spoke, she seemed to use every part of herself. Like most people were given an assortment of expressions. Confused, happy, even silly. Sistine was unlike most people. Her clothes didn't appear to follow any trend. Talking with her was a similarly eclectic experience, as if she'd been given a bonus pack of colors.

She looked completely unfazed that his ass was on Instagram other than to say it was a "complete violation" for someone to do that to him. Then she told him her own embarrassing story about her pants splitting. She'd stooped to pull the rug away when the men delivered her tables back when she opened Knitterly. Laughing at herself, her eyes waltzed around their tiny table. She made him feel less important, which he knew should have been uncomfortable, but in his world where people often looked to him for amusement, it was incredible to be just some guy. Lauren had probably texted him a dozen times wondering where he was, but like a burst of sunlight from a cloudy sky, Cade wanted nothing more than to stay right there in her warmth.

What the heck had gotten into her? One minute she was staring at her budget desperately hoping for an option other than the inevitable. The thought of calling Melissa turned her stomach. Then she was laughing and eating cookies with Cade McNaughton. Cade, whom she rarely saw outside his Tap House and who, despite his over six-foot muscled frame and tattooed arm, looked remarkably at home eating cookies.

She felt bad about the Instagram picture but worse that he'd dated someone who would do that to him. That, of course, led to thinking about the types of women he dated. Her brain enjoyed traipsing down paths it had no business exploring, especially when she was frazzled and tired. She supposed it was a coping mechanism, another way of avoiding the dreaded uncertainty life often threw her way.

Cade was a fun distraction. She noticed when he told her about the picture his cheeks went a bit pink, made all the more obvious by the tough-guy buzzed sides of his hair. Aspen had once mentioned that his hair used to be long. Sistine guessed he couldn't quite let go because the center of his hair was long and slicked back off his face. Sort of a tamed Mohawk. His look was different, which she'd always liked. Now that they had spent more time together, she liked that no matter her chaos, he put her at ease. That was undoubtedly a part of his job that never left him, even after work hours.

"What's in the bag?" He pointed to the paper bag propped between the table and the window. She'd forgotten all about it.

"Oh, I made this cardigan for Mr. Graham down at the hardware store. He opens super early and it's cold, you know?"

Cade nodded.

"The burgundy one he used to wear had holes. But, apparently, our cuddly Mr. Graham is no longer a 'sweater guy' since his recent brush with death. Now he only wears a—"

"Leather vest," Cade said, picking at the brown paper sleeve on his coffee cup. "I noticed."

"Ella says it's normal for people to make changes after going through something like that. He dropped it off with her because he didn't want to hurt my feelings and she stopped here before her shift." Sistine shrugged. "He's a sweet man. I'm okay if he wants to wear a vest."

"Yeah, I hope I'm wearing a leather vest when I'm eighty." Cade smiled and turned to throw out the bags from their cookies.

There went her traveling mind again. Leather, his chest, all the way down the path toward what he must look like under those funny T-shirts. Most women probably imagined one thing or another when they looked at Cade McNaughton. He was a look-and-imagine kind of guy. His body required her to take frequent breaks to avoid staring in fascination at the ridges and angles of him.

He was reaching for the trash can for crying out loud, but the man's back, even clothed, stirred appreciation in a way one might enjoy a sculpture. When he turned back to face her, Sistine's mind went unexpectedly horizontal. Bed, floor, that kind of naughty. She swallowed and quickly looked at the bag, hoping the thought of the cardigan versus the leather vest might help quell feelings she could later attribute to the late hour.

"Can I see it?" he asked, following her eyes to the bag.

"You can have it. Or if you don't want it, Boyd. Does Boyd wear sweaters?" She put the bag on the table. "Or maybe you could hang it on one of those hooks at the bar. People get cold in bars. It could be sort of a community sweater."

Dear Lord, someone save me from my mouth.

He grinned. "Community sweater could work, but who's going to wash it?"

"Hmm. It's cotton and wool so it wouldn't need to be dry cleaned, but it's super soft." She shook her head and pushed the bag toward him.

"I'm rambling. Please, take it."

"Nothing wrong with rambling." He winked and opened the bag.

What was it with McNaughton men and winking? They were all expert winkers, in that they rarely used the normally cheesy gesture, but when they did, it was downright organic. Like the most normal gesture in the world. Cade was McNaughton charm concentrate. Since she hung around the Tap House a bit more now with the book club and her backgammon lessons, Sistine was somewhat immune to the McNaughton charm, but even in a coffee shop, Cade was potent.

"You don't have to take it. I can always check with my dad, although he's pretty well stocked in the sweater department." She sipped the last bit of her tea if only to shut herself up.

He laughed. "Comes with the territory when your daughter owns a knitting shop, I'll bet. Oh, wow. This is great, Sistine." He ran his hand along the soft woven rows of midnight blue and even though she'd spent weeks working on that sweater, it looked different in his hands. He held up her work with an interest and enthusiasm that didn't go with the rest of him. The gentle buzz of too much caffeine tickled along her skin, and she wondered if that was enough to explain her sudden awareness of him.

Two women standing in line were looking at Cade and as if someone had thrown a bucket of cold water on her, Sistine remembered her life. Her building was pitch black, she had no money, and if her gut instinct was right, the committee was not going to select her shop for their expo. Nothing, outside of the warmth and laughter of sharing cookies and conversation with Cade, was going right.

Without realizing, she reached for the sweater and went to put it back in the bag.

Cade held onto it. "Hey, you said I could have it."

"You're not going to wear a cardigan."

"I might. I'll pay you for it."

"I made it as a gift. I'm not taking your money."

"Okay, what do you want?"

A good night's sleep. To stop worrying about money. A meal that doesn't come in a bag, she thought but didn't say. Instead she took their paper cups and tossed them in the recycle side of the bin. The party was over and she needed to get back to the real world.

"Thank you for the cookie. That's payment enough. I need to get going."

Cade checked his watch and seemed to jolt back into his own reality. "Right." He stood.

Sistine put her bag over her shoulder and unplugged her phone, checking to see if she had enough battery to get through the night. He held the door as they walked out of the shop.

"Thank you for the sweater," he said as they both stood by their bikes. Hers pedals and turquoise, his black and powerful even turned off. They stood facing each other in a moment that felt strangely like interest, as if neither one was ready to return to the lives they were so familiar with only hours ago.

She chalked the surreal night up to an exhausting day. "Good night, Cade."

"Night," he said, tucking her sweater into the compartment behind his seat. They were both straddling their bikes when he said, "Hey, do you have Instagram?"

She nodded. "I post stuff from the shop and the occasional picture of Petaluma. Why?"

"No reason. Pedal safe." He gave a hop and his bike roared.

Sistine nudged up her kickstand as he rode away. Exhaustion, she told herself. A good night's sleep and they would both be back where they belonged.

Chapter Three

No amount of charm convinced Lauren to take down the picture, not that Cade was feeling especially charming by the time he arrived at her house. After a numbing hour where she explained that she'd posted the picture to get back at her current boyfriend who "loved her into endless orgasms," she agreed to remove the Foghorn tag as a "gesture."

It took every bit of control Cade had to keep from telling her to kiss the part of him she posted on Instagram, but he managed to keep it together. All in all, even though the picture was still on her account, he guessed that once she patched things up with Magic Fingers, she would take it down for good. He truly hoped things worked out for Lauren, if only because it made his life a lot easier when she was busy messing with other people's lives. After getting home, he couldn't sleep, so he knocked out his post on beer and doughnuts for Foghorn's blog.

Patrick, master of all things annoying as hell, had notified Cade yesterday that the beer pairing was due by the end of the day Friday. Cade had every intention of blowing him off for another week, but in the wake of Lauren's little stunt and the subsequent guilt trip that followed, he decided not to push things. At least for a while.

"Think of it as the ultimate challenge," Trick had said when he "assigned" the post.

"I already have challenges. Dealing with you two." He'd been ballsy enough that day to point at both Trick and his other brother Boyd. "That is enough challenge for one man. I am not pairing doughnuts."

"Fine." Trick had shrugged in that way that riled Cade's need to prove he could do anything.

Growing up, there were two distinct camps among the McNaughton brothers. Boyd and Trick were the oldest, first and best at everything. Cade and West were the youngest, separated by two years. West ran off to Hollywood and now lived in San Francisco. That left Cade to man their camp on his own. All four of them owned Foghorn, but the family pecking order never went away.

Cade had a "gift," as his brothers called it, for pairing food with beer. It was not exactly something he could put on a resume, not that he had one.

"Any food. Any beer," Cade had said years ago, and had never lived it down. A couple of months ago he was asked to pair asparagus. Before that, it was bubble gum, which technically wasn't a food, but they didn't care. His portion of the blog was entertainment anyway. Cade was rarely taken seriously, which never bothered him, but last night in front of his laptop, that persona was suddenly restrictive. Which explained why he'd stayed up until one writing about doughnuts and their newest pale ale. His stomach growled, but at least he'd have the satisfaction of being early for once.

Pulling into the back parking lot of the brewery the next morning, things registered familiar and shifted at the same time. His brothers' lives were different now that they were all married with all these extra people and responsibility in their lives. He got that, but it meant his life suddenly stood in stark and irresponsible contrast.

Cade was the last man standing, as several of their regular customers liked to put it, which up until yesterday had not bothered him in the least. He hadn't planned to be the last single brother in his family, yet it worked out that way and he wasn't complaining. But the picture from last night had made him ridiculous and somehow less focused, less committed, and all-around less than.

All of that sat on his chest as he put his helmet away and lifted the glossy pine of the bar entrance. They didn't open for a couple of hours, but he had a meeting and hoped like hell Trick would focus on his blog post and keep the picture comments to a minimum.

Boyd was already at the bar reading the newspaper. He set it down when he noticed Cade.

"Morning. Rough night?"

Cade shrugged, oddly self-conscious. Shit, he hadn't bothered with embarrassed since Todd Elm jerked a chair out from under him at lunch and yelled, "You broke the chair, McNugget."

"Do you want to talk about it or sulk?"

He poured coffee and refilled Boyd's cup. Taking a slow, deliberate sip, he leaned on the bar. "I'll stick with sulking, thanks."

"Suit yourself."

They drank in silence and Boyd, never one to push, resumed reading.

"She take the picture down?" he asked as he turned the page.

"I thought you were leaving me to sulk?"

Boyd folded the paper and slapped it down on the bar. "Trick and Aspen will be here in a minute. I'd like the inside scoop before we're ears deep in reports and baby talk."

"She wouldn't take it down, but she untagged Foghorn."

"That's good, right?"

"It would have been better if she took it down altogether, but the tag will get everyone off my—"

"Ass?"

Cade made a goofy face in mocking laughter. "You're hysterical and in a chipper mood this morning."

Boyd shrugged. "It's Friday. I'm coming up with our summer brew. Life is great."

There had been a time not so long ago when everything in his brother's life was simply fine. It was nice to hear things had jumped a few levels. No doubt in part due to Ella, Petaluma's emergency room doctor and Boyd's new wife.

"Mase tell you he wants his hair like mine?" Cade asked.

"Not going to happen."

"Why not? I think he'd look good."

"He's in speech club now. He needs people to take him seriously."

"People don't take me seriously?"

His brother eyed him. "No."

Cade brought a hand to his chest. "That hurts."

"No, it doesn't. You're not interested in being taken seriously."

"You don't know that. People change."

"There are few constants in life. You being your loveable, irresponsible self is one of them."

"I'm not irresponsible. I run a third of this place." West was a money partner, but the day-to-day was left to the three of them.

"That you do," Patrick said, setting his stack of papers on the bar and helping Aspen with her bag.

"Is that a cardigan?" he asked.

Cade looked down as if he'd forgotten he wore Sistine's gift. "Yes. Did you read my post yet?"

"No," he said, watching Aspen walk back toward the offices. "Not exactly your usual look. Are you trying to keep things... covered up now?"

Let the comments begin, he thought, finding it oddly comforting that they were putting it out there on the bar, so to speak. He hated the silent treatment.

"Funny," he said. "Nope, I think we can all wear cardigans if we want. Sistine made it for Mr. Graham, but he only wears leather vests now and she thought, who else do I know who's hot as hell and can rock a sweater?" He thunked his head for effect. "Oh, right. Cade." Straightening his sweater, he set a cup of coffee in front of Trick.

Patrick laughed. He looked haggard and was a little more intense than usual these days. Cade imagined that had a lot to do with the pregnancy. He could only imagine the checklists and preparations the two of them had worked up. This kid was going to need her fun uncle.

"I doubt Sistine said that, and even if she did, would we call Mr. Graham hot as hell?"

"Who's hot?" Aspen asked, sneaking behind the bar and grabbing the inventory clipboard Cade kept near the computer. "Are you confused about Tom Brady, babe?"

"You're cute." Trick took his iPad out of his bag. "No, Mr. Graham."

Aspen flipped a page and shrugged. "He has something. I mean he's not Instagram material." She grinned and put the clipboard back.

Cade wanted kudos for his blog post and the sweater gave off an almost mature vibe. It figured they now wanted to joke instead of scolding him like an unruly child.

"Lauren untagged Foghorn." He refilled his coffee.

"We noticed," she said.

"That explains the good mood. Okay, any other comments on my posterior? I'd like to move on. You too, Boyd. Get 'em all out."

Trick and Aspen shared a glance with Boyd and then they all looked at Cade. Aspen produced a piece of beef jerky from some mystery pocket in her dress and chomped down while rubbing her belly with the other hand.

"I've got nothing. You?" she said to his brothers.

"Nope." Boyd thumped his hands on the bar. "Are we going to eat? I skipped breakfast."

"Trick?" Cade heard Javier in the kitchen and turned for a minute to order their burritos. "Any more comments?" he asked, returning his attention to them.

"It's no fun if you confront it like that." Patrick sat next to Boyd.

"Good. Teasing the idiot brother is over. New craving?" Cade gestured to Aspen.

"New sweater?" she asked.

He nodded and put his hands in the pockets. It fit him perfectly. "What happened to the doughnut craving?" Before she could answer, he tapped the newspaper Trick was now reading. "By the way, one more time, my blog post was in early."

"Yeah, yeah, I'll read it." Patrick set the paper on the bar.

"I've eaten more doughnuts in the last few months than I have in my entire life. I guess our little sweetie wants salty now. Teriyaki day and night." Aspen stood next to Trick, who pushed out the stool next to him. She shook her head and remained standing. "Grass-fed, so that's something, I suppose."

She placed her hand on her back with a groan. Patrick scanned his iPad with one hand and rubbed her back with the other as if on instinct. She closed her eyes.

"Clipboard says you're running low on simple syrup," she said after a moment. "Which is odd since we're a tap house, but do you want me to put more on the order?" She slowly opened her eyes. After whatever pain in her back had passed, she leaned over and kissed Patrick. He set down his iPad and kissed her back.

Cade stared as if watching a documentary. "Do you two know you're weird?"

They ignored him and eased apart.

"Good post," Trick said. "Two typos, but funny. Readers will love it."

"And it's early."

"And it's early, good job. I'll get you a gold star later." He leaned over the bar to pat Cade on the head, but he pushed back and flipped him off.

Javier dinged the bell from the kitchen.

"Simple syrup?" Aspen asked, her phone now in hand.

"Yes, but just one bottle. I'm hoping the whole beer-cocktail trend dies soon."

"You and me both," Boyd said, reaching for his burrito and gesturing for the hot sauce still behind the bar. Cade handed it over and his stomach growled again.

Aspen thumbed her phone and on a shallow exhale said, "Order's in. Gentlemen, I'll leave you to handle the meeting. I'm off to a pedicure with my mother." She quickly kissed Patrick. "Here's hoping the chairs are extra large."

"You're beautiful."

"So you keep saying." She touched his cheek.

They exchanged I-love-yous and be-carefuls before she was gone. Patrick's eyes were on the closed door for less than a beat, but Cade was struck by his brother's longing expression. Aspen was round, that was no longer a point for debate, but Trick still looked at her like she was not only carrying their child but doing so in thigh-high boots.

A smile teased at Patrick's lips as he patted the bar and returned to his list. They both seemed exhausted and ready for their baby to arrive, but the love seemed to make it all worthwhile. Cade found that fascinating.

They ate, listened to Boyd share his first thoughts on the upcoming summer brew, and moved on with the checklists and have-tos for the week. Relieved to be over the awkward, Cade was happy to return to what they did best—running a brewery.

He was still thinking about Trick and Aspen even after the meeting. That led to thoughts of Boyd and Ella, followed closely by the life West and Meg had made. It was kind of like when they were kids, but deeper in his chest. Cade wanted a life, a love, like his brothers.

He wanted a woman to look at him that way. To know her so well that he rubbed her back without asking. He wasn't certain how to make that happen, but for the first time in his life, he wanted to be up to the task. Wanted to offer a part of himself and have the gesture returned. All of this went far deeper than the surface of his current life, but hell, he submitted the blog post early, which meant anything was possible.

Patrick peeked around the corner. "Sistine is coming in to get some work done. I told her she can have the back table all to herself. No one ever sits that far away from you." He fluttered his eyes and Cade shook his head. "I guess the Wi-Fi at the coffee shop is down. Amateurs." He slapped the wall and was gone before Cade could ask what was wrong with Knitterly's internet.

He'd never known Sistine to be away from her shop for long during business hours. As far as he knew, she *was* that shop. As his mind drifted to the other things he knew about Sistine, Javier called him back to the kitchen for one of his you-gotta-see-this-shit moments, which were rarely good news.

Her contractor finally called Sistine back as she washed her face with freezing water in her dark bathroom the next morning. Yes, her electrical was shot. And, no, it wasn't an easy fix like a fuse. Beyond that, he said he would be happy to take a closer look sometime next week.

"Some of your guys are already at my place working on the patio. Can't they see what's wrong?"

None of them were electricians, he'd explained. She didn't have a week. Sistine had seriously entertained going back to bed, but she heard her father's voice saying, "It's a bad day, not a bad life."

She'd been on all fours patting around for her other shoe when Keith, the guy Aspen had recommended, called to say he would be at her shop within the hour. It was as if the universe thought she might start crying and tossed her a bone.

Clearly the universe was short on bones, because that's where Sistine's luck stopped. After several grunts and what-the-hells, Keith emerged from the back corners of her building to deliver his diagnosis.

"Most of this is original wiring from nineteen whenever this building was built. You've got overlamping, that's what finally blew things up. Most of these sockets can't handle what you're plugging in. Hell, they can't handle plugging in anything from this decade."

Oh, nice. Keith had a sense of humor, exactly what she needed. He went on, careful to point out workarounds that would save her some money before delivering the bad news that if she didn't fix most of the issues, her building would never pass inspection once the back patio was done or if she ever wanted to do additional remodeling. She thanked him and was told he'd email her a tiered quote—what was critical, what could wait but was still out of code, and what she needed if her building was going to "survive the long haul."

She was no longer convinced she was going to survive the long haul, so it didn't much matter if the building was up to code. Finishing what was left of a stale box of Cheez-Its and calling it breakfast, she canceled her Friday and weekend classes and then called Aspen to ask if she could work from the Tap House. That eliminated the need to pay for overpriced tea lattes in exchange for Wi-Fi.

In her best handwriting, she wrote a sign explaining Knitterly was closed for renovations and would reopen shortly. She added a smiley face she was not feeling and taped it to her shop door.

She normally posted any changes to her usual Monday through Sunday hours on social media, but if there was a small chance the expo committee still wanted her, she didn't want to set off any alarms. Depending on the quotes, maybe she could ask Keith to start work tomorrow. He mentioned his team could have at least the urgent list completed in four days.

Pedaling her bike through town, she tried to appreciate the breeze on her face, the beautiful clouds. She reminded herself that life wasn't all about money even though it seemed every move she made put her deeper into debt. At least she had friends and the Tap House had air conditioning, she thought as she parked her bike in front of the giant warehouse-looking structure.

She grabbed her bag from her bike basket and checked her phone for the quotes, which had arrived. Staring at the email bold and unopened in her inbox, Sistine took a deep breath and tapped the screen.

Six thousand, seven hundred and forty-six dollars. That was the price tag for the urgent items. If she were independently wealthy, she could go for the full package and spend—her hand went reflexively to her chest—nineteen thousand dollars. There was some change there, but to aid in her sanity and to keep from bawling in public, her mind rounded to whole numbers.

Melissa. The name popped into her head like a lifeline. A lifeline tied to a shark, Sistine knew, but there was no way she had six thousand dollars, let alone nineteen. She was barely getting by and even if by the grace of some higher power, the committee chose her shop for the expo, they wouldn't give her the deposit for another month. She couldn't afford to have her shop closed for a month.

Pulling open the massive front door of the Tap House, Sistine went directly to the back table. By the time she'd settled herself in and plugged in her laptop, she'd made up her mind. She had been raised amid the ups and downs of running a business. Her parents owned the Crab Shack and two crabbers since before she was born. The family motto—Whatever it takes—was all but tattooed on her subconscious. Small business owners had to make tough decisions all the time. Sacrifice things in the name of survival. Dignity be damned, she booted up her laptop.

Chapter Four

The lunch crowd started to trickle in around eleven. Sistine was wearing the same sweater she had on last night at the coffee shop, which was unusual. Cade couldn't recall ever seeing her in the same anything since the day they'd met. She still had the same weight in her expression too as she flashed a barely-there smile and nodded in his direction. No question, something was up.

He poured a club soda, balanced two limes on the rim of the glass, and tucked a menu under his arm before letting Tina know he'd be right back.

"Everything okay?" Cade asked, setting the drink on the only piece of table not covered by papers and her laptop.

"Thank you." She lowered her screen. "Sure. I... have, need to have some electrical work done in my building." She was doing a great impression of a person stressed out by the everyday mess of owning a business, but Cade recognized the exhaustion.

"Only your shop or the apartment too?" He had never been inside Knitterly, but he knew from Aspen and Ella that she lived in the apartment behind her shop. The building was one of the originals in historic downtown. Having suffered through Foghorn's remodel, Cade knew firsthand what a nightmare buildings with character could be. He'd gone through it with his brothers. She seemed to be dealing with everything on her own.

"The whole building." She squeezed the limes in her water and let out a strained laugh.

"Damn. I'm sorry. Did you call—"

"Keith? Yes. He was out in an hour and already sent me quotes. He's great." She sipped. "I'm sure Aspen threatened his life."

Cade laughed and had no doubt. "Electrical is expensive. What are the repairs going to cost you?"

She touched a finger to the lime floating in her glass and Cade registered that she was uncomfortable.

"Sorry. None of my business." He handed her the menu. "I was told to get your lunch order. Strict orders to feed you while you're here."

"I'm fine."

"Aw, come on. It's on the house. It's the least I can do for my awesome sweater." He gestured, hoping to make her smile.

She shook her head. "I didn't even notice my own work."

More strained laughter that now tugged at a need to protect he had not realized was possible outside of his own family.

"It looks great on you."

"Right?" He tapped the menu on the table. "A few days of free lunch. What's your poison?"

She glanced down. "BLT."

"Fries?"

Her brows rose as if the answer was obvious.

"Should have known." He took the menu.

"You really should have."

Cade stepped away and Sistine opened her screen again.

He turned back on instinct. "It's going to be okay. You know, in case no one has told you that yet. We'll figure it out."

A grin teased at her lips. No lipstick today, he noticed. He had no idea why he was suddenly invested in Sistine's business, that barely-there smile. Maybe it was because without even knowing it, she'd been there for him last night. Or maybe caring for other people was part of his new improved-and-responsible Cade routine. Whatever it was, the smudges under her eyes clashed with her usual flower barrettes and funky shoes. He wanted to see her back in her revolving wardrobe of colors.

The "we" had thrown her for a second, and she hoped she'd covered it up well. The last time Sistine had trusted a "we," things had gone all kinds of awful. She knew in her heart that Cade and all of the friends she'd made since moving to Petaluma three years ago were nothing like Melissa, but that experience had turned Sistine into a "me" person, and she doubted anything would change that.

She'd gotten the small business loan on her own and even as she made friends, she kept her business to herself. She didn't even discuss money with her family. They had their own troubles—everyone did. Vienna owned a small business she seemed to manage with ease. Ella saved lives and certainly didn't have time to hear about Sistine's inventory woes. Aspen was having a baby, and Bri was saving lives right along with Ella. Everyone had their "stuff."

Sistine could have stayed home and worked for her family, but she wanted something separate. That was her choice and her responsibility, so while she appreciated Cade's "we," Knitterly was her problem on a bad day and her piece of the American dream, a gift to a community she loved, on a good one.

It would not fail. She would make sure of that. Unable to listen to Melissa's voice at that moment and certain she'd go to voicemail anyway, Sistine texted her instead.

I'll do it. I want twenty-five thousand up front and five thousand a month.

Sistine giggled at her audacity. She'd asked for ten thousand more up front and double what Melissa had offered when she'd called a month ago. There was no way she was going to—

Melissa: Done. Trying on this hideous dress, but I'll transfer the down and the first month as soon as I get to the car. TINY!!! I LUV U, I LUV U! I'll email everything tonight. Thank you! I owe you one.

Her mouth hung open. She knew they had vastly different lives after Melissa screwed her over the first time, but the degree of different was still shocking. Heart racing, she reread the text, searching for a catch or a loophole. Old habits and all. Once she realized what she'd done, her mind scrambled to make sense of it.

Okay, this isn't so bad. You're going to save your shop and then get out as quickly as you got in. Everything will be fine.

Sistine didn't make a habit of telling herself what she wanted to hear, but the shock of having secured enough money for Keith's ultimate package and a cushion for her monthly expenses with one text message must have jostled even her practical gray matter.

She'd sold her soul to the she-devil, that was the honest truth, but after she received the email from her bank that thirty thousand dollars had been deposited into her account, she decided going through hell was Knitterly's only chance and emailed Keith back.

"This will get your mind off things." Cade set silverware on her table and refilled her club soda in a way that said he could serve people in his sleep. "See the guy at the middle of the bar with the woman in the white blouse?" She realized how hungry she was once he set her sandwich and a basket of fries in front of her.

"Yes, I see him." She snatched one fry despite the niggling from somewhere in her childhood that it was rude to eat during conversation.

"Apparently this is a lunch first date." Cade scrunched his face. "Not the best idea, but he's giving it his all, so I'm rooting for him. She says, 'It was so refreshing when we met that you didn't approach me with some cheesy line.'"

Sistine was unable to hold back one minute more, so she bit into her sandwich and wiped her mouth.

"To which he says, 'You were so beautiful, I forgot my line.'" Cade leaned on the back of the chair across from her.

Her eyes widened and finished chewing another bite.

"Right? That might be the best line I've ever heard, and I've heard them all."

"As lines go, that's a good one." She wiped her mouth and managed to part with the first delicious sandwich she'd had in a while. "What did she say?"

"Nothing. She smiled 'the' smile. He'll get a second date."

"What's 'the' smile?"

Cade hesitated.

"Oh, come on. I knit. I'm not a nun. I'm only confirming that the smile is the he's-getting-lucky smile."

Cade nodded and wiggled his brows. His eyes were pine, maybe moss. A cloud must have moved off the sun because the midday light streamed in from the mostly glass roof of the Tap House, and she knew pine or moss wasn't going to cut it. She saw all of his colors now. Cade's eyes were Oasis 5222 40/60 blend. The base was moss, but the edges were dappled with lighter shades and sprinkled with deep blues. It was like the name suggested, all the colors of an oasis.

Wow, she needed to lay off describing eye color based on her yarn order. Yet another clue for why she might still be single in the sea of her married or almost-married friends. Where the heck did that thought come from? She didn't care if she was single, hadn't thought about it since she moved to Petaluma, and sure as sugar didn't need to be thinking about it now that she had the Melissa thing to figure out. Cade had beautiful, colorful eyes. She'd leave it there.

"What's the worst pickup line you've ever heard?" she blurted out as Cade turned to leave.

"There are so many."

"There has to be one that stands out."

He hesitated and stood closer. "Okay, this one." His face went all sleazy and he leaned on the back of her chair this time, right at her ear. "Was your mother a beaver? 'Cause damn! Or no, no, this one." He leaned in closer and she smelled the mint on his breath. "Did you just fart? Because you blow me away!" He thumped the back of her chair and they both laughed. "Yeah, that's the worst."

"Someone did not say that."

"Heard it with my own ears." He tapped his head. "Unfortunately, so did the poor woman sitting next to him."

"That is the worst. Well done."

He pumped his arms overhead and returned to the bar. She wondered if he knew. Did he practice showing off those arms in the bathroom mirror, or those awful floor-to-ceiling things at the gym? She hoped not but wouldn't be surprised. They were lovely arms.

She went to jot down the pickup line but stopped. The idea swimming through her mind now was possibly the stupidest one yet. Cade was her friend. He'd offered her a "we." If she was determined to fix things alone, she'd need to retrain her flirty side without help too.

Chapter Five

*P*rior to his recent Instagram awakening, Cade's neighbors had asked him if he wanted two of their chickens. Foghorn Brewery and the Tap House ran out of an old egg-processing plant. His neighbors Greg and Sandy thought he might like to have some real chickens.

"Fresh eggs," Greg had said.

At the time, Cade thanked them but said he didn't want the responsibility. A mere two weeks after showing his goods on Instagram, and he was putting the final touches on his backyard coop. He'd decided on two hens to start. Greg was bringing them by after work. Cade had been up most of the night researching backyard chicken care, and he emailed Trick. He had some ideas he wanted to talk over, ways he could be more involved in the brewery and contribute in his own way.

Henny and Penny, that's what he'd decided to call the hens, would be mascots for the brewery, and he wanted to include them in the website, blog posts, and even on Foghorn's Instagram.

He hit pause on the grammar podcast he was listening to and took a swig of water. It was warm for March and his T-shirt stuck to his chest. Wiping the sweat from his forehead with the back of his hand, he skipped back a few minutes in the podcast so he could re-listen to the part about figurative and literal. Those two had always confused him in school.

Cade tried to keep a few podcasts on his phone. He liked learning things, and while he couldn't listen to someone talking while he worked out, he tried to fit in podcasts during his commute and when he was screwing around at home.

After attaching the latch to the front of the chicken coop and fencing in a sizable area for them to roam, he jumped into the shower to wash off the *literal* sweat of his chores. Maybe Foghorn should include an educational piece on their website or a monthly podcast. He totally believed technology could enhance lives. It was a shame some people wasted it on stupid garbage.

The embarrassment of his private life out there for everyone to see had been a wake-up call and he was ready to project a different image, different energy. Even Lauren had moved on. According to Brandon, who now followed Cade's ex on Instagram, which was weird, but to each his own, she had removed the now-infamous picture. She also appeared to be back with Magic Fingers. Perfect. Lauren enjoyed taking pictures of herself more than anyone else anyway. Men were practically irrelevant so long as she had the right filter.

Cade appreciated a less-is-better philosophy when it came to sharing his private life, which was only amplified when his younger brother went from actor to celebrity. West at one point lived with every move he made on display. Now that he and Meg were married, West stuck to indie films. "Some of them are even good," their dad liked to tease. Likes and trends were fickle, and West was happy to be off-trend.

Women rarely saw past Cade's looks. He certainly wasn't the prettiest McNaughton—that honor went to West or Trick—but he knew he had a particular look that attracted... Who did his look attract? He swiped the fog off the mirror, ran his hand over his two-week-old beard, and smoothed long bangs off his face. The sides of his head, normally clipped close, were growing out.

He touched his arm, the green vine traveling from the middle of his forearm and wrapping around his bicep. The curls and curves of his tattoo had taken three trips to Aaron at Halo Arts and hours in the chair. Jack and the Beanstalk, that's what Cade had said he wanted three days after he graduated from high school. Aaron had outdone himself. Cade's arm was a work of art. He loved it and had loved the time in his life that it represented. Until about twenty-one, his decisions had mostly been about stepping out from the middle of the McNaughton clan and telling the world he was his own man. If his brothers went one way, he went the other, and in the end, his physical appearance had become about being different. It suited his lifestyle, but which one?

Staring back at himself in the mirror, he wondered for the first time since he sat in Aaron's chair if it was time to tone things down a bit. If he wanted to be taken seriously, if he wanted to find a partner as his brothers had, someone who respected and loved more than his body, maybe it was time to change things up. He held the long center strip of his hair in one hand.

Shit, it had taken him years to grow it out.

He shrugged. "It's only hair." Grabbing the scissors from the drawer with his other hand, he cut it all off.

Cade ended up buzzing everything, even the sides, until he had time for a proper haircut. When he got to the Tap House, Patrick was in his office on a conference call. He saw Cade through the window and waved him in. As he stepped inside, Patrick was finishing up.

"Sounds good. We'll touch base. Please tell Aspen we'll be thinking about you both," an older man's voice said through the speaker.

"Will do. Appreciate it, Clyde. Talk soon," Patrick said and disconnected.

Cade leaned against the wall, hands in his pockets. Being in his brother's office felt formal. Crossed t's and dotted i's. Everything in Trick's world seemed to have a spot. Sometimes it was hard to believe they were only two and a half years apart. Normally happy to point out that he was the fun brother, Cade found himself wanting to focus on what they had in common.

"So," Patrick looked up from his laptop, noticing but not mentioning Cade's hair. "I love your ideas for the website and the chickens. Aspen and Boyd do too."

"You've already talked to them?"

"I called Boyd on my way in. We're all on board."

"Great." He walked closer and grabbed the back of one chair opposite his brother's desk.

"I do have one concern."

"Of course you do."

"Hear me out. Branding for Henny and Penny, the blog, and our social media are the way we connect with our clients: people who buy our beer, businesses that stock our products."

"I'm not two, Trick. I don't need to be told what goes into our business."

"You already have a lot on your plate with the Tap House, and I've had to keep on you just to get one blog post a month."

"That's because those posts are stupid. These will be worth reading, and I have Max now to help out behind the bar. I can do this, and you or Aspen don't have what I have. I'll be better at it."

His brows went up. "You going to tell her that?"

"No."

They both laughed, and Cade sat down, resting his elbow on his knees. "I can do this."

"I know you can. It's not a matter of can, it's a matter of consistency. People will expect new content, it's not something you can do on a whim and then when you're bored, Aspen and I have to clean it up."

He should have been pissed, but the truth was his track record on consistency wasn't great. Everyone grew up, though. He was pushing thirty-three, proud of the Tap House, damn proud of his family, and ready to contribute more than a wink and a smile. "All I can do is take it and show you. Remember when you wanted to bring in someone to manage the Tap House?"

Trick nodded.

"We're at least a fifty-percent-revenue center in less than two years. I manage all of it and people love us."

"No question. Okay, let's get down to it. How's this going to work?" He slid a pad across the desk to Cade, and it reminded him of the early years when the three of them, with the help of funding from their movie-star brother, hatched a plan for the best brewery in northern California on scraps of paper and napkins. Swallowing a lump in his throat, Cade laid out his plan. Posts to introduce Henny and Penny as their new mascots, linking the past and the future through chickens, some videos, and maybe even a podcast with the three of them or a guest brewer in the future. Cade talked collaboration with other businesses in downtown and cross-promotion. Patrick listened, expanded, and encouraged.

By the time he left, they'd agreed to a weekly social media schedule. They'd all see the posts on Friday and agree before the week started. Patrick showed him the shared drive and explained what they had for stock photography, as well as who to contact for new images. Cade hadn't been this excited since opening night for the Tap House. He knew their business model better than anyone. Hell, he lived the culture they were selling. With everything he had planned for the brewery, one stupid picture would be history in a matter of weeks.

There was a thirty-minute wait and a packed bar before happy hour even started. Cade was relaxed, telling jokes, and defining "intrepid." It was weird how Lauren's post gave him this new way of looking at things. Boyd always preached life was made up of good and bad. Every tough spot held a piece of good, a lesson learned. Not for the first time, he thought his brother might be on to something. If his ass hanging out was Cade's worst, he'd take it, and he was more than willing to work for the good.

Sistine had money in the bank and her shop was better than ever. Keith changed out all of her light switches, swapped out her work lights for more energy-efficient models, and even took down the ancient fluorescent lights in her apartment and put a skylight in its place. She could see the stars at night and the sunrise every morning. It made her place seem a little larger, like there was more room to breathe.

She'd cleaned up her apartment and even bought some vegetables. Maybe she'd make a salad. Her first try at filling in for Melissa had gotten her a late-night text message regarding her "lack of enthusiasm." Sistine would admit to being a little rusty, but she wasn't the person she'd been in college and certainly didn't have access to the same... skill set.

Trying to focus on her day job, Sistine greeted her ten o'clock Sunday knitting group, which also happened to be composed of her best friends and was affectionately named Knit, Bitch, Knit. Name compliments of Bri. Aspen walked in first, followed by Ella and Bri, both in scrubs having worked the night shift at the ER. Vienna had called and said she would be a few minutes late. Bri was the self-proclaimed singlehood expert, although she'd been dating Joe for over a year so Sistine was up for that title.

Plugging in her phone and turning on the overhead speakers, compliments of Keith, Adele began singing about giving up or chasing pavements and everyone applauded that they didn't have to listen through the static of her tiny portable speaker. She loved everything about her shop before the electrical overhaul, but she would admit that now it was a much better experience for her patrons.

That reminded her that she had not heard anything from the expo committee despite leaving a voicemail yesterday, which meant they'd probably moved on to other newer shops. It seemed like most people took the easiest path between two points. As much as Sistine would have liked the committee to see past her building's bumps and bruises to its history and splendor, she could understand the light debacle throwing off their confidence.

Aspen, Bri, and Ella took their seats while Sistine handed them each a new knitting cheat sheet before going through the door that separated her shop from her apartment to get the sangria. When she returned, Vienna had arrived and they were all huddled together and laughing.

"What's so funny?" Setting the drinks on the table, she joined them.

"We are laughing because Ask Amy put this idiot in his place. Do you read *Cosmo*?" Bri said.

Sistine knew her friends had placed her in the good-girl friend category. She owned a knit shop and rode a bike around town. She was currently sporting a gecko pin on a tomato red sweater she'd made years ago and purple jeans she'd found at the thrift store. Add in book club moderator and she understood all signs pointed to cat lady, so she was flattered Bri even asked if she read *Cosmo*.

"I don't have time to read anything. What's this one about?"

"This woman wrote to ask if it was reasonable for her husband to ask for a weekly minimum in their sex life."

"Like a guarantee?" Sistine asked, handing out glasses.

They all nodded.

"Who are these people?" Vienna opened the pastry boxes.

"You'd be surprised what people think is normal." Ella poured ginger ale and handed it to Aspen before ladling sangria for the rest of them.

"I think my favorite part is when Ask Amy says, 'Perhaps if your husband worked on his form, things would naturally exceed the minimum,'" Vienna read.

They all hooted and clapped. Sistine took a bite of her cinnamon roll.

It *was* a great line.

Setting her roll on a napkin, she brushed her hands together and reached behind the counter for her needles.

"Okay. So last time we met, we'd started working on the yarn over. Remember this is what we use when we want to increase the number of stitches, which will get us ready to make our first blanket."

They bobbed their heads to acknowledge they were listening in between eating and sipping, but they barely had needles in hand before Sistine lost them again.

"Would you put up with that from Thad?" Bri asked Vienna. "A minimum?"

Aspen groaned. "Ugh, please. I'm about to pop here, and haven't we all heard enough about my brother the wonder lover?" She used aggressive air quotes. "Before anyone says another word about his hot body or some new detail I'll never be able to unhear, please remember I am with child."

"Oh, believe me, honey, there is no possible way to forget." Bri moved the yarn through her needles in a fluid motion, and Sistine was impressed. "It will be over soon. For all of us."

"What?" Aspen got tangled and put her needles on the table. "I have been a great pregnant person."

They all looked at one another, nodded, then shook their heads in exaggeration. Aspen had not exactly taken to the limitations of pregnancy. She seemed to think she could barrel along right up until the birth and got testy around six months when she realized that wasn't going to happen so smoothly. She also read every pregnancy book ever written, which only gave her more information than she needed.

"I never get tired of hearing about Thad," Bri said.

"Well, let me tell you, I'm always tired, ladies." Vienna pursed her lips and batted her lashes at Aspen.

There was more laughter, as Aspen feigned gagging and took a big bite of her beef jerky stash.

"While I would love to go on about my gorgeous fireman, I think we all need to shift gears to appreciate the beauty that is Cade McNaughton's body." Vienna held up her phone and then passed it around the table.

"It is something." Bri handed the phone to Sistine.

She tapped the screen to bring the light back on and took in a quick breath at the image of a beautiful sun-darkened man asleep on white sheets. She'd heard of the picture that night in the coffee shop, but seeing him asleep stirred feelings she didn't realize she had. Apart from the physical beauty of the photo, she was struck again by the betrayal at being photographed without his knowledge.

"Hasn't that been deleted yet? How awful."

"Sweetheart, that is not awful. That is the way The Almighty intended man. And it has been deleted, but Pam grabbed a screenshot first. She's the most efficient employee." Vienna laughed along with the rest of her friends and topped off their sangria.

"Well, I think it's ridiculous. What kind of person does that? And, I'll remind all of you that if this were gender flipped, you'd be losing your mind. Man or woman, he's a person and this is such a violation."

They all stared at her, blinking like she'd introduced an algebra equation.

"What? It's wrong." She glanced at the phone, and dear God he was something straight out of a magazine, but it was Cade. She knew him, and she didn't care how prudish it sounded, it was wrong.

"Okay. Leave it to Sistine to put us all in our place," Ella said, looking at Aspen. "You're right. He's our brother-in-law."

Aspen could barely manage a nod as she stood and rubbed her back. "He did take it pretty hard. We should show some respect," she said.

Bri and Vienna looked at one another and then back at the phone. "Well, we are not related, so one more time: the man is beautiful. Agreed, it was crappy that his ex posted it, but the caption is accurate. Damn."

"I will second that," Bri said.

Sistine shook her head and tried to redirect the class back to the yarn over, but the sangria was flowing now. At this point, there was no controlling the Bitches, save Aspen, who'd barely touched her ginger ale and was now pacing.

Vienna held the phone up to Sistine again. "This man is single. You are single. I think you need some of this, sis."

"Me?"

They all nodded, even Aspen, who lowered herself back onto the padded rocker seat.

"He wore your sweater again yesterday," she said on a grunt.

"What?" they all said.

"The sweater she made for Mr. Graham. Cade wears it at least every other day."

"The cardigan?" Ella said.

Aspen bit her lower lip after putting her hand on her back again.

"Are you okay?" Ella asked, reaching over to touch her hand.

"Yes." Aspen stood again. "I'm... the baby feels super low and—" Before she could get another word out, she let out a long moan and when they all looked up, her cute little maternity capris were soaked.

"My due date is tomorrow. First pregnancies never arrive on time," she said, clutching the table.

"Honey, if you thought a baby you and Patrick made was going to be late, even one day, you're not paying attention," Bri said. She and Vienna went to Aspen's side and Ella called Patrick. Sistine stood there, needles still in hand like she'd been caught unprepared.

"Oh, crap. This hurts." Aspen closed her eyes.

"Breathe, Aspen. Slow, deliberate breaths. Almost like you're blowing into a man's ear. Can you do that?" Bri said.

Aspen leveled a glare. "Seriously? I don't want to think about that right now. Blowing into a man's ear is what got me here in the—" She grabbed Bri's arm and opened her eyes wide. "Oh. My. Gawwd."

"Okay, bad image." She removed Aspen's grip and drew her close. "Steady breath in, slow exhale."

Sistine helped Bri pack up Aspen's bag, and both of them shared a look that expressed the excitement of knowing their friend would be having a baby in a few hours. Moments later, they were all in Aspen's car and Bri was comfortably over the speed limit en route to the hospital. Sistine reached from the back seat to rub her friend's shoulders. Aspen's eyes were focused on some point through the windshield and it was clear, like everything else, she was not going to let labor pains win.

Chapter Six

Hattie Pane McNaughton, named after Aspen's beloved Grand, Harriet, arrived three minutes after midnight on her due date, which Cade thought was appropriate given her obsessively punctual parents. His face hurt from smiling as Patrick handed out doughnuts in honor of his "Gorgeous, perfect, spectacular, and so damn brave wife."

Patrick quickly recounted the birth. In the middle of contractions, Aspen was still running down the list of things she'd gone over with him a hundred times. Then there was the moment she yelled and gripped his hand with equal parts need and anger. Cade laughed at the story until his brother's eyes welled up and he told them about Hattie. How she was quiet at first when she came out, but then let out a McNaughton wail and they knew everything was all right.

"She's so tiny. Well, not exactly. She's eight pounds and four ounces, which isn't tiny, but my God." He took their mother's hand. "Four times, Mom. You did that four times. And we never even thanked you or had a proper party." He kissed their mom on the forehead. "Well done."

She wiped her eyes and kissed Patrick on the cheek, having to stand on her toes to reach him. "This is all the thanks I need. I'm so proud of you and Aspen. Now"—she dropped back down to her own height and wiped her eyes again—"when do I get to see my second grandchild?"

Cade held his niece and wiped a few tears of his own. She was tiny, and her little lips were perfect. Her eyes were searching and even in her first hour of life, she looked like both her gorgeous mother and his well-dressed brother. What must that be like to create not merely a piece of furniture or a drink, but a human being? To know that little bundle would be looking to them for the rest of their lives the way Cade and his brothers still looked to their mom and dad. Cade shook free of his own thoughts as Hattie's eyes closed as she slipped off to sleep in the crook of his arm. He loved his niece instantly. It had been the same way when he'd first held Boyd's son Mason. He knew right there that if he never had children of his own, it would be easy to give all his love away to his brothers' kids.

Volunteering to step out when West and his wife Meg arrived around one o'clock, Cade headed to the vending machine for coffee. After getting lost on his way back, through sheer luck, he found the waiting room and noticed Sistine sitting in the corner knitting, eyes up to the muted television near the window.

"Congratulations, Uncle Cade," she said, glancing at him, hands still knitting away as if they worked on their own.

"Thank you." He sat next to her. "I would have gotten you a coffee if I knew you were here."

"That's okay. I only drink tea."

"Huh, I'll remember that."

She did something with her yarn and met his eyes. "You don't need to remember. You got your hair cut."

Cade ran his hand over his head as if reminding himself. "Yeah. You like it?"

She tilted her head and returned to her knitting. "It's different."

He didn't know how to respond. He'd been up since five o'clock yesterday working on Henny and Penny's first blog post. Different good or different what-the-hell-were-you-thinking? Cade didn't ask. He never asked what people thought about the way he looked. So much for never because lately he was interested in Sistine's opinion on a whole slew of things. "What are you making?"

"I'm almost done with Hattie's blanket. I want to finish so she will have it tonight. Those hospital blankets are so hospital-like." She gathered her work from the large bag next to her and Cade was once more blown away. It was yellow, a deep summer flower yellow with black and white sheep all over.

"How do you make those, the sheep?"

She smiled. "Not easy, but they are each a series of stitches. Different colors and a pattern."

"That's incredible."

"Lots of practice and patience. Sheep represent innocence and vulnerability. I wanted them on her blanket." Her eyes welled up.

"Hey, are you okay?"

Sistine shook her head. "I'm great. I cry. It's something I do when things are good. I get this feeling, this full and grateful feeling. It sometimes spills out of my eyes."

Cade put his arm around her. Her hands were still knitting. He swallowed his own emotions even though it seemed safe to share them with her.

"How'd you pick the color? I think it's great you didn't go with pink, but that's not even a typical baby yellow."

What the hell? He was a baby color expert now? There were a million things he could have said. Charming conversation was his game. What was it about her that brought out the chubby kid he was in sixth-grade science club?

"It's daffodil. The flower for people born in March. I had a feeling Hattie would be born close to her due date. Not quite this close, which is why I am a little—" She moved her sticks, or needles, around a few more times and the blanket was somehow off the needles. "There. All done and ready for that sweet baby." She smiled, and Cade realized his arm was still around her, that they were closer than they'd ever been and that she smelled like candy. At least he thought it was candy. There probably wasn't a candy perfume. Their eyes met and her breath seemed to catch before she cleared her throat and stood with her blanket.

"I didn't know daffodil is the flower of March. Does every month get a flower?" Cade asked, hoping things would tilt back to normal. He had not eaten in a while; maybe his blood sugar was off.

She nodded and folded the blanket a noticeable four full chairs away from him. Never one to crowd, Cade stayed put.

"What's April?" he asked.

"Daisy or sweet pea. Each month actually gets two flowers. It depends on where you look."

"Not exactly badass, either one. I guess I'll go with the daisy."

She smiled, holding the blanket to her chest. "You were born in April?"

"Yup. The sixth."

"Aries."

"Trouble, right?"

"I was going to say honest. I suppose that can be trouble in the right situation."

He smirked.

"Daisies are purity. Sweet peas are blissful pleasure."

Cade hung on that word—pleasure—like it was the first damn time he'd heard it. The pull to her was more than low blood sugar. "I should probably go with the sweet pea then."

"Purity not your speed? Even with the new haircut?" She gestured to her own hair.

Cade stood up, intrigued by her sarcastic layer. Maybe late nights did things to prim and buttoned-up Sistine too.

"Nothing wrong with purity." He stepped closer. "Pleasure is a better word. Better concept." There it was, the McNaughton charm front and center. Finally.

To her credit, she didn't step back. Probably because she had a baby blanket between them. Only an idiot would hit on a woman in a waiting room after she finished knitting a baby blanket. Wait... was he hitting on Sistine? That made no sense. They were friendly, friends even, but she was not the type of woman to be hit on. Jesus, was he tired? What the hell did that even mean? One more step and he was inches from her. She seemed to be clenching the blanket a little tighter, but her eyes stayed on him as if she expected nothing.

"Pleasure is a lovely word, but..." Her glance shot directly over his shoulder. "Hey, how is she?"

Cade turned to find Boyd and Ella, both looking bloodhound curious. He stepped back, shoved his hands into his pockets, and met his brother's eyes. Never let them see you sweat.

"Great. They're both incredible. How's everything going in here?" Ella asked.

Sistine held up her blanket. "Good. I finished Hattie's blanket. Cade and I were trying to decide if purity or pleasure is a better word."

"Is that so?" Boyd smirked, folding his arms across his chest.

Sistine scrunched her face and turned to grab her bag. "That came out wrong. Sorry. Can I go in and see Aspen now?"

"Yup, we're here to switch with you. I'll show you the room," Ella said. Sistine followed her out.

Cade gave her space but regretted that doing so left him in the room with his brother.

"So, how are things?"

"Things are good. Hattie is beautiful." Cade treaded lightly.

"She is." Boyd took a seat and rubbed his eyes. "Were you doing your move on Sistine? And what the hell did you do to your hair?"

Cade went with the easier answer. "I cut it."

"Looks better. So, new haircut but still the same moves?"

"I don't have a 'move.' It's past your bedtime and you're cranky. She was showing me the blanket she made. Settle down."

Boyd ran a hand over his beard. Sort of like a mountain man looking to chop something.

"Cade, are you coming too?" Ella asked, peeking back into the room.

"I am. Later. Get some rest, old-timer."

After a fair amount of fawning and ogling over the perfect Princess Hattie, Sistine found herself again in a dark parking lot with Cade.

For a moment, she'd forgotten how she arrived at the hospital and then remembered Bri and Vienna had left and Aspen's car was staying with Aspen. Stopping on the sidewalk, right beyond the sliding doors, she took out her phone.

"I can give you a ride," Cade said, holding out his helmet.

"No, thank you. I'm not used to a bike with an engine."

"I'll drive. All you have to do is hang on. Have you ever been on a motorcycle?" He walked back toward her.

She looked up from her Uber app. "Yes."

"Really?"

"Why are you surprised that I've been on a motorcycle?"

"I don't know. I guess... I just assumed."

"I'll bet there are a lot of things you assume about me."

He tilted his head. "Probably. Let me take you home, Sistine. I promise I'll drive slowly." He extended the helmet again.

It wasn't the bike that scared her. She was attracted to him and if the energy between them was any indication, touching him would be a mistake. She could explain none of this to him, so she took the helmet and when he guided her arms around his waist and drove them off into the late night, she tried not to notice the slope of his back, the curves of his body, or how freeing it was not being the one in charge.

Cade parked in front of her shop and everything felt surprisingly like a date, so she quickly handed over his helmet and thanked him for the ride.

"You're welcome." He got off the bike and she stepped back. Not out of fear, well, maybe it was fear. It was late and he wasn't the fun-loving equal opportunity flirt she knew from Foghorn. The man shoving his hands in his pockets and walking her to the door of her shop, which was only steps away, was rumpled and heavy-lidded. He was a tired uncle, a guy beaming with love for his family. These new sides of Cade were too much for Sistine's frazzled life to handle.

"Did you make all of these?" He gestured to the front window of her shop as she searched her bag for her keys.

"Most of them. My godmother made this big blanket on the chair as a shop opening present and—" She stepped back from the door because she couldn't seem to remember her own display. "June made the baby bonnet and—" Cade was looking at her with such interest that her chest squeezed.

What the heck was going on? I've been in this town for years and now, you choose now to stand with me in the moonlight and talk about my shop?

As if he could read her thoughts, Cade's lips curved into a middle of the night smile. "It's a great shop. You should be proud." Before she could answer, he touched her arm briefly and was on his bike.

"Thank you, I am," she finally managed.

He nodded, that unnerving glint of interest still there as the roar of his bike cut through the blackened silence and he was gone.

The last thing she wanted to do when she got into her pajamas a little after two was get on her computer, but if she didn't get to work, she'd miss the schedule cutoff and she was already on thin ice. She assumed Mel wasn't going to end their arrangement. Honestly, who else did she know in her upper-crust Washington world who would be willing and able to keep it a secret? That's what she'd needed when she called: someone to handle her dirty little side business now that her husband was a senator. Sistine was convinced she had some power, some control, but she had a history of landing on her face anytime she was too comfortable around Melissa, so she wasn't taking any chances.

Making a cup of tea, she dropped onto the couch with her laptop. The glow of the moon poured through her new skylight. She glanced up to find a full and glorious moon. Sweet Hattie was born under a full moon. Good luck for a stunning little girl and her equally amazing parents. Sistine realized she hadn't even turned on a light and her apartment was washed with magic. Hattie's magic. The aging plaster of her walls softened into antique and even the chipped Formica of her kitchen counter sparkled as if it were diamond encrusted. Sistine knew they were just pockmarks in the surface, but under Hattie's moon, every flaw was more than fine.

Faced with watching the magic or working what had now become her second job, she closed her laptop and lay back on her couch. She had never thought about having children, well, not in any sense that went past playing house with her neighbors or wheeling a baby carriage. She would be thirty-one at the end of the year and had never heard the ticking clock her mother loved to bring up when she visited home. Muriel Branch was twenty-four when she had Sistine's brother Drake. A year later, she had Jules, and two years after that, Sistine was born. Three children before thirty. Sistine had never thought about her mother's life in relation to hers, but if there was a baby-making timeline, she was behind.

Eyes growing heavy and not able to muster the energy to pull her bed down from the wall, she grabbed the blanket off the back of her couch and imagined herself running her shop pregnant. Having her own business would allow flexibility most moms didn't have. Her laptop dinged with the notice of a new email, but Sistine ignored it. She would always have things to get done in reality and wanted to spend a moment more under the magic of Hattie's moon.

Speaking of moments, her next dreamy thought was of Cade and whatever that was in the waiting room before they were interrupted. Pleasure. What had he said about pleasure? She was so tired. There was an easy mix of humor and meaning every time she was around the McNaughtons. She understood why Aspen and Ella had been drawn to their partners. Sistine didn't know Meg well but guessed she fell in love with the McNaughton side of West instead of the movie star. The way they moved together, leaned on one another, was lovely and didn't seem to have strings.

Sistine came from a great family, but she often felt like an appendage rather than a separate being all her own. Maybe Cade felt that way too, but nothing appeared to bother him. The haircut was interesting. He'd have to work at looking bad, but truthfully, she'd liked the long, crazy Mohawk.

Sistine snatched the blanket up over her shoulders and closed her eyes as the nagging feeling that getting involved with Melissa again had been a mistake. Resolved that she had no other choice and relieved that her shop and her building were now safe, she welcomed sleep and let it take her under.

Chapter Seven

By Wednesday, Cade already felt the added responsibility. Now that Patrick and Aspen were home with baby Hattie, Boyd and Cade divvied up the responsibilities Trick wasn't able to reschedule or handle from home. Boyd had received the delivery on Tuesday, checked everything off, and emailed the paperwork to Aspen. Cade hoped she wasn't checking email yet, but he wouldn't be surprised.

For his part, he had gotten in at six to meet with the tech guys who were there to fix Foghorn's back bar computer system. It felt like they were going to run smack into the lunch crowd without a register thanks to the "new and improved upgrade," but when the guy rebooted it one more time, everything came alive. Crisis averted, Cade texted Trick and went right into serving.

Max, who was thankfully a great addition and willing to take on more shifts, would be in at four, so Cade could get home, feed the chickens, and start work on next week's social media schedule. At the moment, though, he was handing out food and pouring soft drinks and the occasional beer faster than Tina could serve it. When he looked up again, it was already one o'clock.

Sistine took a seat at the end of the bar. Her chin-length brown hair was pinned back off her face and she wore a sweater that made her look like the host of a kid's television show. Pushing her sleeves up toward her elbows, she caught his eye and made a gesture with her hands like she was cracking her knuckles. She was ready for backgammon battle.

Cade made her a club soda with two limes and set the board on the bar before the ding of the order-up bell called him away. He felt a pull to get back to her and realized his draw to Sistine had always been there. It may have grown lately as part of his search for more substance, but from the minute he'd been introduced to her, he'd wanted to be around her. She had an energy, a clear and genuine beautiful mind that matched her beautiful outside. And she got him, seemed to see right through his flash to his center.

"Lunch?" he asked.

"Sure. Why not. How about some of those incredibly overpriced fries with the cheese."

"You're Drunk, Fritz."

She laughed and there went his blood sugar again.

"That's what we named them." He pointed for her to check the menu.

"Clever. Yes, I'll have those. And I think I'll have a beer. You pick."

He shrugged, suddenly feeling like some high school show-off. "That's an easy one. There's rum in the chili sauce that comes on the side, which I know you'll try because, well, because you seem to like colorful things."

"I do," she said, tapping her fingers on the edge of the board. Cade wasn't sure why everything she said since the night of Hattie's birth sounded like an invitation. Clearly he was losing his mind. "So"—he cleared his throat—"with the cheese and the kick of rum you'll need an IPA, correction, this year's IPA because Boyd went heavy on the apricot, but it's still bitter."

"I thought bitter was bad for beer."

"Balanced bitter. The cheese and fries are heavy, so you'll need it. Something has to cut through all that richness."

She put the menu down. "You're the expert, so give it to me."

Her eyes, light brown and dusted with gold, were locked on his for less than a second. Holy shit, he needed a sandwich.

After rolling the dice to see who went first, Cade moved his checkers and left to clear some glasses and wipe down the bar. "Does anyone know what a flock of crows is called?" Joe at the other end of the bar asked. He was sitting with two guys Cade hadn't seen before wearing Petaluma Electric shirts and playing some game on his phone.

"A gaggle," one of the other guys said.

Cade shook his head. Mindy from the dog grooming place three stores down from Sift offered, "A pack?"

Cade refilled her Diet Coke and returned to see where Sistine had moved.

"Come on, people, I only have six seconds left."

"A murder," Cade and Sistine said at the same time, eyes on the backgammon board.

"That's right! Damn, you guys are in sync."

Cade watched Sistine roll the dice and couldn't tell if she'd ignored Joe's comment because she was so into her move or if, like him, she felt the charge between them grow stronger every time they were together.

"Hey, Cade. I had this drink once," Mindy said. "And I have never been able to figure out what it was."

Never one to turn down a challenge, Cade asked questions while he played his turn and handed the dice back to Sistine.

"Beer or mixed?" he asked.

"Both. It was Guinness, I think. Some kind of cream and something else."

He ran through the possible combinations while Sistine rolled again. The cream was throwing him, but it could be de Menthe or Irish cream. Yup, that was it. Happy to see the lunch crowd heading back to work, he pointed to where he thought Sistine should move before clearing dishes.

"The third ingredient was whiskey. I'm guessing you had what used to be called an Irish Car Bomb." He followed a wince with a smile as Mindy's eyes went wide. "There's a new politically correct name for it, but I'll have to look that up for you, so let's call it an Irish Bombshell."

"Perfect. If I didn't have twin poodles and a golden retriever waiting for me, I'd ask you to make me one of those. Maybe I'll come back after work. Do you make those kinds of drinks?"

"For you, Mindy, I will corrupt a perfectly innocent beer."

She licked her lips and nodded, pulling her bottom lip between her teeth. Cade smiled and took Mindy's credit card for her lunch. Smiling was automatic, he'd decided a long time ago. It was part of the job.

"I'd use our Stout, Big Brahma, instead of Guinness." He pointed to the chalkboard overhead. "And a local single malt for the shot. It'll be better. In the meantime, you need to either Google the PC name or we'll have to come up with something."

She handed her credit card slip back, slid off her stool, and pointed at him. "I'll be back, McNaughton."

"Looking forward to it, Mindy."

Cade fell in love with the entertainment factor of tending bar when he worked at Flips right out of high school. The dim lights, the background music, the noise, and the women. At eighteen, the women might have been the biggest draw. Back then there was something in their glossy eyes and low-cut shirts as they leaned into the bar that had Cade filling out an application and convincing Tim that an eighteen-year-old bartender was exactly what he needed to "breathe some new life" into the small bar area of his restaurant.

Tim had sort of bought his pitch. Cade worked as a barback and washed dishes for that first year. During that time, he learned everything. How to pour, mix, and the twin arts of eye contact and conversation. He grew up watching men with far more facial hair than he imagined possible back then and women who could reduce a man to a boy with one well-placed stare. After his nineteenth birthday, Tim gave Cade his own shift and he'd never looked back. That was almost fourteen years ago. Cade knew he was a good bartender. He wasn't the smartest McNaughton or the prettiest, but he knew beer and he loved food. Everything else was trial and error.

He could not remember a time in his adult life when he didn't want to tend bar. From the time he was old enough to look in the window of a restaurant or corner bar, he wanted to be part of that energy, to be around people coming together in more good times than bad. Granted, he'd never imagined everything they'd accomplished. He was living his dream. Of course, he had never pictured awkward blog posts or endless meetings as part of that dream. The meetings killed him. But that's what it took to keep things running. Work was how a person made money in order to have a life. For him, his life was the bar.

But he wanted more professionally and personally. Turned out he liked responsibility and the growing feelings he had for the woman about to split double sixes when she should play it all on two checkers.

Sistine knew she'd lost before all her checkers were even home. Running a finger along the wooden edge of the board Cade brought in when she asked him to teach her backgammon, she cringed as he returned and met her eyes.

"Game's not over."

"Oh, don't baby me. We both know I lost."

He leaned on the bar.

"I think Mindy the dog groomer has the hots for you. Any comment?"

He glanced up. "Are you trying to distract me?"

She feigned shock. "Is it working?"

He removed two checkers and set them next to him. "Your move."

"You know, it seems busy now on Wednesdays. Maybe we should cancel these lessons."

"Not a chance. He loves Wednesdays," Boyd said, squeezing behind Cade. Boyd was wearing a leather apron over a flannel shirt and jeans. His baseball hat was on backward and he appeared confused, or in thought, Sistine couldn't tell.

"What's up?" Cade asked.

Boyd shook his head and refilled his thermos with coffee.

"That's old. Do you want me to make you a fresh batch?"

"No. I'm good. When was the last time we used pecan?"

Cade twisted the red straw in his mouth and right when Sistine expected him to say, "How the hell would I know?" he answered, "2015 Toasted Brissel."

Boyd's eyes widened as the memory seemed to dawn. "That's right. With the coffee." He raised his thermos to emphasize. "I'm going to use pecan again, but this time with biscuit," he said, seemingly dismissing Cade from his mind with a tilt of his head. He mumbled something completely to himself that Sistine couldn't make out and turned back. "Ella thinks we should have a party for Aspen. Something about celebrating that she survived birth. Trick mentioned it at the hospital. Can you get that rolling?" he asked, and before Cade answered, he was gone.

"Did he say biscuit? Like biscuits and gravy?" she asked after she finally removed two of her checkers. She was still behind. At this point, she'd need doubles to catch up to him.

Cade chuckled. "No. Biscuit is a malt. Boyd speaks in code. Hasn't Ella filled you in on that? He's in the middle of creating a new batch. He usually stays in his cave, but now and again he wanders, and we get to see the genius at work."

"I don't think I've ever seen him like that."

"It's a rare seasonal sighting. He's like Bigfoot."

Sistine laughed and realized she did that a lot around him.

"I love the party idea. I'll talk to Ella."

"I'm meeting West tomorrow at Sift and I'll mention it there too."

"Look at us coordinating the couples," she said, still hoping for doubles.

"Someone has to keep them in line. Might as well be the clear-headed singles, right?"

She nodded and Cade excused himself again to cash someone else out. He refilled and chatted and joked with Javier all on his way back down the bar.

He loves Wednesdays—Boyd's comment rolled around in her mind, and Sistine knew she did too. Before her deal with the she-devil, before he'd offered a "we." She'd enjoyed being around Cade since the beginning. Did that make what she was about to do right? Probably not.

Cade rolled double sixes and took his last three checkers off the board. Sistine crunched the ice from her water glass.

"Before you pout, we were three checkers apart. That's incredible. You're getting better."

She shrugged, put one of her lime wedges into her mouth, and flashed a big green smile that made him laugh. The lunch crowd was gone now, leaving only one man toward the end of the bar who was finishing up a salad while watching baseball on the television over the bar.

Three checkers. Sistine saw her opening and took it.

"Speaking of three. What are your thoughts on threesomes?"

Cade's hand slid off the bar and he nearly smacked his face on the surface. Regaining his composure, he searched Sistine's expression for sarcasm. When he found genuine interest, she couldn't read his expression.

"I... why are you asking?"

She used her straw to move the ice around in her glass, suddenly unable to look at him. "Conversation, you know, bar talk."

She sounded like a misfit. A perverted misfit. She fully expected him to blow her off and never play backgammon again, but as was his habit, Cade surprised her by leaning back and putting his hands in his pockets.

"Well"—he tilted his head as if pondering a great mystery—"I like to pay attention to one thing at a time when I'm in bed with a woman. Even if it's only sex, there's a respect and I guess a need to please."

Sistine was struggling for breath, intently focused on her ice like some gawky teenager. Make that gawky misfit pervert teenager. "Interesting, so as a guy you would never say... participate in a threesome?"

When Cade didn't answer, she peered over at him.

He smiled. "What's this about, Sistine?"

She let go of the straw and decided to act like an adult. "Nothing. I'm curious. I'm interested in—"

"Threesomes?"

"Yes," she managed, certain her face was at least yarn color 221 Lipstick 50/50 blend. "It's a work question."

"Is that so? Knitterly's getting pretty racy these days."

She was spiraling toward total humiliation. Why she expected the guy to simply blurt out his experience and advice on threesomes was beyond her at that point. Maybe he wasn't even all that experienced. His ex posted a sexy picture and every woman, literally every woman, swooned all over his bar, but that didn't mean he took any of them up on their smoldering looks. Maybe Cade was a turn-in-early guy, a big reader, and she'd insulted him by assuming he—

"I think threesomes can be fun if all parties are comfortable and there's no real relationship with either of the women. I think convincing yourself that you're going to spice up a committed relationship with another woman is asking for disaster." He checked the bar and when seemingly satisfied things were under control, he leaned in to face her. "A friend of mine was about two years into his marriage and things had started to settle. He talked to his wife about inviting another person into their sex life to try it out. She said she was game, even chose one of her single friends they'd had dinner with a couple of times."

If Sistine could have started recording this on her phone, she would have. With every detail, she wanted to thank him, tell him he was so being her "we" in that moment, but instead she listened to him relay a story he'd probably only shared with a few people.

"Anyway, they were divorced less than six months later. So, I think it only works in a casual setting, and even then, I think it would be tough to find the right people."

She stared at him. Her expression must have broadcast her next question because he shook his head and grinned in a way Sistine felt deep in her stomach.

"No. I have never had a threesome. I'm sure you thought I had or you wouldn't have asked the question."

"I wasn't... I didn't think that."

"Sure you did. It's okay. I'm flattered you came to me with your... work question." He nodded and was off again, probably thrilled to move on to the noncreepy patrons at his bar.

She grabbed her bag and left without saying goodbye. Pedaling back to her shop, she had what her father often called a "slap yourself" moment. What the hell was she doing? She'd completely stirred up her life and relationships with people she cared about, for what?

Parking her bike in front of Knitterly, she opened the front door to the sound of Adele saying her lover wasn't going to go. It reminded Sistine why she was willing to make a fool of herself in front of Cade. She needed lights, music, electricity. Without them, she returned home a failure.

After her four o'clock Knitting 101 class wrapped up, she sat alone at the lesson table and checked her emails. As if the universe knew she was reeling from what already felt like a bad decision, she opened an email from the Stitches expo committee. They appreciated her time, blah, blah, blah. They would be "expanding their reach" for a suitable venue. Knitterly was still a "consideration." Sistine closed her laptop and pressed her forehead to the table.

She was no longer desperate for the expo thanks to the new side job, but she'd wanted it. While both brought in the money she needed, the expo felt like something she'd have won on her own merit. Her arrangement with Melissa was cheap and stepping backward no matter how she rationalized it. Maybe the committee would still choose her. Being a "consideration" wasn't exactly bad news. She sat up, rested her hands under her chin, and stared at the bulletin board. Specifically the picture of a shirtless Ryan Reynolds with the text "Hey, Girl. It's killing me that you have to frog all those rows. Let me make you a cup of tea."

Vienna had found that on Pinterest a few months ago. She'd recognized the term "frog" from a knitting cheat sheet Sistine had handed out in class. It wasn't often knitting was made sexy and Sistine smiled every time she looked at it.

"Frogging," she had explained to the group, "is when a knitter makes a mistake and has to undo rows, essentially undoing hard work. It's not something we like to do, so thank you, Vienna, for bringing Ryan in to ease our pain."

"Yes, thank you." They'd all nodded and then laughed as Sistine pinned Ryan to the board for eternal inspiration. Her bulletin board was filled with bits and pieces. A keychain one of her customers made, funny cartoons, a picture of a lamb that read "I love ewe," and a printed schedule of each month's classes. Even with technology, some customers still liked to see things in print.

Deciding to be a big girl and not pout over something out of her control, she began rerolling the balls of lesson yarn. Since she was thinking out of control, she naturally thought of Cade. The mischief, concern, and intelligence all seemed at home together in his eyes. Setting the yarn in the basket on the table, she locked the front door and flipped her sign. Now that she was under contract, she needed to get ready for tonight. While she was at it, she needed to pack away any growing feelings for Cade McNaughton.

To her surprise, Cade was the type of man a woman who hadn't sold her soul for new electrical work could easily trip and fall in love with. So, it was good she'd probably freaked him out with her random threesome discussion. Picking up her laptop and the half-eaten bag of pretzels she was calling dinner, Sistine shut off the lights and went into her apartment to get ready for her second job.

Chapter Eight

The line at Sift, typical for the weekend, was almost out the door. Cade scanned the line looking for West. He'd arranged to meet his brother for breakfast before West and Meg headed back to San Francisco, their phones full of pictures of their new niece.

He didn't see either of them, so he got in line behind a couple and their toddler daughter. The little girl wanted a brownie for breakfast and while the man holding the curly-haired beauty in his arms was negotiating, his husband was not having it. By the time they made it to the counter to order, they'd agreed carrot cake was technically a breakfast cake and were rewarded with kisses and "Thanks, daddies" that had the entire line, including Cade, smiling.

He was ready for love—that explained why he was aware of every couple... why he was captivated by the picture-perfect two people who came together and became a family like the couple in line. It was clear they adored their daughter as she twirled the bright pink ribbon holding her hair off her face. He tried not to stare, but he was filled with a need to have what everyone else had. It sounded like he wanted the latest phone or flat-screen TV, but wasn't falling in love, getting married, and starting a family a matter of choice and therefore similar?

Glancing around the bakery, Cade felt like the only single guy late to a party he might not have been invited to, and the idea socked him deep in the chest. What these two men had, what Vienna and Thad had, what every one of his brothers now had suddenly seemed out of reach rather than a matter of choosing. Like maybe he was relegated to threesome questions and nothing more. He refused to accept that.

As the little girl dipped a finger in her carrot cake breakfast frosting and the ideal little family of three made their way to a table, Cade wondered if he needed to approach falling in love with the same determination as say a marathon. Marriage was for a lifetime. He'd witnessed his parents' effortless marriage. The two of them were made for one another. Nothing was out of reach. He'd already started training, and he was closing in on the kind of woman he wanted with him at the finish line.

"Hey, Cade." Vienna waved her hand in front of his face.

He'd zoned out into somebody-love-me-like-that land and ignored that maybe women never looked at him as the settle-down type. Maybe guys like him weren't given the adorable curly-mopped child. No. That was defeatist. Cade didn't believe in that crap. If he wanted the love of his life, kids, and a dog, he was going to have it. If his brothers had managed it, there was no reason he couldn't have the same luck.

"Sorry. Hey, Vienna." Habit had him pushing at bangs he no longer had while he tried to remember what he was doing. "How are you?"

Vienna smiled in that frazzled, small-business owner way and let out a breath as if he was the first person to ask how she was since she'd opened. "I'm well. You seemed like you went somewhere else for a minute."

"I've been dreaming about your oat fig bars." He smiled and in a flash, the persona he'd built for himself slid right back into place.

"You are the only man who appreciates my figs," Vienna said. "Two?"

"I'm having breakfast with my brother—the former sex symbol. Better make it three."

Vienna stacked three fig bars on a white ceramic plate with blue dots, then slid the glass to her case closed. She set the plate on the counter. "You could easily give him a run for his money," she said, fanning herself.

He shook his head. "Instagram?"

"Honey, I love Thad more than cake flour, but damn."

Cade laughed. Vienna had a way of turning something so annoying into light and fluffy. He wondered if that was something Thad loved about her.

"I'm actually looking to go in a different direction, so thank you for the vote of encouragement, but I'd like to be more than—"

"A hot piece of ass?" she whispered, handing him his bars and a cappuccino. "Lauren's words, not mine. Totally accurate, but not mine."

"Something like that."

Vienna gave him his change and turned the line over to Pam, her now full-time employee, before stepping over toward the freshly baked bread with Cade.

"Does Thad get sick of... that sort of attention? I mean the guy saves lives, they all do, and it seems like women only want to see their abs on a calendar."

Vienna stared at him for a beat like he might be joking before she appeared to realize he was serious. "I think it does bother him sometimes. He's never come right out and said anything, but he gets on some of his guys who are working more of the hot firefighter angle. Maybe it comes with age and..."

"Wanting something real?"

"Honey, being beautiful is real. There's nothing wrong with the way you look. I was a bit sad to see the hair go and my oat bars aren't giving you those shoulders. That's work."

"I guess. Sorry to take up your time," Cade said. "Oh, have you heard about the party for Aspen?"

"Yup. We were thinking next Tuesday. Can we close the Tap House for a private event?"

"We can. I'm on it."

"Perfect. Sistine is in charge of decorations. Ella and Bri are charming Javier into making the food, and I'll do the cake."

"What do I do?"

"You're in charge of securing the venue. Oh, and if Trick asks, it was your idea to close up and lose revenue for a party."

"Perfect." He shook his head. "Exactly what I need, more Trick angst."

Pam called for Vienna.

"Hang on, I'll be right back." Vienna pointed over his head. "Looks like another winner in the gene pool that is McNaughton finally showed up."

Cade turned to find West weaving his way through the tables.

"Did you get me anything?"

Cade shook his head. "I got three for me." He sipped his drink.

"Ass."

"I see what you did there. Any more?"

"Nah, that's it for now."

"Hot water with lemon," Vienna handed a cup over the counter. "Are you going with the 'I'm an actor' bran muffin or the 'I'm like everyone else' cinnamon roll?"

West looked at Cade's plate and rolled his eyes. "I'll be the normal one today. Thanks, Vienna."

After she handed West a giant cinnamon roll and he slipped two twenties into the tip jar when she'd suddenly gotten too busy to take his money, Cade found a table in the corner.

The little girl had finished her carrot cake breakfast and was pulling for both of her dads to "furry up" so they could go to the park. Cade remembered pushing Mason on the swings when he was little and playing pirates in their parents' pool during the summer. As the family cleared their table and left, Cade thought about sweet Hattie. Someday she would be that age, and while only a few days ago he'd thought being the best uncle was enough, now he wanted a playmate for Hattie or a little boy who would look up to a teenage cousin.

"Holy shit," he said on a huff and shoved an oat bar into his mouth. Was he allowed to say shit if he became a dad?

"What? You realized some of these people might not have seen you naked?"

Cade finished chewing. "What is with you guys? It's like you're obsessed."

"Hey, Boyd used to be obsessed with my waxing habits and you never defended me. Fair is fair. It's your turn to be pretty."

"Yeah, well that's the last shot of my body anyone will see on Instagram. And she took it down weeks ago."

"Oh, come on. I think you have a few good years left in you. There could be another picture."

"I'm changing things up."

West licked frosting off his finger and Cade thought the two women at the table next to them were going to slide off their chairs. What was it with the women in this town?

"The haircut part of the big change?"

Cade caught himself before he touched his head this time. "It's easier."

"Uh-huh, and the cardigan?"

Cade raised a brow.

"Boyd and Patrick told me."

Cade nodded and finished off his second oat bar. "Maybe the cardigan is part of it, a sign that I'm looking to love someone, make babies of my own someday."

"Are you now? Thinking you'll stop by the store and pick up the love of your life? It's not that simple."

"Seems to be. You're younger than I am and already married. If all of you can settle down, I should be able to find my soul mate. I'm tired of being the joke."

"You're not a joke. You're you, Cade."

"Well, I'm tired of that too."

"Tired of what?" Meg said as she came up behind Cade and kissed him on the cheek.

West stood and kissed his wife, nowhere near the cheek.

The women who were previously sliding off their chairs were now sighing.

Cade thumbed the remaining crumbs off his plate, put them in his mouth, and grabbed a chair for Meg.

She sat with her jacket across her lap. "So, what are you tired of?"

"Nothing. How's my perfect niece?"

"Still perfect. And she smells so good. My goodness, the smell." Her eyes met West's and Cade recognized the unspoken conversation going on between his brother and his sister-in-law. His parents had similar conversations all the time when they were growing up.

"What?" Cade asked.

West shook his head.

"Nothing." Meg adjusted the coat in her lap and stole the last piece of West's cinnamon roll.

It took Cade longer than it should have. His head was all clogged up with his damn feelings, but after an extra beat of silence, he knew.

"You're pregnant," he said, louder than he'd meant to.

"Oh, my Lord. Seriously?" Vienna said after she delivered a French press to a table near the door.

Meg exchanged glances with West and then they both beamed in tandem. Cade's chest warmed, and he stood to hug Meg once Vienna was through with her kisses and congratulations.

Holding on to Meg, emotions washed over him again. The feeling that his family was growing and the sense he was being left behind.

"You weren't going to tell me?" He hugged West.

"You seemed preoccupied and I didn't want to—"

"Forget that. I'm never too up in my stupid head to find out that I am once again going to be the favorite uncle. Damn, you two. You're going to be the best parents."

"Thanks, Cade." Meg sat back down as Pam circled by to clear their plates.

"How far along?"

"Look at you go with the lingo."

He shrugged. "Professional uncle."

She laughed, and West took her hand in that way couples did when they couldn't stand to not touch each other. They were so good together. Everything from the wrinkles in his rolled sleeves to the cargo jacket in her lap. They were a match and Cade meant what he'd said: they would be fantastic parents.

"A little over three months."

"We didn't want to move in on Patrick and Aspen's time."

"And, it's bad luck to announce before three months anyway."

"Well done keeping the secret from Mom." Cade bumped his brother's arm. "She's usually a bloodhound when it comes to babies. Do they know now?"

West nodded.

"Aw, man." Cade ran a hand over his face to distract from his emotions. "This is incredible."

"You're the last man standing."

"Right? I better get on my game. I need to find a woman with twins in the family, so I can double down."

West laughed. "You'll be okay. Let's work on finding you a nice woman."

"Without an Instagram account," Meg added. "I can't believe her. Did you even—"

"Time's up on that topic. Cade doesn't want to talk about it. He's changing things up."

Cade nodded to a slightly confused Meg. "Nice woman without an Instagram. Done."

"Yeah?"

"Anyone I know?" West asked.

"You're married to the only nice woman you know."

"True. Are you serious, have you met someone?"

"Working on it," Cade said as they all stood, waved to Vienna, and walked to their car.

He was bluffing. There was no nice woman poised to slip on a ring and make babies with him. All he had at the moment was a new sweater and a fascinating knitting store owner with an electrical problem. He liked Sistine. He liked that during the first time they'd met, she asked him what he was reading. A couple months later she asked him if he knew how to play backgammon. Now they had this friendship built on what came out of his mouth instead of what he could do with his body. He could be his whole self around Sistine, and he hoped she felt the same. Maybe he should ask her.

After watching his younger brother drive off, lovesick grin now permanent on his face, he pushed his hands into his pockets and wondered if there were any great love stories that started with board games.

Chapter Nine

Sistine could have sworn she ordered size six carbon needles and another box of the cute strawberry stitch markers, but she'd gone through the box delivered yesterday and didn't see either one. She emailed her supplier right before her contractor arrived to show her around her new and expanded patio and, of course, collect final payment. She had handed over her business VISA with confidence.

Melissa had texted last night that according to an email from her client, who Sistine imagined was now her client, that her latest attempt was, "fantastic." Managing to convince someone, well, a lot of someones, that she was the opposite of a stereotypical knitting store owner, brought an interesting tinge of accomplishment, but mostly relief.

Sistine had spent the last hour walking around her new outdoor space. Tile, comfy chairs, and even a fountain in the corner. They'd covered the seating section with Plexiglas and wood so on the off chance it rained, she and the guests in her shop could sit out and watch the rain. It was perfect, and she couldn't wait to add more succulents and create a couple of classes with a nature theme. First though, she needed to work on Aspen's party decorations before her two thirty with the Blue Hairs knitting group. June, Gracie, and Bess made up the group, which used to include Aspen's Grand up until she passed away almost a year ago now. The Hairs, all in their "bonus years" of life as June often called it, were incredible women and despite their age reminded Sistine to be youthful and have fun— something she rarely made time for these days.

She had knitted an entire scarf last night from Oasis 5222. It was a stress knit, or a guilt knit since guilt was now part of her stress. From the time she'd learned to knit, she had used it as a stress reliever. When she was in college, she made every girl in her sorority an infinity scarf and when her first and only real boyfriend broke up with her when he found out about the Melissa thing, Sistine had made an entire sweater in three days and then wrapped herself in it to cry.

There was no question why she chose the color she did. She'd felt ridiculous bringing up the threesome with Cade and awful that she'd used his suggestions without his knowledge. When she agreed to fill-in for Melissa, Sistine thought she'd be able to draw on her previous experience, but somehow she wasn't that woman anymore. When Melissa left and took their business with her, Sistine shut off her playful side, her sexy self. Grabbing the scarf now, she decided to stop by the hardware store for some rope and other party supplies. If she had time, maybe she'd run by the Tap House and give Cade the scarf. Was that weird since she'd just given him a sweater?

Adjusting the clock hands on her Be Back Soon sign to give herself forty-five minutes, she secured the flap of her backpack and walked her bike down to Mr. Graham's store. She slid the front wheel of her bike into the yellow painted rack outside the hardware store. Usually, she didn't lock up her bike, but all it would take was one out-of-towner or an after-school teenage dare and she'd be out her only means of transportation. She *really* did not need that at the moment, so she clipped her lock on.

As she reached for the brass door handle of the hardware store, her phone vibrated. Her mother's Bitmoji, which looked eerily like her, smiled up from the screen.

TAP

"Hey, Ma."

"Sweetie, could you please tell your father that our chowder does not need more paprika."

Mr. Graham noticed her, so Sistine held up a hand that she'd be right back and moved down the street. Her mom's phone calls were rarely brief.

"Just last week your father decided the chowder needs more paprika. Like we suddenly haven't been making the chowder right all these years."

"Change is good, Muriel. We need to spice it up. Hello, my daughter who abandoned me," her dad said loud enough for Sistine to hear.

Her heart squeezed at the sound of her father's booming voice. The comfort of it was something she hadn't realized she'd missed so much. "Hi, Dad," she said into the phone, even though neither of them was listening. Conversations with her mother were often this way. It was as if being on the phone with Sistine gave her mom the ally she needed to speak her mind. Her older sister Jules referred to it as "using her lifeline," which was a reference to some game show Sistine didn't watch.

Her parents spent so much time together running their business that Sistine imagined many things went unsaid out of sheer exhaustion. Today must be the day to discuss some simmering issue disguised under the veil of paprika.

"Well, I guess now that your father is sixty and lifting weights in the garage, he thinks everything needs more spice."

And there it was, the real issue.

"Ma, I'm going to go so you and Dad can—"

Followed by the giggle she could have also predicted. It was the way every argument or tiff, as her mother put it, ended. Her dad would scoop her mom up in his arms, bury his face in her neck, and make her laugh. Somehow, in the laughter, whatever it was they were arguing about didn't matter. In her entire childhood, Sistine could only remember one time when it took her parents more than a couple of hours to work it out while still serving customers at the Crab Shack, and that time, she later learned, was because of a lie.

77

That time, it had taken her parents three days to make up. Drake and Jules, her older brother and sister, still teased their dad about the Fourth of July weekend he spent on the couch.

Now, after a longer-than-necessary story about her mom's "funny feeling" regarding Drake's new girlfriend who "never goes to the grocery store" and convincing her mother that no, they didn't "all need to be concerned as a family," Sistine ended the call and tried to remember what the heck she was doing before she swiped answer.

Turning back toward the hardware store, she saw Cade standing by her bike and looking so gorgeous that her breath came to a screeching halt before slipping back into its usual in and out. Resisting the urge to pull the scarf from her backpack and yell, "Here, I made you this and I'm sorry I don't have sex anymore and I used you for..."

"Hey," Cade said as she approached, the deep thrum of his voice snapping her out of another odd frenzy.

"Hello. I almost didn't recognize you outside of the Tap House." A smile teased his lips.

"I was going to buy some rope and these tacks I saw the other day."

His eyes went wide and playful. "Should I get my shovel? Rent a van?"

Sistine laughed and knew she'd be knitting again tonight. Cade held the door open and they walked through the narrow aisles to gather her supplies before chatting with Mr. Graham. He apologized for the sweater and when she said she thought he looked great in leather, he blushed.

Sticking the stuff in her backpack, Sistine remembered the scarf but packed the supplies on top as if doing so meant she could shut down everything other than being in the early-morning sun with Cade McNaughton.

When had she started thinking about him past his fun sense of humor and those arms? She'd remembered a few of his stories, but she'd never imagined him the way she was now as they walked toward the park at his suggestion. They discussed the food Javier was making and whether they should have it in the main area near the bar or in the beer garden. Deciding on the beer garden, Cade explained that Boyd had finished the recipe for the summer brew. They were thinking about doing a taste test at the party.

"I meant to ask you the other day—"

"You mean the day I'm now calling threesome backgammon?"

She felt her face flush and didn't bother to hide it. "Yes, that day."

"The day you drilled me, pun intended, about my sexcapades and then bailed without saying goodbye."

"I had to get back to the shop. I left a tip."

He grabbed at his chest. "I feel so cheap, so used."

She knew they were playing, but the truth of it hit her and he must have noticed.

"I'm kidding. Back to your question," he said, saving her embarrassment once again.

"When Boyd asked you about using pecan. How do you remember all your beers? Even the years?" She adjusted her backpack.

Cade shrugged. "I don't know. I remember things. Always have. How did you learn to knit?"

"My godmother Nikki taught me. She's also my mom's best friend. She taught all of us."

"Us?"

"I have an older sister and brother. You met Drake when he delivered your glasses before the Tap House opened."

"Hold up, the guy who saved our grand opening at the last minute, that guy knits?"

She nodded. "He does. I'm better, of course." She looked at her watch as if needing to remind herself casual conversation with Cade while walking through a park midmorning was not her reality. Cade was the guy who owned the local brewery with his brothers. He was brother-in-law to two of her best friends. He was the guy who taught her to play backgammon on a whim, and he was nothing more. If he was, then there wasn't enough knitting in the world to... She needed to get back to her shop.

"Hey, would you like to get dinner?"

She stumbled and he held her arm. Putting her hand on top of his as if to confirm he was there, she allowed herself a moment of having someone at her side and then his question registered.

"I had breakfast already."

When he grinned, she removed her hand and stepped away, mindful that alone suddenly seemed like less than it had only an hour ago.

"I didn't mean right now. I meant some other time. I'd like to take you out... on a date."

They crossed the street back toward the hardware store. She tried to pick up the pace, but he was easily twice her size and kept in step with little effort. Why now, she wanted to ask. She'd been in Petaluma for years and he'd never—she'd never...

She stopped walking and turned to him. "I'm on a juice cleanse. I tried this frozen vegan chickpea creation for dinner the other night and it didn't sit well. So, I'm not eating dinner until I get myself right." Sometimes the TMI her mouth was capable of was staggering.

His expression held as if there was more to her made-up story. If he liked made-up, boy did she have a doozy for him someday. Cade was asking her on a date. She let that little nugget sit in her heart for a minute.

Did he even date women who sometimes forgot to shave? More importantly, with or without her current runaway bus of a life, did she date men for whom the words rippled and yes-one-more-time were invented?

They were standing in the middle of the sidewalk, in the middle of the day. It all seemed perfectly routine, save Cade in front of her, one eyebrow arched over Oasis 5222. Sistine could be witty, even downright funny when she worked at it, but nothing was coming through at the moment. Without witty or clever, she was often left with honesty.

"I lied."

"Okay, about what?"

"About the juice cleanse. I eat all the time."

"Great. So dinner?"

"No."

"I'm trying to follow."

"I know, sorry." She looked up. "Thank you for the invite, but I have... prior commitments."

Cade let out a breath and shoved his hands into his pockets. "Damn. Sorry, I didn't know you were seeing someone."

"I'm not. I meant my shop and... other things." She started walking and Cade was at her side again.

"Besides, even if I didn't have other things, I knit," she said, trying to justify why they would never work even if she wasn't tangled up with the nonknitting things. Why was that again?

"What does that have to do with dinner?"

"It means I'm a knitter. I love socks and I dilute my essential oils with coconut oil because they're too strong by themselves."

"I... don't like socks, but that doesn't seem like a deal breaker. Unless you're like crazy obsessed with them, I think we could still share a meal."

They were finally back at the hardware store. She took off her backpack and unlocked her bike.

"Cade, you're great and I enjoy our end-of-the-bar chats, but I... have soft parts that I like. I ride my bike everywhere, except on rainy days when my hair is uncontrollable, but that's to trick my body into exercise. I do think a strong heart needs maintenance, and that way, I don't have to buy new clothes every year."

"That's a great way to sneak in exercise, and please don't say I'm great when you're rejecting my dinner invite. No guy ever wants to hear the words, 'You're great, but.' That is what you're doing, right? Rejecting me?"

"As nuts as that sounds, yes. Thank you, but I don't have room for anything else."

And I can't start liking you any more than I already do, or I'll have to explain some things about my life and I don't know how to do that.

She tried to help him understand. "I noticed an ink stain at the bottom of my favorite purse. Now, I know you're thinking, how hard is that to wash? But that leads to my washing machine, which I'm all but certain was the first washing machine ever made, and the insane noise it makes on the spin cycle. That's assuming it spins at all and doesn't sit there, tub full of water, sticking its tongue out at me. I have a lot going on and I still can't find the size six needles I know I ordered, and I'm not date ready. I can't remember the last time I waxed anything, or hell—" Her hands were flailing, so she took a breath and tried to step off the crazy train. "Cade, you are great. You're an Aries for crying out loud. But great is inconvenient right now. I needed electricity, so I chose a 'me' over a 'we.' Do you understand?"

"I am... trying. Why does Aries matter again? We're all assholes?"

She eased her bike from the rack. "No, they're a perfectly lovely sign, but they never give up. They crave the chase and I'm saying you need to chase somewhere else. I'm flattered you asked me out, but no."

Walking back toward her shop, she didn't know what else to say.

"Huh." They stopped in front of Knitterly. "Can't say I've ever been rejected quite like this, but okay."

"Have you ever been rejected, period?"

"Oh, yeah. I'm not every woman's cup of coffee, or tea in your case." He smiled and she wondered how that was possible.

"Although, I do try to gauge things, so I don't get too beaten up. I thought there was something between us that we might want to... But you seem happy with your 'me', so I'll be non-Aries and step back." He laughed and she found herself trapped between what she knew she had to do to keep her distance and the certainty she was making a mistake.

"Backgammon lesson on Wednesday?" she asked as she locked her bike in front of her store. Hopefully she could ease things back to where they were before he acknowledged what they were both feeling.

He glanced at her, hesitated, and nodded before walking away. As he crossed the street toward Sift, Sistine wanted to call after him, but June's large, putrid yellow town car that was at least three decades old parked in front of Knitterly, and Sistine was again reminded she did not have the luxury of Cade McNaughton.

Chapter Ten

*C*ade spent the rest of the week tending bar, answering emails from Trick and Aspen, and fielding questions about Henny, Penny, and his new rooster Cocky, who were overnight celebrities. He was having T-shirts made and the feed store asked if Foghorn wanted to do some cross-promotion. Things were going well, but he still couldn't figure out what happened with Sistine.

She didn't want to go out with him, which wasn't all that shocking. He'd meant what he said. He'd been rejected before, but it was the way she turned him down. Why did it seem like she was always running in ten different directions? The electrical in her shop was fixed, but the crease between her eyebrows remained. Maybe there was something Foghorn could do to help drive business to Knitterly, although the idea of knitting and beer was almost as nuts as beer and doughnuts.

He wanted to help, be there for her even if it was only as her friend. And, he would tell her once the awkwardness of asking her on a date dissolved, they weren't all that different. Or maybe they were. Hell, he needed to stick with what made sense.

"Hey, please don't tell me I need a vegan option for Aspen's party," Javier called from the kitchen.

Cade assured him that vegetarian was as far as he needed to go. Javier had vegan angst that made all of them laugh.

Patrick told them Aspen was already up and about, color coding everything in the house, so it seemed like the right time to celebrate. Placing an orange slice on the rim of a glass of beer, Cade noticed the rain tinging off the metal roof of the beer garden followed close by the first roll of thunder.

He was looking forward to the Mother of All Baby Celebrations, as Mase, his nephew, had put it. Princess Hattie already owned all three of her uncles and one extremely cool cousin. They'd gone over yesterday to bring Trick and Aspen groceries. Cade had to admit it was cool helping Wonder Woman and the brother who never seemed to need help.

Hattie was more alert now and the McNaughtons were clearly a family of men because they were stupid when it came to Aspen too. When she stood to go to the bathroom, they all rose and guided her until she finally stopped them at the bathroom door. "Back. You are not coming in here with me."

They'd close tomorrow after lunch and open again for a late dinner crowd. Patrick would lose his mind if they shut the Tap House down for an entire evening. Cade was restocking the bar and smiling at the memory when the front door to the Tap House opened.

He'd managed to play it cool around Sistine despite her shutdown of his dinner invitation. Wednesday's backgammon game started off formal and odd, but by the end, they were joking and almost back to normal. She was due back in again today, although with decorating for the party, he doubted there would be much time for games.

The Tap House had been busy all week, and Cade kept his eyes open for any other smart, adorable knitters who rode a bike, had sexy eyes, and might agree to date him, but it turned out that particular blend was tough to come by.

He'd all but decided that she must not be the one for him if she wasn't even willing to go on one date, when the front door opened and there she was. All of his mental work went right out the window. The woman was in overalls, one leg rolled up. She'd obviously been on her bike in the rain and her hair was dripping in her face. He turned away to hide that he was smiling like a fool as her Converse squished their way toward the bar. When she took off her backpack, dropping it and another bag on one of the stools, he grabbed a stack of bar towels and handed them over while she pushed her hair off her face.

"Downside to riding a bike, eh?"

"Thank you." She wiped her face. "It came out of nowhere. Usually I check the weather and this morning there was a—"

"Twenty-five percent chance, I know."

"If I had a twenty-five percent chance of dating Robert Downey Jr. that would never happen." She kept wiping and then stilled. Cade saw the awkward in her expression when she slid the towel down her face and appeared to mentally kick herself.

"So, Robert Downey Jr. is your type. Good to know. Isn't he a little old for you? And short. He seems kind of short."

Sistine smiled and he was glad for it. He didn't want her to be weird around him. Glued to her every word, he didn't care if she agreed to go out with him or not. He would simply piece together these moments with her until he was satiated.

"What's in the bag this time?"

She hung her coat on the hook and shook her arms to reveal a white blouse with the slightest hint of lace near her neck. His eyes tripped on that lace before he remembered to reel in his attraction. They were intellectual partners and this, even though she had not agreed to a date, was a mature relationship. The lace kept teasing that Cade was a bigger fool than he knew.

"I made garland." She removed a long, knitted strand of flowers in the same yellow, marigold if he remembered correctly, twisted together with bits of shiny stuff and leaves knitted out of a green so vivid they matched his tattoo. She kept pulling. There were yards and yards of garland that looked like something out of a magazine. When she reached the end of one strand, he recognized the rope they'd bought at the hardware store. Unbelievable. Didn't most people pop over to Party City?

Everything she did was a twist on the usual and Cade reminded himself that she didn't want him. Maybe he could ask her out again later when she'd fixed the crease between her brows on her own. He wanted so much more than backgammon. He wanted her opinions, to know her ideas, to know what she did when she wasn't working. Yesterday, he wondered where she got her bike serviced. He was clearly losing his shit.

"That's incredible," he said, helping her lay the strands across the large table at the back of the Tap House.

"Thank you. I thought maybe they could use some of it in Hattie's room. I hate buying things that are thrown away after one use."

Nothing helped ease the need. He kept hoping she'd say something to convince him they had nothing in common.

"Where do you find the time to do all this?" Cade asked, shoving his hands into his pockets to keep from moving a wet strand of hair off her face.

"I don't sleep." She stepped into the closet off the bathrooms and brought out the step ladder.

"I can help you with that."

She held up her hand. "I've got it." She kicked the legs of the ladder open and grabbed the end of one strand before reaching into the pocket of her wet overalls for a box of tacks.

Cade balled his hands and kept them in his pockets. She didn't want his help, didn't want to even share a meal with him.

"So, you don't sleep. Vampire. I had a feeling."

"Is it the pale skin that gave it away?" She secured one end to the beam in the ceiling and stepped down, pushing at her wet hair.

He laughed, and as he did, her eyes went from playful to something... else.

She didn't want a "we." That's what she'd said. She had commitments and wanted what they had: backgammon and shared friends and nothing more.

All of that had been clear until those eyes, he realized now were caramel, changed and her rain-soaked lips parted like she had something to say but couldn't find the word. That might have been the

86

first time he'd seen Sistine at a loss. Commanding himself to get back to work, he nodded and went back to the bar. His signals must be off again because it definitely looked like she wanted more.

Sistine wobbled on the step stool as another clap of thunder shook the Tap House. Sheets of rain swept over the glass roof through the intermittent light show between the beams where she continued hanging the garland. It was good that the party wasn't until tomorrow. Hopefully the weather would settle down by then, although rain, even torrential downpours like this one, were good luck. Aspen and Patrick seemed to make their own luck, so sunshine would work for them too.

Sistine needed all the luck she could get at the moment. Her mature resolve that made her choose not to mix the tangle of her life with the pleasure every moment with Cade promised was slipping. He acted like nothing happened and she wondered if he asked women out all the time. Maybe it was an odds game with him and he'd moved right on to ask any number of women lined up around his bar. Reaching overhead, she let the garland slack a bit and then secured it to the beam with a tack. The industrial lights that normally hung from the beams were softened by her work, and she was filled with love for her friends. That was the joy of making things for people. It was a way of harnessing her feelings into something tangible. She reached up again, forming another loop.

"Sure you don't need some help?" Cade asked, clearing dishes off a table. "It's a lot of work and I'm taller."

"I'm almost done," she said, straining on her tiptoes while nudging her damp sleeve out of the way.

Another clap of thunder, this one louder than the rest, partnered with a full light show from Mother Nature right as Sistine reached to secure her final piece of garland. Up on her toes, one more push at the tack and it held, but as she stepped away, she lost her footing as the stool wobbled on the uneven concrete floor. She managed to avoid falling by balancing her feet like a skateboard, but thunder clapped again and the entire Tap House went dark save the candles still lit on the tables. At the shock of being thrust into darkness, Sistine let go of the step stool and because she'd never been much good at skateboarding, lost her fight with gravity.

Remembering some article she read about staying loose and protecting the head in a fall, she ducked her head into her chest and prepared to meet solid concrete. She had always been clumsy, so tripping, stumbling, and occasionally falling were familiar. Eyes cinched closed, she did what she often did in life—hoped for the best. Feet and arms flailing, she'd managed not to hit a table on her way off the stool, but before the moment of impact with solid ground, she was enveloped by solid muscle.

Last week, Sistine had tripped over a box on her way to pick up the ringing phone. She'd fallen back into the mountain of yarn not yet reshelved. Her butt hit the pillow of rainbow colors and she almost bounced. Alone in her shop, she let the phone go to voicemail and laughed for a good ten minutes, scared for a moment but grateful it was the yarn wall she'd chosen to reorganize instead of the needles.

Cade saving her, she knew it was him even with her eyes still closed, felt nothing like yarn. When her hands clenched his arms, there was no give. He was almost as solid as the concrete floor, but warm. His pulse thrummed beneath her fingers and the now familiar mint of his breath tickled her nose. Distant voices searching for flashlights and more candles barely registered as the rest of her senses returned and his chest moved in a soothing but rapid rhythm.

Sistine opened her eyes to his face, close and illuminated by the candlelight. She touched his cheek, as she had his arm in the park, to again confirm he was there. The roughness of his unshaven jaw seemed to welcome her cold hands and she was again aware of her damp clothes. He met her gaze and panic thinned into relief. He was different in candlelight, his eyes more the muddled colors of a well-worn sweater than the defined strands of new yarn. He held her with strength she knew could crush her, but still her heart charged right at him. She didn't want him to set her down. Didn't care about her shop or Melissa, if anyone was watching them or if wanting Cade was right or wrong. All of her energy languished in the wonder of a man she was now certain she appreciated physically as much as she did his back-gammon skills. He shifted her in his arms and set her on her feet. With his arms now at her waist, his expression was still searching.

"I put almond milk in my tea," she said. One more time, exactly the wrong words to say when a beautiful man was holding on tight.

"Okay. Black's too strong? Are we circling back to diluting our essential oils?"

She nodded, impressed at the common theme she had not no-ticed.

"And." She allowed her hand to explore the curve of his shoulder, the shape of him as she searched for another reason staying in his arms was a bad idea. Carefully, she stepped past the obvious choices because that meant she had to let go. "I have not seen any of your brother's movies. I don't like those kinds of movies."

"You're missing out."

God, the way he looked at her was like a promise. Promise of a good time or promise he'd catch her, Sistine didn't know but in that instant, she'd watch one of those damn action movies if she got to do it with him.

"You are decorated." He touched the stitch work on her overalls, one arm still wrapped around her waist. "And so am I." He gestured toward his tattooed arm.

Her lips were open only enough to keep her lungs working. His breath caressed her ear and his mouth was right there. He was again giving her a path toward a "we." All she had to do was reach out and take it.

"You've been thinking about this."

"I have a hard time giving up on something that seems right. We're not that different, Sistine. Can you see that?"

"I can't see much of anything."

His chest rumbled with laughter as the rain grew louder. She knew there were still a few people scattered throughout the darkness, but the only things clear were his mouth and the weight in his voice she recognized as need. How had he come to need her? More distressing, when had she started not simply looking forward to seeing him, but needing him? Lord, need scared Sistine like not much else. She had no business needing. He wanted the Sistine he thought she was, the woman who ran a successful knitting shop. The woman his brothers' wives hung out with, the quirky Sistine who knitted a sweater for the hardware guy. He didn't want the bumbling, lying mess she was; he didn't even know that woman. Her hands should have listened to her thoughts and pushed away, but without permission, they moved across the front of his shirt and traced the edge of where T-shirt met warm neck.

"Can I kiss you?" he asked softly.

Four words, the formality and simplicity of which completely eased her doubt. She nodded and Cade's hand slid along the back of her neck. He held for a beat before his lips softly took hers as if he might only get one kiss. Sistine didn't know if she'd been so absorbed in her shop or her worry, but she'd never seen him coming. If some-one had told her Cade McNaughton wanted to kiss her in the way currently melting her bones, she would have laughed in their face. And yet, there they were.

Sculpted from head to toe, he was decorated, as he put it, in a way that invited a woman's hands to wander. That would be enough, but he was also inquisitive, funny, and gentle when he surely had the power to command.

Every word left Sistine's mind except one — soft. Like the finest Italian cashmere kind of soft. She couldn't stop touching him, wanting him to touch her. Cade kissed like a poet who instead of sitting at the back table of a coffee shop smoking cigarettes and penning words in a tiny notebook was front and center putting years of prose into action. He was a man Sistine might have dreamed about if she were the sort to dream of men. That was her last thought before his tongue slid past hers one last time and the lights flickered back on.

Chapter Eleven

*C*ade pressed his hand to the small of her back as if to confirm he was indeed kissing Sistine Branch. Her overalls were still damp and the fringe of her hair tickled the tops of his hands holding her face. Her skin smelled like soap and outdoors. When she grabbed his shoulder, bunching the material in her fist, Cade thought he might be in trouble. When she wrapped her arms around his neck and took the kiss deeper, he was lost, unable to find his way back to the fun, spontaneous request for a kiss. Her mouth, her body, and the force of her now seemed destined and dangerous. He wasn't merely kissing her; she was kissing him back, wanting him too, and that realization made his heart pound in his chest.

He had meant to get to know her on an adult, long-lasting level, and yet there he was still kissing her even though the lights were back on and at least a handful of people were surely watching them. He should ease back, regain composure, but he couldn't let go.

Touching her was too good. The way she kissed him was even better. He was ruining his plan. This had nothing to do with mature conversation and everything to do with physical connection, but the taste of her stopped his brain from functioning properly.

She'd returned his kiss, hesitant at first and then with a determination that snatched the breath right out of his chest. His entire body was on alert as Sistine twined her arms around his neck, her lips tugging and nipping in a way that made him moan into her mouth. He shifted her for better access and took over the kiss. He hadn't figured Sistine for the type to take the lead. As her tongue reclaimed the kiss, he couldn't remember why he assumed she'd be timid. She was a business owner, an all-out free spirit in a way he rarely encountered. Knitting was clearly no longer for little old ladies.

"Holy shit." Cade registered his own voice through the fog of lust.

Sistine drew back and must have found his expression amusing. She smiled, and his entire body tightened. Lips raw, her eyes weren't heavy or smoldering. They were shining, playful, and ready for more.

"Are you okay?"

He nodded because it was honestly the only gesture he could manage.

"Sorry. I... enjoy kissing." She looked around, as if the few people left might notice and tattle on them.

"Enjoy? People enjoy the theater, a Forty-Niners game, pizza, lots of people enjoy pizza. That was—"

"Enthusiastic. I know. I've been told." She stepped back, her cheeks flushed. "Now that the lights are back, I should probably—" She tugged at the bib of her overalls. "Eh, I think I'm starting to mildew. I should—"

"Don't." He took her hand and hauled them into the storage closet. "Don't ever apologize for enthusiasm." Locking them in, he took her mouth again, this time prepared to get as good as he gave, if not more. Her body shifted to rest against his and her hands moved over his back. Moments later every inch of his body was ready, which normally led to clothes on the floor and any sturdy surface until neither he nor his partner could stand.

Cade knew how to do lust, how to read a woman's body whether she wanted him to bring her up slow and easy or fast and flying in the space of lunch break. He wasn't arrogant. It simply came down to how he excelled in every area of his life—practice. That and he truly loved women.

Growing up amid an excess of testosterone, Cade always preferred talking with his mom's friends at parties. In school, his friends gave him a hard time for having friends who were girls. Girls liked talking to him, but they didn't want to do what Sistine was so skillfully doing until around his junior year of high school when he got in shape. Growing up, he was "chubby" or "thick," as his dad suggested. So much so that even with Patrick a good two inches taller than him, Cade's nickname was "Big Guy."

It didn't bother him until around thirteen when the great hormone shift sent the boys to one side of the world and girls to the other. Girls paired up with the athletes and the popular guys. Cade liked science back then. He rode bikes with his friends and worked on projects with his dad in the garage. All of this relegated him to the funny chubby guy, which suited him until the football coach wanted him on their defensive line. Cade saw it as a chance to be involved and noticed he was getting in shape. That's when things changed and suddenly girls wanted to be with him. He'd admit it was heady for a while, but the talking stopped. Conversation turned shallow. Once he started working in bars, it got worse.

Sistine eased away, but brushed her lips across his mouth. It should have been the end of the kiss, the conclusion of a hot make-out-in-the-closet moment that allowed them to both come back, but she kept going. Soft kisses across his lips, down his jaw, and around to his ear. Lust mixed with delicate, and Cade knew it was nuts, but he felt worshiped. Her hands traveled down his chest and lower before he carefully took her wrists and held them to the wall on either side of her. He knew himself, and new responsible outlook or not, if she kept inviting him with her touch, he would accept the offer.

Sistine was a mash-up of the girls who used to have lunch with him before they discovered his abs and the women who wanted to climb him like a tree after one smile. It was unnerving. He didn't know it was possible to have both.

She ended the kiss and rested her forehead on his chest.

"Do you think we can have dinner now?" Cade said, surprised at the audible strain in his voice.

"It's not a good idea."

"But this was?"

"I didn't say that. I couldn't control myself."

He could breathe all he wanted now, but that kiss was going to stick. He'd replay the moments with her in his arms, the taste of her lips for weeks. Leave it to Sistine to knock him over one more time.

Sistine had practically attacked him. What happened to previous commitments? That had been such a mature response back before she found herself in his arms. Her mind kept replaying the whole scene from "Can I help you?" to "Can I kiss you?" What was with him and the alluring questions? Why did everything about him have to be so right? Sistine aimlessly walked the aisles of Beasley's Mini-Mart.

She should be home getting ready for her client, but she couldn't settle down. If she'd rented instead of purchasing the building that had an electrical breakdown, maybe wanting Cade would be possible. If she'd waited to hear about the expo before jumping the gun or if she accepted that her shop was failing, maybe she could sleep on Cade's... couch.

So many things could have gone differently and allowed her to simply go to dinner with him, but nothing since she left home had been simple. She was beginning to wonder why. People opened businesses all the time. Why did it seem like she kept stumbling? She stopped in front of the chips and grabbed two bags. Screw the vegetables in her fridge. She'd crossed the line, let him kiss her, and kissed him back. Now she knew what he felt like and couldn't have him. That was a barbecue chips kind of screwup.

People clapped after the lights came back on. She could have stepped back at that point, but no, she'd gone more than willingly into a closet to finish what they'd started. Had he started? Oh, yes. She remembered the question now. The twin tinges of surprise and regret in his eyes only fed the spinning in her stomach. He'd explained that he hoped to "take things slow with her." She didn't catch that last part before they were back at it again like two teenagers after the last person left and he'd locked the front door.

It was as if all the time she'd spent with Cade, every moment of laughter, every exchange, had been sitting in wait for an unexpected rainstorm, a spark, and Dear Sweet Jesus, that tongue. That everything. His hands on her body, the angles and the controlled simmer of him made her crazy. That's what it was.

She paid for the chips and strapped them down in the basket of her bike. If she'd lost her mind in a moment of lust, then there was a chance he had too. Granted, he'd asked her out to dinner again after the kiss, but maybe that was his way of... being polite? Wow, she was even lying to herself now.

It was a kiss, she told herself, licking the barbecue off her fingers. For all she knew, he kissed lots of women like that. There was no need to panic at this point. She could certainly control her urge to kiss him again.

Sistine grabbed her bag of groceries and entered through the front door of Knitterly. She locked the door behind her and collapsed onto one of the front room chairs. Sometimes she thought about what it would be like to give up. She could sell off the building and Knitterly's inventory, close the doors, and work at Sift or maybe the bookstore. Nowhere was it written she needed to own her own business, pull her hair out trying to make things work, stay ahead of the trends, and deal with a piece of Petaluma history. Maybe she could find a roommate.

Because that had worked out so well the last time, some ugly, resentful voice whispered. Sistine's imaginings and reality rarely reconciled.

In hindsight, things had started out so simple. Another roommate match that grew into a budding college friendship never meant to survive the trials of growing up and apart. Melissa was an explosion Sistine needed at the time, but while she thought they might be friends forever, they hadn't survived past graduation.

Melissa moved away and once the lawyers got involved, what used to be simple and fun turned into complicated and downright awful.

Their relationship dissolved fast. Sistine hadn't realized it at the time, but she never once missed Melissa. Not in the way one should miss a friend, even a friend who had brilliantly screwed her over.

Sistine blossomed, as her mother enjoyed saying with fluttering hands, after college. She cut her long hair and finally invested in a small collection of tennis shoes instead of the heels Melissa always insisted made her legs look longer. In effect, Sistine found her preferences without her friend's constant commentary and relaxed into herself.

For her part, Melissa moved to DC. Based on the last photo in some newspaper, she was as shiny as ever, her teeth still perfect. Not that Sistine googled the DC mover and shaker when she was feeling beaten up by her own life. That would be pathetic.

Besides, she had almost managed forgiveness and acceptance when she'd heard from Melissa a month before her electricity shut off. When she transferred money to her account in under an hour after Sistine texted her, all was forgiven. What did that say about her? Sistine had never imagined herself materialistic, even in college, but lights were important.

Rolling up the bag of chips and hiding them under her register, she walked back to her apartment. She couldn't work for anyone else. This shop was her place, this city was her home. Her feelings for Cade were new. New things fell apart all the time.

Although, that kiss was not going to wait until her side job went away, she admitted to herself as she crawled into bed. She hadn't thought about how long she'd be willing to keep Melissa's secret, if that was the right term for what she was currently doing to make money. The electrical work was done, and she had enough to pay for her patio. What was her plan for wrapping things up? She wasn't even sure if wrapping Melissa up was possible or if there'd ever be a way out.

Whatever her options were, that kiss was a right now type of kiss. It was a kiss that promised things. She'd have to tell Cade. Tell him that she was... She stuffed the pillow over her face because suddenly she had no idea what she was doing, let alone how to explain it to anyone.

Chapter Twelve

The day of the party, Cade held the Tap House door open as Thad brought in a cake that looked like something out of a fairy tale. A tree, tiny flowers, it was unlike anything Cade had seen at Sift.

"That's a cake?" Cade asked as Thad set it down on the center of the table.

"Right?" he said, brushing his hands on his jeans. "She's been working on it for two days straight."

"Unbelievable."

"Thanks. I'm happy we got it here in one piece." Vienna circled the table to review her work.

"How did you get the frosting to—"

Sistine walked through the door holding wrapped presents and balloons. She was wearing a black blouse, no sweater, and a white-and-black skirt. Her arms were bare amid what looked like ruffles and some sort of embroidery at her shoulder. He had not meant to stop speaking, but it was as if kissing her had flooded his brain on sight and all other functions were momentarily turned off.

Setting the presents down and tying the balloons to one of the tables, she joined them, kissing Vienna and hugging Thad. She smiled and nodded in Cade's direction but then focused on the cake.

"Wow. You've outdone yourself," she said.

Vienna glanced from Sistine to Cade but said nothing at first. She bumped Thad, whose eyes then traveled the same path.

"You're blushing," Vienna said after what looked like a visual conference with her towering fiancé.

Sistine put her hands to her cheeks. "Am I?"

Vienna shook her head. "Not you. Him." She tilted her head toward Cade and it took him a few beats to realize she was talking about him.

"Sorry?"

"Don't sorry me. You were midsentence until our beautiful knitting goddess walked in, wearing a killer ensemble I might add."

"Thank you." Sistine gave a little curtsy and touched the embroidery on her blouse, which Cade now realized was two birds on a branch. Again, where did she find this stuff? More importantly, was the urge to touch her, to run his hands along the bare skin of her arms, to kiss her all over again ever going to ease to normal? Vienna obviously didn't notice his dilemma or didn't care. She continued her interrogation.

"Anyway, you straight-up stopped speaking and now you're blushing."

"I don't blush."

Vienna nodded. "You do now."

Sistine was super intent on the cake and no help at all, so Cade looked to Thad for some male support.

Their fire chief, Aspen's brother and men among men, shook his head. "You're screwed, man. She's on the scent and you are blushing. Pull it together."

Cade leveled a glare. "Thanks."

Thad laughed and shrugged.

Vienna circled behind Sistine and took her gently by the shoulders, then forced them both to face Cade. "So, why would Cade stop speaking when you walked in, sis. Any ideas?"

Sistine swallowed and shook her head, saying nothing, which was a good strategy had they been dealing with anyone other than Vienna.

The woman baked for people early in the morning. She'd seen people at their worst and during their happy times too. Birthdays, break-ups, weddings, and parties. They all wanted her, and that meant she knew everything.

She leveled a stare at Sistine. "Don't make me call the rest of The Bitches over here. Why is Cade blushing?"

Sistine looked like she had something distasteful in her mouth, but then her eyes locked on Cade's and the edges of her mouth crept up.

"I have no idea. Maybe he thinks I look nice."

"I do," he said, not bothering to break eye contact or to care who noticed.

"Or maybe he's excited to celebrate his sister-in-law."

"I am." He grinned at the thought of Hattie and hoped Aspen would be surprised.

"Or maybe," Vienna took over, "according to Ray, who works with Thad, the lights went out last night at the Tap House and when they came back on, you and Cade were not playing backgammon."

"That," Cade said, unable to control his smile when Sistine met his eyes. "That's definitely it. You look beautiful by the way. Nice isn't enough. The birds are on point."

Her smile grew, and she tilted her head in a playful way he'd never noticed before. "Mason teach you that expression?"

Cade nodded. Thad, appearing not nearly as invested in who kissed who, joined Boyd at the bar.

Before Vienna had a chance to dig further, the guests of honor arrived, and the Tap House exploded with applause and cheers as Patrick and Aspen made their way through the crowd.

Sistine was gone in a flurry of celebration.

The party dwindled before happy hour. Cade and Boyd cleaned up the beer garden and kissed the tiny foot of their sleeping niece one more time before Cade put on his apron and slipped behind the bar.

Sistine sat at the end of the bar flipping through Cade's camera at images of the party. There was a close-up of Aspen's face, her eyes wide with surprise and laughter. It was such a beautiful reflection of her friend boldly entering a new phase in her life that Sistine instinctively held her hand to her heart.

There was a shot of Patrick, glass raised, toasting and thanking his friends and family for "making the most special woman feel even more so." Thad and Vienna laughing, June and Gracie holding the baby, and Mr. Graham in his leather vest handing his wife a flower from the center of the table. Boyd and Ella helping serve cake. Bri drying her eyes and clapping at the same time. One of Cade talking with Mason, baby Hattie on his shoulder as if right at home in the center of so much love. He'd taken several pictures of Sistine too. Close up when they'd stolen a few minutes together and several of her laughing with her friends. It was different seeing herself through Cade's lens. She was more interesting, prettier, and somehow less tired in the images he captured of her.

The happy hour crowd began taking their seats at high-top tables and at the bar. Max had offered to tend bar that night, but Sistine heard Cade tell him at the party to "head home and spoil Patti." Sistine learned that Max's wife was also pregnant. They'd been trying for a few years and after some tough times were hopeful. Sistine was constantly amazed at Cade's ability to empathize with people. She wondered if being a bartender had brought that out in him or if he was a great bartender because of who he was.

Glancing up from the pictures, she watched Cade serve two women sitting center bar who had the familiar melted-butter look in their eyes. While she was certain he enjoyed the attention, she'd never seen him exchange more than flirtatious banter. She'd heard that he dated, a lot, but she had also heard from Aspen that Lauren had been the one to break things off after six months.

The woman in the green dress extended her hand to touch Cade's arm and they both laughed. Sistine wasn't naturally flirty, nor was she the smooth woman men went out of their way to pick up in bars, get into their beds, or marry even. She was a sporadic mix of cute and spastic. Back in college, Melissa had done her best to sexify Sistine, but ultimately, the girl who used to play in the bait tanks on her dad's fishing boat won out.

The other woman wore a purple off-the-shoulder angora sweater that Sistine wondered if she made before catching herself. Rarely did women make their own sweaters and while she knew she was judging, she would bet this particular woman only wore designer brands.

They must have been discussing Cade's hair because both took turns feeling Cade's newly buzzed head. Sistine tried to focus on the pictures, but if it was clear Cade had cut his hair, what was the point of touching it? As if summoned from the underworld, Melissa's voice popped into her head. *Who the hell would pass up a chance to touch that man?*

The purple-sweater woman pursed her lips in a perfect pout and flashed a smile that all but guaranteed fun before Cade turned from them back to the register. Melissa would have been impressed, and if she were honest, so was Sistine. She knew the time and effort that went into being what men like Cade wanted.

Heck, she'd spent more time in the details of what men and women wanted than she'd ever care to admit. Both women were gorgeous and if it wouldn't have been super awkward, she would have offered a high five and "well done, ladies."

Sistine never understood why women didn't unite. Why some spent time tearing others down all in the name of male attention. If women spent less time in some invisible competition, they could run the world. Melissa used to enjoy "assessing the competition," as she put it when they would go out, which was Thursday through Saturday back in the day. She was often the one pulling down the hem of her all-too-tight dress and exclaiming, "This isn't a horse race."

She was never drawn to the guy everyone else wanted. Her types sat out parties and went on to get master's degrees.

Melissa liked to counter with "Type has nothing to do with a good time."

Urging herself back to her present, Sistine returned to the pictures, flipping through two incredible shots of Cade with all his brothers and their father.

"Hey, dude, you work out?" Some man sitting two seats down from the gorgeous women said, slapping his hand on the bar.

Cade smiled and set three beers on Tina's tray.

"I'm serious. What d'ya lift?"

The man's T-shirt was entirely too tight and Sistine was a bit mesmerized by the mole over his ear. It looked like a raindrop was stuck to his face.

Cade plucked more orders from the printer. "There's no way I lift more than you do, man."

The guy nodded, stood next to his girlfriend, and lifted his skin-tight T-shirt to reveal his abs. Sistine glanced over at the band to keep from laughing.

"That's a shit-ton of work. Well done." Cade served a salad and a grilled cheese that the two women shared and then met the fist bump of the guy who had still not put his shirt back down.

"Your turn." He finally covered up. "My girl here thinks you may be in better shape."

At that, Cade laughed and served the matching Hawaiian shirt guys. "I don't show and tell. Can I get you two something to eat? Coffee?"

"Aw, come on," the gorgeous women purred after sipping their cocktails.

Cade turned to the register and when his back was to the bar, Sistine could see him rolling his eyes. This was ridiculous, and she was filled with an unexpected urge to rescue him.

"Excuse me, sir," she said, leaning up from her stool.

He smiled, his back still to the bar, but from her seat, she could see the grin. He glanced at her. She waved and he walked over to her.

She was standing on the metal rim of her stool so she could speak at his ear before she lost her nerve. "Does this happen often?"

He shook his head.

"I mean, at the knit shop I get this sort of behavior all the time, but here at a nice neighborhood brewery, I was not expecting this kind of blatant objectification." She plopped herself back down onto the barstool and was rewarded when he laughed.

"First threesomes and now abs. I need to look into knitting lessons."

"You have no idea. All those… balls of yarn." She fought back the laughter in her throat. "If you talk with me for a couple more minutes, it looks like glistening abs over there is about to redirect. His girlfriend wants to dance."

"Glistening. Good word, descriptive." Cade moved to look, but she touched his cheek. Warm. "Don't you know anything about surveillance? Never look over."

"Do you know about surveillance?"

"No, but I read a lot."

"About surveillance?"

"Not specifically but crime novels. I love a good murder followed by a stakeout."

"I swear, every time you sit down at my bar, I learn something new, Sistine."

"Me too," she said and tried to dial back the beer-buzz enthusiasm.

"Yeah, like what?" He leaned into her.

"Like you don't pull your shirt up."

"I do not. Hopefully that guy doesn't either when he's sober. Alcohol does strange things to people."

She had to agree.

"You'd probably make more tips. The women over there seem awfully interested in what's under your"—she craned her neck—"'Beer: because good stories don't start with a salad' shirt."

"I'm not interested in tips." He grinned. "And, I don't charge to take off my clothes."

Sistine's swallow of beer went down the wrong pipe and she coughed. A hacking grandma cough. Perfect. She patted her chest.

Cade chuckled before taking her hand and kissing the top. It was chaste, but the comfort and ease with which he touched her now made her stomach flutter. He'd certainly kissed more than her hand before, so it wasn't the kiss, it was being with him in this new and familiar space.

Before she could overthink it, Sistine decided to enjoy the new. How often did a grown person get butterflies? Less and less, she imagined, so she was grateful for the flutter and watched him return to work with an uncontrollable grin. The two women were now leveling death stares in her direction.

The one in the purple sweater scrunched her face in that bitch way Sistine knew from years with Melissa.

"Are those birds on your blouse? Seriously?" She giggled and sipped her beer.

Sistine touched one of the embroidered birds at her shoulder to protect a blouse she loved. There it was—that woman-against-woman poison. She channeled Melissa if only to protect her bird blouse.

Tossing her head back in a fake laugh, she stood from the bar. "They are birds. Are those your actual boobs in your blouse? Seriously?" She mimicked her voice.

Cade glanced over, but was quickly drawn away again.

At the gasps and other nasty words from the women, Sistine walked out of the bar. She'd barely pedaled out of the parking lot and felt bad. She didn't speak that way, but she was tired of being pushed around. Usually, she made a point to defuse bitchiness, but that had been a blatant insult after the woman saw Cade's kiss. Sistine wasn't about to let another woman make her small while Melissa was already doing such a bang-up job in that department.

Chapter Thirteen

Cade woke up the next morning with nothing to do and nowhere to be for the first time since they'd started building the Tap House. Max, his new relief bartender, was handling opening and the lunch crowd. He was hired so Cade could have a life, as his brothers put it. Since Max started, Cade had had more time to work on some projects around his house. Recently he'd been building a table for his backyard and had planted dino kale in his garden, compliments of Pamela, Tina's wife.

The blender stopped, and he poured his smoothie into a mason jar. His brothers teased him that he was turning into Martha Stewart and now with the extra time off, he was starting to believe them. He needed the gym and he needed it now before he started making his damn bed and cleaning the gutters.

Rinsing out the mason jar and willing himself to leave it right there in the sink instead of putting it in the dishwasher, he put on a sweatshirt and grabbed his helmet and keys.

The first quarter that Foghorn made a profit and it seemed like they would be around longer than a year, Cade traded in his old Triumph for the Harley Dyna Super Glide he now rode. He'd splurged for the custom handlebars, and the bike was another extension of his personality. Much to his mother's disapproval, he'd ridden a motorcycle since he was eighteen. He wasn't the type to zip through traffic or display his need for speed. He wasn't compensating for anything. He simply liked riding a bike—the weather on his back and the immediacy of everything when he was on the road. Once, over dinner, he swore to his parents he was a better driver because of his bike. They weren't buying it, but he knew it was true.

Following an hour and a half of getting his butt handed to him by Myles who was Cade's trainer and ex-military, Cade had new appreciation for the word "enough." As soon as feeling came back to his legs, he took a quick shower. He needed to hit the grocery store and to pick up some wood Graham's hardware had ordered for him to expand the chicken coop.

It was a gorgeous day and he wasn't feeling the grocery store. There was no way he was getting the wood home on his bike, even if his order had arrived. Having rationalized his way out of his remaining have-to list, he thought about Sistine and her quick exit from the party after the stare down from the two women at the bar. He couldn't imagine she was intimidated by much, but maybe he needed to ask.

Maybe the whole scene was keeping her from going out with him. Granted, knitting and drinking were on opposite sides of the adult recess field, but the Tap House wasn't a typical bar. Besides, she hung out there and until they'd opened the place back up for the dinner crowd, there'd been family, friends, and an incredibly cute baby. Telling himself he was simply checking on Sistine and not that he wanted to see her, he headed toward Knitterly.

Cade parked his bike in front and looked in the window of her shop. He didn't see Sistine at first until he caught a flash of yellow movement and realized she was lying on the floor. His heart jumped, but when he craned his neck, he realized she was fine. Eyes open, wearing bright yellow shoes, she stared up at the ceiling of her shop. He knocked gently and she sat up. Her hair was tied off her face today. He wondered how many times he would need to see her before her outfits started to repeat. Did she ever wear the same things the same way? He'd seen the narwhal sweater a couple of times, but everything always looked different. A new color of pants or a skirt, something clipped in her hair or on her sweater.

She got up off the floor, smoothed the scarf holding her hair, and adjusted the sweater that had fallen off one shoulder. She was so easy to want now that he was paying attention. Appearing a bit apprehensive, she smiled and pushed open the door.

He walked into the blue morning light and lavender scent of her shop. She stood, hands clasped tightly in front. They'd progressed past backgammon and she seemed unsure of her next move. Sistine locked the door behind him.

Suddenly unclear of his own strategy, Cade went with the first thing that came to mind. He went to the spot on the floor and lay down. After a moment, she joined him, both of them staring up at the light-strewn branches hanging from her ceiling.

"You left last night without saying goodbye," he said, more than aware of her body next to his.

"I needed to get back. Keith added these when he redid the electrical. I hung the branches on the ceiling when I first designed my shop, but now they twinkle."

"Is that why we're lying on the floor? Taking in the new twinkle?"

"I suppose. I lie on the floor at least once a month."

"I can see why. I like it down here."

When she turned to face him, Cade stayed, eyes to the ceiling for a minute, hoping to collect himself before taking in the image of Sistine's lovely face as she lay on the floor next to him. He took a breath and looked over. Her shoulder had fallen out of an oversized sweater in a pale, almost white blue. Bits of the same color were in the scarf on her head. She didn't have any makeup on, the blank canvas making her eyes and her lips more prominent. She was a washed-down and maybe a little tired version of the Sistine he knew from the Tap House. He pictured her routine. Did she make smoothies or toast? Finding he liked mornings with her, he wanted to know.

They said nothing for several breaths.

Sistine cleared her throat. "Good morning."

"Good morning, Sistine." He reached between them and took her hand. Her fingers were delicate or his hand was clumsy. He couldn't decide which.

"Why the sudden interest?" she asked. "I'm not hookup material and you're not exactly looking to make waffles before dropping our little towheaded children off here on your way to work." She was still turned to him. "Or maybe you are now. Is that it? New haircut, knitting shop girlfriend?"

Cade started counting the lights, hoping for something charming and clever to pop into his head. Something that would change the direction of the conversation because when she put it that way, he sounded absurd. A guy didn't wake up one morning and decide to take his life in a different direction, or did he? Why not? People changed their lives all the time. At first, he may have been drawn to her because she was the opposite of where he'd been, but now they were lying together on the floor, her shoulder to his shoulder. He didn't want to leave; he wanted more, wanted to take her out, make her laugh, take her to bed at that last moment when neither of them could stand it one more second. If waffles were all it took, he'd buy a waffle iron after work. But while he was working a checklist of ways to legitimize his life, he knew there would be work. The waffles were a damn metaphor.

"I like you. I like talking with you. I look forward to seeing you and I liked kissing you."

"I like you too."

He squeezed her hand. "You know the key to a great kiss?"

Sistine closed her eyes. "Please don't tell me."

"Why not?"

"I'll Google it."

"Nah, Google is sterile. Everyone—especially guys—makes a big deal about sex and it is the big show, but kissing can be more intimate, don't you think?"

What the hell was happening? She thought she'd figured him out. She was a novelty for his new image. It made sense after the Instagram embarrassment. Ask the knitting woman out. What could be safer, right?

She'd planned to call him on it. Tell him that while she was flattered to be part of his plan, she preferred to go back to the way things were. Her sitting at his bar, talking sexy things, and him flirting with other women. Sure, he'd kissed her, which was a twist considering his new cleaned-up image, but she'd fallen into his arms and it had been raining. All of that could be explained away as lust.

But now he was at her shop and lying with her on the rug she'd loomed with her own hands. He was as gorgeous and genuine as he was behind that bar or holding his new niece in the hospital. She didn't need all these extra pieces of him.

Who looked that good early in the morning? Didn't the man need to warm into the day like the rest of the world? She would have appreciated at least some dark circles under his eyes.

And here she was, calling him out, poised to put an end to this little fling and get back to backgammon and business, and he surprised her with the I-like-you card. No one simply said they liked someone anymore. Nor did they ask for a kiss. People took what they wanted and hid their desires behind sarcasm and games.

Men, in Sistine's experience, did not hold a woman's hand under twinkling branches and plainly state their feelings. Not charming, beautiful men who ran tap houses and had tattoos and a killer wink. Those men were trouble or a great one-night stand. All of this would be so much easier if he could stick with sexy bad boy bartender.

Her mind paused, and her heart took over when she faced him and found he was already looking at her. Horizontal Cade was even more enticing than Storage Closet Cade.

"Did you know that I have chickens?"

"I... real chickens?"

He nodded. "Henny, Penny, and my rooster, Cocky."

"I thought those were made-up mascots for Foghorn."

"You're obviously not following our social media. Did you read my blog post? If you're not a big reader, there are three pictures of them on Instagram. I watched this YouTube video on Instagram tips and apparently I need to pick a filter and color scheme. It's more pleasing to the eye."

She couldn't help but laugh. "Where did you get the chickens?"

"My neighbor. I bought Henny and Penny first, but then he brought over Cocky a couple weeks ago and said I could have him. He didn't realize roosters crowed at all hours of the day, not only in the morning. His wife Sandy informed him it was her or the rooster."

"He chose well."

"He did. So, now it's the four of us at my house. I take care of them and they give me the best eggs I've ever tasted. And bonus, they fertilize my two fruit trees and my vegetable garden."

"You don't cook. Please do not tell me you cook."

"I don't cook, but I like smoothies and salad, so now I grow my own. I make a mean scrambled egg, but that's where my cooking skills end."

"Thank God."

They both looked back up at the lights.

"Why are you telling me about your chickens?"

He squeezed her hand and brought it to his lips. "I was thinking that our... What did you call our kids?"

"Towheaded?" She crossed her legs at her ankles.

"That's blond, right?"

She nodded.

"I think my hair was lighter when I was younger, so blond is likely. Anyway, I was thinking our kids could help with the chickens in the morning before I drop them off at your shop. Would that work for you?"

She laughed. "One of us will have to learn how to make waffles."

"Did you know you almost close your eyes when you laugh?"

She nodded again and felt a lump in her throat. She was so tired, and there he was offering to make their imaginary kids waffles and introduce them to his chickens.

"I can't believe you don't follow us."

"I thought I did. I'll have to check. Do you follow me?"

"I... am not sure." He grinned. "I'll check too. Do you have a blog?"

She untangled her hand from his. "For my shop?"

"Sure, you know, the life of a knitter?"

She sat up. "Do people truly want to read that?"

"Probably. At least a few people out there are reading about beer and doughnuts."

"What's your latest one?"

"Perfect beers for lazy days."

"You are turning into a social media mogul."

He laughed and sat up too.

"Did you know your tongue touches your teeth when you laugh?"

He nodded and there they were now, sitting in the center of her shop like two people on a picnic.

"Is it the bar scene? Is that why you won't go out with me? After the party, those women at the bar."

"There are often women at your bar, Cade."

"Right, but they don't sit at the end of the bar like you do, and they definitely aren't there for my sparkling conversation and back-gammon skills."

"They want your body."

"Sometimes."

"And you want theirs."

He let out a breath. "Wow, that is a lot of yarn."

"It's my Wall of Yarn," she said in a booming announcer voice she hadn't used since she was a kid. Drake and Jules liked to play WWF wrestlers and Sistine was the announcer.

What the hell? Why?

Cade chuckled. "Sounds epic."

"It is. I'm proud of the yarn."

"Did you pick all of those out or is there like a standard yarn stock?"

"Are you changing the subject?"

"Trying." The corner of his mouth quirked in that way that warmed the back of her neck.

"Okay, well, some women shop for shoes, some shop for makeup or purses. I buy yarn."

Cade nodded. "Lots of blue."

"I'm partial to blue and neutrals. You can never have enough shades of neutral, especially 90/10 cotton blend, you know?"

"I don't, but I'll take your word for it. How do you know which color to pick?"

"Sometimes it's project driven, but usually I choose my color based on my mood."

"Lots of moods."

"You have no idea."

"I'd like to know."

Their eyes locked, the sun filling Sistine's front window now and washing out the twinkle of the branches. She lay back down.

"I have in the past," he said after joining her back on the floor. "To answer your question about my body. I have wanted and been wanted in the past."

"But now your only desire is to lie on the floor of my knitting shop and hold hands?"

His expression grew uncharacteristically serious. "Is that why you turned me down? The scene and women who might not be wearing sweaters?"

"That would be awful if that was why I wouldn't go out with you. You clearly love what you do and the women in your bar are as entitled to have as good a time with their hot bartender as they are in my crochet class."

"Okay. But you don't want to go out with the hot bartender?"

"Don't women drive you nuts sometimes?"

"Yes, yes they do," he said.

"Let's take those two women in the bar who asked if I had birds on my blouse. They'd barely noticed me until you kissed my hand and then they had to rip on my blouse. One of my favorites, by the way."

"It is a good one."

"See, that's the problem with women. The Jimmy Choo wearers take issue with the Converse women, and the jeans and T-shirt women rip apart the tiny dresses. When it's all a matter of working what's true for each of us. When I was in college, Melissa was a dance minor. She walked around our apartment all the time half-naked, and when we went out, she rocked the tiny dress. She was the most comfortable-in-her-skin person I'd ever met and probably still is."

"Who's Melissa?"

What was she doing? It was as if her subconscious was edging her toward honesty. There was no reason for her to ever mention Mel's name, and yet there she was.

"My roommate in college."

"And you're not close anymore?"

"Why would you say that?"

"You said she probably still is. If you were still friends, you'd know, right?"

"True. Well, she lives in Washington DC. She's... different. We grew apart." Sistine concentrated on the snarled tangle of the branches. Over, under, twist. Cade cleared his throat and she snapped back. "What were we talking about again? Oh, right. Why is what a woman wears some type of commentary on who she invites into her bed or how many times?"

He had that look men often got when they weren't certain where something was going, but there were few things that set her off more than women messing with other women.

"At the same time, if I wear birds on my blouse, why do people assume I'm not up for frantic wall sex with the hot bartender? My birds are a joke because those women chose push-up bras. See what I mean?"

When she faced him, his mouth was hanging open. "Can we go back to the wall sex? And, am I said bartender? Because I like the birds. Love them actually."

She sat up again. "I'm serious. Men wear out-of-the-hamper flannels and that's hot. A guy in a suit, he's hot too. What the hell can a man wear that means he's easy or giving it away?"

"A see-through shirt." Cade stood up and offered his hand to Sistine. "Like mesh, or anything made out of rubber. Plastic, plastic is a no too. I don't want to be in that guy's bed."

"You're funny. I'm not afraid of women like Lauren or the women who come into the Tap House. I turned down your dinner invitation because I had a lot going on. I didn't plan on kissing you or enjoying it so much. I was thinking about my shop and not much else."

"Was? Past tense?"

She nodded and ignored both her racing heart and her whispering mind. She wanted to go on a date with him, wanted the feeling of hopeful and fun. She'd go as far as telling herself she deserved Cade if she didn't know expectations led to disaster. So, while she wasn't entitled to him, she wanted a date. One night of fun and feeling special instead of the shoulder-creeping sense she was in over her head.

"You lay down on the floor with me and held my hand. I'm different now."

"Me too. I wasn't really into you until those branches."

She laughed. "Still funny."

"You should see me on a date. I'm downright magical."

"I'd like that."

"Seriously? How about dinner?"

She nodded.

"Great. Tomorrow."

"That's... wow, soon."

"I don't want you to change your mind."

She grinned. "I'm not going to change my mind, but you need to text me. If you don't leave now, you'll be surrounded by a group of twentysomethings, some of whom you may know or even have dated, who are arriving for Knit and Chop."

"I don't date nearly as much as people think."

She crossed her arms and held her comment.

"Fine, I no longer date as much as people think."

Sistine snickered.

"What is Knit and Chop?"

"Lunchtime knit class. We bring in chopped salads and work on basic skills."

"Great idea. What kind of salad do you like?"

"Oh, no. I do not partake in the green stuff. Although I did recently buy a head of lettuce. It's still in my tiny fridge."

"In your tiny apartment?" He nodded toward the adjoining door.

"The very one. I should show you the new patio. There's a fountain." Sistine realized she was bursting to share with him.

She'd shown people the courtyard. Bri stopped by yesterday after work. Vienna had come over right as they were finishing up. People she cared about in her life had seen the patio, but she wanted to share it with Cade, which was new. Holding hands and allowing someone into her excitement was definitely new.

Following a lengthy discussion about her succulents, he kissed her by the fountain, the tinkling sound of water and the man she had no business falling for ruined her new patio forever. Every time she walked out there now, she'd think of him. Even after things fell apart and it was only a matter of time. Desperation or not, no one liked feeling used. Sistine knew that from personal experience.

By the time he kissed her again when they had walked back into the shop, she had convinced herself another way was possible. She'd simply stop now that her electrical work was paid off. It's not like this was the mafia. She'd text Mel and say she couldn't do it anymore. Right, that's what she was going to do, and she'd be guilt free to date Cade all she wanted.

His last kiss should have been a simple goodbye, but he was so early-morning clean and male that before she could remind herself to behave, she grabbed the front of his shirt and hauled him away from the front window of her shop. When his back hit the wall of beginner books and crochet needles, she kissed him with desperation she rarely let surface. A growl sounded low in his chest as his hands fisted in her hair, sending her bumblebee barrette flying before she practically climbed him.

When the front door jingled, she jumped back and adjusted her sweater. "This doesn't count as the date. I'm expecting big things from you, Cade McNaughton," she whispered.

"Is that so?" His brows danced as his smile grew lethal.

"Not what I meant. I'm intrigued by all the substance behind the McNaughton magic."

"Surprised I'm more than a pretty face?"

"I am."

"Excellent. I love being more."

"More what?"

He shrugged. "Anything. More anything, I guess." He nodded at the women filing in with brown bags and bent to pick up Sistine's clip.

She fully expected him to leave without acknowledging they'd been plastered against the crochet section, but he put the clip in her hand and kissed her on the cheek.

"I'll text you," he said softly in her ear and Cade McNaughton, master of the Tap House and hot as hell by anyone's standards, bowed his head like a kid who'd secured his first date ever and walked out of her shop.

Chapter Fourteen

*L*auren's perfume wafted in before Cade glanced up from pouring beer and found her, arms splayed out on his bar like a picture frame for her breasts. He thought about collapsing on the floor and feigning an attack of some kind, but if she was the same ex who broke up with him because he didn't understand the "impact she was meant to have on the world like Tyler did," she would leave him writhing on the floor. After taking a picture and hashtagging the hell out of it first, of course. Mulling the caption over in his head while he handed Tina her drinks, a smile tugged at the edges of this mouth.

This guy was so excited to see me he collapsed.

#hotflash #desperateforattention #imnotleavinguntilhesreallydead.

"What can I get you, Lauren?"

"You didn't call. Not even a text. I took the picture down. No thank you?" The woman didn't undress him with her eyes, she ripped the clothes to shreds.

"Rumor has it you and Magic Fingers got back together. That's why it came down."

"Pfft. You can't believe everything you hear."

Cade raised a brow. "Truer words."

"Let's see what your funny little phrase is today." She scanned his chest. "This weekend, I've decided to do a juice cleanse. And by juice, I mean beer." She giggled that jingly way that made her boobs bounce to the edge of her blouse, and he wondered if she practiced that in the mirror. "That's a good one."

"Thanks. What'll you have?"

"I like your Insta. Noticed you have quite a following." She sat down.

Christ. Where was a packed bar when he needed one?

"It's Foghorn's Instagram. It's business."

"So is mine."

"Interesting. What is your business?"

"I'm an influencer."

Cade grabbed a ticket off the computer and set two glasses on the bar.

"Do you know what that is?"

"I do not."

"I'm in the business of people wanting to be me. People send me stuff, and I make it all look good."

"Interesting. Good luck with that. Are you here for something or just dropping by for a chat?" He felt bad for a second that he wasn't his normally friendly self, but the woman was a double shot of crazy.

"I'm here for you."

For not the first time since he'd met Lauren, Cade was baffled that she'd been the one to break things off. Why had he not noticed they were nothing alike? Was Lauren just another accessory, like his bike? Had he been that stupid and shallow? He exhaled.

"Here's the deal, Lauren. You had me, remember? And then you dumped me and then you posted your little picture of me sleeping, naked, on your Instagram. I guess if I were in high school I might find that flattering, but high school is over."

"Babe, there was nothing little about that picture."

"Thank you. I've already heard that one at least a dozen times from my brothers and customers, so much appreciated. I didn't call you and didn't text because I'm trying to pretend it didn't happen."

"Is the yarn lady helping you with that?"

He shook his head, wondering how she knew about Sistine, but not wanting to ask.

"My sister takes her little salad and string class. She saw you there and you were... kissing the weird knitting lady. Seriously? Are things that rough?"

"Watch it."

"Ooh, someone has a crush."

Henny had gotten stuck in the coop that morning. Cade rescued her and had the crap pecked out of his hand for his trouble. This felt like that, but worse because at least he loved Henny. Damn it, he thought he'd recognized one of Sistine's knitting students. Meeting Lauren's wide eyes, he laughed.

"This is nuts. Shouldn't you be preoccupied with making people want to be you?"

"That's why I'm here." She pursed her lips as if she couldn't stop posing. "I thought we could get back together. Combine our followers."

"Huh. Well, as fun as that sounds, I am going to be thirty-three tomorrow and I already know what I want to be when I grow up. So, thanks for the offer, but I have customers."

"You know what?" She stood and adjusted her blouse. "I'm going to give this some time. You'll miss me and realize we're still a hot item. Now that you're on board with Insta, we could be a power couple."

Cade didn't respond and excused himself to give out menus and take drink orders at the other end of the bar.

"I meant what I said in that post, Cade."

"That you miss my ass?" His back was to her as he typed in the drinks.

"Yes. Come on, baby."

When Cade turned around, he felt like one of the gazelles in the *National Geographic* videos Meg, his sister-in-law, liked to post.

"Great. I'll let you know if it starts missing you."

"It will."

Cade started to laugh and bent to get some more coasters. If he thought for one minute Lauren cared about him he would never laugh, but she cared about practically everything more than she did about him. He hoped it wasn't too long before someone else caught her eye.

Turned out Melissa *was* a bit like the mafia.

"You can't pick and choose, Tiny. I was there for you when you needed money."

Melissa's turning the disguise of her politically incorrect past into rescuing Sistine in her financial time of need was an example of the Mel Dunn brilliance in full force.

"Besides, after your rocky start, things are going well now. You're on time and they love you. Why mess with what works? It's not like anyone has to know. No one cares what goes on in your little village. I'd still be doing it myself if I wasn't in this stupid fishbowl."

That was another part of her skill—tapping into Sistine's need to be good at something. Melissa played her like an instrument, and who was she kidding? She loved Washington and the fishbowl.

"I'm sorry. Things have changed on my end, so I'll take care of things this week, but then I'm done."

Melissa chuckled, sinister and society mixed like a chilled drink in a delicate glass.

"Please don't make this difficult. I'd intended to take things off your hands, but my life has changed."

"You can't get out of our agreement."

"I can. I'm telling you, I'm not doing it anymore."

"I hear that, but those few clicks in the email I sent you were acknowledgment, an agreement. You remember contracts, don't you, Tiny?"

Sistine pulled the phone away from her face as if Melissa's nasty manipulation could reach out and grab her.

"Hello? I don't have all night."

"I can't believe you. I have no idea why I'm surprised, but I am."

"You thought I was going to hand over five thousand dollars a month without a contract? I'm a lawyer from a family of lawyers, come on."

"How could I forget?" When they were in college, Melissa used to inform anyone who would listen that both her parents were lawyers as were her grandparents before them. Her grandfather was a judge. Sistine used to find the ease with which Melissa accepted she was a dependent and needy blossom on a much larger tree fascinating. She had no issue calling her father when things didn't work out to "fix it" for her.

Sistine was the opposite. There was nothing she wouldn't do for her family, but the moment she turned eighteen, she wanted her own things to talk about, her own accomplishments to bring home for discussions on holidays. When everything had imploded the first time with Melissa, Sistine swore she would never, ever, rest on someone else's connections. She left college wanting no one. If her close friend could so royally screw her over in the hallowed walls of university, she needed to pay attention in the real world.

And now, here she was in the real world having fallen, once again believing that Melissa Dunn had helped her out this once. Technically she had and if Sistine were able to be objective despite her clenched jaw, she would admit Melissa was right. She had paid her a crazy amount of money and it was right to want a guarantee. Sistine had only been at it for a month.

"How much to get out of the contract?" she said.

"Oh, let's not do that. You've got the hang of it now. I don't want things to get ugly again."

"How much, Mel?"

"All of it. If you back out, you have to pay everything back with interest."

Sistine would not cry and she definitely wasn't going to beg. As with so many things in her life, she sucked it up and did what she had to do. Doing what it took was what got her into this. It's not like she wasn't making money. She'd focus on that and ride it out.

"When does the contract end?"

"Two years, and there's a confidentiality clause so you can't go blabbing."

"I would never do that."

"I know, but it's been a while since we worked together."

"Is that what we're doing?"

"Don't be pissy. I hate it when you're pissy."

"Goodbye, Mel."

"You're the best, Tiny. Maybe you should treat yourself to a great pair of sexy boots or something. Take a trip into San Fran. Have lunch, get some sexy boots and a massage. That's what you need."

Sistine covered her face with the pillow. Melissa never did quite understand what it took to run a business. She loved all the rest, but the day-to-day, the have-tos had always landed on Sistine's lap. Hanging up before the thought of an actual massage made her cry, she plugged in her phone and went to bed.

Hours later, she was startled awake a little after two in the morning. Grabbing the water bottle next to her bed, she tried to understand what had prompted her subconscious to create such a jumble. In her nightmare, she was hanging off a cliff in nothing but a thong. She was so focused on pulling herself from certain death, she couldn't see the thong. It was freezing, and she remembered thinking the raccoons had her pants, but they kept asking her where she'd put the barbecue chips.

She leaned back on her pillows. She *had* finished off a bag of barbecue potato chips while she was talking to Melissa, so there was that. The rest of it was as good as anyone's guess. Chalking it up to exhaustion, she reached under her sweatshirt. After a few strategic pulls, she removed her bra and tossed it on the chair. She should get up and wash her face, brush her teeth. Maybe even put on her clean pajamas that were folded right there on the chair, but she had the Blue Hairs at nine o'clock tomorrow sharp. That meant she needed to be up by seven thirty at the latest. She needed sleep more than clean pores, and her teeth would have to hang on for a few more hours.

Sistine checked her laptop for confirmation and set it on the floor to keep all things thong-related out of her dreamland. Sinking into her pillows, she summoned only happy thoughts, and of course, the darkness behind her closed eyes filled with the warm wonderfulness of Cade.

"Thank you," she sighed into her soft sheets. She needed a good dream. And that's what he was, wasn't he? A few moments of fun in her anything-but-light-and-easy life. She rolled over and tugged the covers.

They'd go on a date. Dinner, maybe more climbing up his body, and then she'd go a couple more months with the Melissa thing. Savings would be nice and maybe she could fix the sink in her apartment.

She opened her eyes and Cade's face was gone. Was she lying to herself in her own tiny space? If a woman couldn't be real in her own darkness, then where could she be real? She was stuck with Melissa and she was falling for Cade. As she drifted off to sleep, she replayed the scenario where she simply told Cade. That made her close her eyes tighter.

The next morning, Sistine was a half hour into her class with the Blue Hairs and explaining to Gracie that she had a "tangled mess" because she started her project from a hank of yarn and hadn't rolled it into a ball.

"So what does that mean? Can you fix it?"

"We'll have to cut it, but it will be okay," Sistine said and looked up when the front door tinkled.

Aspen walked in with a blanketed bundle strapped to her chest, followed close behind by Mason. He was carrying her black leather diaper bag, which was definitely clashing with his cool guy persona.

"Aw, sweet Hattie." Bess dropped her needles and rushed to Aspen, carefully lifting the blanket.

"I miss Harriet too, Bess." June looked up as if she was expecting an out-of-world visitor. "Darling, our Hattie is shopping at the Heavenly

Kingdom Costco location." When she realized everyone was huddled around Aspen and baby Hattie, not her dear departed friend, she bonked herself on the head. "Of course, sweet Hattie," she said and joined the others after sending a wink to the heavens for Aspen's Grand.

Sistine knew that kind of bond. She felt it full force when she was with her girls and couldn't imagine losing one of them. For a moment she imagined the four of them sitting around a table one day chatting about the latest gossip or discovery online. She was working on not looking too far in the future, but she hoped for that moment one day.

"Hey, Mase," Sistine said, joining the group. She leaned forward and kissed her sleep deprived but over-the-moon-happy friend. After putting some hand sanitizer on because, hello... germs, she offered a drowsy Hattie her finger. "Hi, sweet girl." She met Aspen's eyes. "How are things?"

"Good. We are working on a schedule."

"Well, if anyone can give this baby a schedule, it's you."

"How's it hanging, Mase?" Gracie asked, and teenage indignation was all over his face for a minute before he had a chance to remember he was polite.

"I'm good, Mrs. Nathan. Did you mean what you said about Grand, Mrs. Holt? Holy Kingdom, you think that happens?" He looked to June.

She glanced around the group. "What the heck does that mean, does it happen?"

"Like, you believe that? You think Grand is somewhere in the clouds? At Costco?"

"Of course, I do. Heaven isn't a matter of opinion, young man, it's... it's heaven. Where do you think Grand went?"

He shrugged. "I'm tossing around the idea that we all return to the earth's energy, but I'm pretty much agnostic."

"Ag-what?"

"Agnostic," Sistine offered. "It means he's still questioning where we go. He doesn't know."

June looked to Bess and Gracie for a beat before they all started to laugh and walked back toward their table. "I'll tell ya, you kids crack me up. You're all about what you see on the internet, and the real stuff you can't figure out. Grand *is* at the Costco in the sky. Know that."

Sistine caught Aspen's expression and ached for her friend's loss and the new joy she was bouncing as Mase joined the Blue Hairs and continued his rousing debate.

"How's your day?" Aspen asked, sitting in one of the large chairs in the front.

"Never dull. Do you want some coffee?" At Aspen's pained expression, Sistine remembered she was off coffee while she was breastfeeding. "Sorry, that was cruel."

"It was."

"We have some delicious herbal tea."

"Oh, yay," she said, glancing over her shoulder. "Hey, Gracie is hitting your candy drawer again."

Sistine turned to find the little woman shoving a Kit Kat into the pocket of her dress.

"Gracie, those are for the children who visit."

Her lips made a raspberry sound. "Candy is wasted on the youth. They should take care of those perfect teeth while they can. Mine are gone." She reached into her mouth as if it was perfectly normal, removed her top dentures, and smiled. Sistine looked back at Aspen, who was pulsing with laughter.

Gracie put her teeth back in and stole a Milky Way and a package of Nerds before returning to the table and dropping the candy in the center for her friends.

Sistine made tea and went back to sit with Aspen.

After a few sips, she lay back with Hattie resting on her chest.

"So," she whispered, "I heard a rumor."

Sistine froze midstir as her mind flooded with excuses. I needed the money. Melissa was a friend from college and while it looked super bad, it hadn't started out that way. There was a contract and she had no choice. Deciding she was paranoid, she took in a steady breath. There was no way Aspen had time in her life to snoop around, and why would she or any of the people in Sistine's life bother? They weren't the schemers or manipulators of her past.

"You, Cade. You're going on a date."

Oh, that rumor. The good rumor. Yes, she was going on a date with Cade. A smile teased her lips and the air felt less stifling at the mention of his name as if the flutter in her stomach could fix the churning over a far larger secret.

"We are. I... know it seems strange on the surface, but we have quite a bit in common."

"I don't think it's strange. He is interesting. Absolutely quirky, but you are too, and he talks like you do."

Sistine was taken aback at the easy assessment of their attraction. "What does that mean?"

"You know, like you're strolling down a path. You both talk that way."

"And how do you talk?"

She huffed. "The fastest line between two points is a straight line. That's how I talk. You and Cade meander."

"Great word."

"See, that's what I mean. You two could go off and meander for an hour. You suit each other."

"Let's not get crazy. It's one date."

"A date on his birthday. That's a big date."

"What? Why would he..."

Aspen's eyes went wide. "Obviously he wants to take you out."

"He didn't want me to change my mind."

Aspen laughed and must have remembered a sleeping baby was attached to her chest. She automatically started a gentle bounce. Sistine was not surprised that her friend, who was a badass in everything, had also mastered mommy movements in record time.

"Cade can be... persistent. He likes you."

"I like him too."

"He's growing up. I don't know if it's watching his brothers, or Patrick and me having a baby, but suddenly he's... normal. Well, not normal because he still wears those ridiculous shirts, but tame. I think you two work together."

Sistine had finished a men's cardigan a few weeks back to sell on Etsy. Like Mr. Graham's, this one was Cade's size too, but it was oatmeal and had leather patches on the elbows. The sweater was wool and cashmere. It had taken her months to make and it was the perfect birthday gift. Especially given the conversation they had about Mr. Graham and his leather vests. Knit and leather. It was only their first date, but she imagined that combination fit Cade perfectly.

"Let's see how the date goes. Did you and Patrick have..." Sistine was at a loss for how to describe it. Did you two have challenges sounded stupid. Every couple had challenges. She almost wanted to lean on Aspen and say, "Help me. I'm going to screw this up because I've already screwed up and I can't find a way out." For both their sakes, she said nothing. Aspen had a new baby and more important things to worry about. Since moving to Petaluma, Sistine had worked out her life on her own, and she would find a way out of her deal with the she-devil too. On her own.

Chapter Fifteen

*C*ade picked Sistine up at her shop. When he walked in, the place was empty. He called out and a muffled voice answered from the back. Following the noise, he went through the door into her apartment.

"So, this is where you live."

"Yup. I'm sort of like a mouse in the wall," she said, still out of sight. "Sorry, I'm running late, but June from my Blue Hairs group needed..." Her voice faded and then with a grunt, she practically fell out of the closet into Cade's arms. She spun around and her hands, one of them holding something knitted, went to his chest.

"Oh boy. You smell great." She closed her eyes and leaned into him. Cade was about to kiss her when her eyes flew open and she patted him on the chest before stepping back. "Sorry. My closet is out of control and I wanted to wear this wrap with"—she threaded her arms through what looked like a group of stretched cotton balls, not that he was going to share that with her—"this blouse." She huffed. "There. All I need are my shoes and we're off." She disappeared back into the closet and emerged with a pair of yellow shoes, the second closet experience seeming far less traumatic. Cade couldn't remember ever seeing yellow shoes before and wondered where Sistine bought her clothes.

"Sorry," she said, slipping on her last shoe, brushing the front of her outfit, and stopping in front of him. "I didn't want to rush, but I tend to lose track of time when people ask me to help with their projects, you know?"

Cade had not said one word; there'd been no room. He couldn't tell if she was nervous or always like this before a date. How much did she date, anyway? He'd assumed not much because, well, she appeared busy with other things, but that was an assumption.

"You look beautiful." He quickly kissed her before she flew away again, and he handed her a succulent in a painted jar. He was going to mention the name but couldn't remember. He would need to brush up on cacti and succulents if they continued dating. They had not even left her apartment and he already wanted another date.

"Oh, you brought me pork and beans." She held up the plant, turning the pot to see the design.

Cade laughed. "I don't think the woman at the flower shop called it that, but if you're excited about it then yeah, I brought you pork and beans."

"Technically it's a Sedum rubrotinctum, but no one uses that name. She may have called it jelly beans."

"I don't remember. I was sort of overwhelmed. A lot to learn."

She smiled and for the first time, Cade took in her outfit. Dark jeans, a mustard-colored blouse, and big necklace with so many colors it reminded him of looking through a kaleidoscope. He loved those things when he was a kid. Her hair was smooth and pinned to the side with a small flower. She had color on her lips and cheeks, but it didn't look artificial. Her skin was glowing, and she smelled like summer.

By the time he got to the yellow shoes with the lemon-shaped buckles, she had squeezed his arm and said, "Thank you." She set the plant on the small window ledge by a refrigerator that looked the size of the one in Aspen's office. Everything in Sistine's place was smaller, like a livable dollhouse. Cade peered around the corner looking for another room but found nothing.

"I like your place. Quick question, where's your bed?"

She pointed to the wall behind them. "It pulls down."

"Huh, that's cool."

She shook her head. "Not so cool when it gets stuck, but it's fun when it works." She flung a large leather bag over her shoulder and huffed out a breath as if to collect herself. "Are we ready?"

Leaving through the still-open door, Cade turned as Sistine locked her apartment. When she whipped around, they were both in the tiny bit of hallway that led to her store. Fun, that's what she'd said about her bed. Her closet was "not behaving."

Who the heck was Sistine Branch? And why did the entire world suddenly seem so much more interesting?

She was still, both of them with their backs on opposite walls and inches from the other. Cade's mouth curved into a smile and he reached out to touch one of the earrings dangling like a hanging garden. She was incredible. His fingers touched the soft skin of her cheek and he didn't have to lean far before he was kissing her. She made a little sound and was now on his side of the small space. Wrapping his arms around her, he kissed her until her sweet smell mixed and danced with his own familiar scent. She seemed like the type of woman who wasn't looking to take over a room—she simply made everything look better.

Easing back from the kiss, she touched his shirt.

"Handsome." Her voice broke before she cleared her throat. "You look handsome."

Cade suddenly felt unprepared for this date. Here he thought he was taking sweet, innocent Sistine from the knitting shop on the date of her life. In less than twenty minutes, she had flipped everything to her taking poor, shallow Cade, who spent far too much time at the gym and not enough time with succulents, on a date with colorful and full-of-life Sistine. He hoped he was good enough.

"Thank you." That was all he had in him as her eyes, more dramatic with makeup, blinked up at him and her full tinted lips smiled in that way that once again knocked him right over.

They drove through the gates of Windrush Farms, and Cade knew he'd achieved the element of surprise. He'd hoped even with all her whimsical flair that Sistine would not expect to be taken to a sheep farm on a first date. Rounding to the passenger side of the truck he'd borrowed from Patrick, Cade grinned at her expression, a mixture of awe and confusion. He opened the door and took her hand.

"This is our date?" She stepped out, the gravel crunching under her lemon shoes, and kept hold of his hand.

He nodded. The property, right outside Petaluma in Chileno Valley, was green and gold. Rolling hills and weeping trees seemed to reach down to greet them. In the distance, dozens of sheep grazed near a white farmhouse with several other buildings in the same style. The parking area led to a gravel path bordered by railway ties and small lights barely visible in the early evening glow.

"This is Windrush Farms." Cade tucked her hand under his arm, feeling pretty damn proud of his choice, and led her toward the house. "They do a farm-to-table dinner and I thought you might want to meet the sheep."

She beamed, her face tipped pink by the cool air. "You're good, Cade McNaughton." She squeezed his arm as they approached an area canopied by two massive trees. The tables were lit by giant candles and antique lanterns peeked through the branches overhead.

"That's the rumor." He brought her closer. Her laugh, the one he was already craving, echoed in the massive space. She kissed his shoulder and for the first time, Cade imagined years ahead. More dates, trips they might take.

Reining it in, he focused on the here and now. Even if Sistine managed to reason her way out of a second date, he still had tonight. She was with him, smiling and breathtaking, on what would always be their first date, and he planned to enjoy every minute.

Moments later, they were seated at a picnic-style table with cushions tied to the benches. There was a glass carafe of water on the table along with long, thin breadsticks in a clay jar and a dish of olives.

Sistine pointed to the branches above. "More branches. Did you plan that?"

"I would like to take credit, but I didn't know about the lanterns in the trees." He held her hand across the table.

After they ordered what the waitress called their Little Bit of Everything board and two beers, they talked about The Tap House and how being in the business tended to ruin the simple pleasure of eating out for all of the McNaughtons.

"We can't help it. We're either noting things we do better, or texting things we need to improve."

Sistine laughed. "During the date?"

"We try to keep it on the DL."

"Mason's lingo?"

Cade nodded. "You know my family so well. Tell me about yours," he said once their beers arrived and the waitress poured water into mason jars.

"My brother lost his arm in a motorcycle accident." She sipped her water and shook her head. "I have no idea why I chose to lead with that."

"That explains the hesitation to get on my bike."

"No. I'm not afraid of bikes. I wasn't quite ready to wrap my arms around you that night." She smiled and managed to lighten what he was certain was an ordeal for her brother and her family with humor. How often did Sistine do that in her life? He knew running a small business wasn't easy. He couldn't imagine doing it alone.

"I did notice the Iron Man arm when I met him."

"Oh, don't call him Iron Man. He already thinks he's superhuman."

"I'll keep it to myself. But that reminds me, you all knit?"

She nodded. "My sister Juliet was last. Drake and I started one day when we were bickering about candy, I think. It was the second or third year after my parents opened the Crab Shack."

The waitress put a large board at the center of their table with olives, cheese, and different kinds of bread and crackers. They thanked her and she complimented Sistine's shoes before moving to serve another table.

"My Auntie N, well she's my godmother, but we call her Auntie N. Like the *Wizard of Oz* character."

"Wasn't that Auntie Em?"

"Her first name is Nikki so we must have improvised. *Wizard of Oz* is her favorite movie and she has spiky hair. Practically begs for a cool nickname."

"Understood." He handed her a small plate.

"Anyway, Auntie N threw her giant knitting bag over her shoulder, grabbed me by the arm and my brother by the ear, and brought us to the edge of the water." She put food on her plate while she continued. "We sat on this big cluster of rocks in the shade and she gave us both needles and a ball of yarn. 'Life is full of chaos,' she told us. I'll never forget. 'Like the sea, you will need rhythm to survive.'"

"Huh, I like that. Auntie N isn't dead, is she?"

"No. Why would you think that?"

"I don't know. Sometimes these life stories have a tragic twist. The wise and inspiring godmother with the cool nickname who taught you to knit by the seaside was then plowed over by a delivery truck, and that's why you moved away from home to open a knitting store in her honor."

Sistine shook her head. "She's alive and well. You are crazy."

"That's probably true. We had an aunt. She was closest to West, but she was pretty cool. She did die. Has Auntie N been to your store?"

She nodded. "When I opened and last summer. I'd like to get her to stay for a week sometime and teach a master class."

"Maybe I'll stop by to meet her."

"You would like her. She dyes her hair. It's almost exotic plum, but with more mulberry, you know?"

"I do not. Is that purple?"

"Sorry. I see the world in yarn colors."

Cade was gone. One date, surrounded by gorgeous scenery, and he could not take his eyes off her. Her hands were animated as she explained her godmother's dark, almost black-purple hair. She went on to say that it took longer to teach her sister to knit than it did Drake and by the time they ordered, his mind was already conjuring a second and third date. He tried to stay in the moment. After all, he wasn't guaranteed anything past one date, but something about being with her already promised a tomorrow.

"Does Nikki dress like you do? Is that where you get your style?"

Sistine looked down at her blouse. Her clothes never seemed all that remarkable to her, but she'd gotten used to comments.

"I didn't mean there was anything wrong with the way you dress, but you... make a statement with your clothes, don't you think?"

She shrugged. "No more of a statement than yours." She pointed and then realized he was in a button-up shirt and a jacket for their date. "Well, normally. Your T-shirts. This"—she gestured up and down—"is not your norm."

"True. I guess we have that in common."

She couldn't help it and her eyes stayed on his chest, which fit beautifully in dressed-up date clothes too. How did he do that? She loved picking out clothes when it was only her and her mood for the day, but the idea of dressing for a date, for someone else, seemed a bigger nightmare than the thong-raccoon one.

"Is that why you wear the shirts? So women will check you out?"

He laughed and choked a bit on his beer. "No. I like words. It drives my family nuts. I've always been interested in different ways of saying the same thing, funny puns or tongue twisters."

"Riddles?"

"I love riddles. I completely forgot about them. I'll bet there's a riddles app or something."

"Did you know there's a MadLibs app? You can fill in the words like the old school paper ones."

"No way. Is it any good?"

She shook her head. "I downloaded it and it's the same setup as the paper, but maybe I'm over how funny 'three hundred cups of urine' or 'he had twelve thousand cats' sounds."

He smiled, and there it was again, that look of interest. She liked him and loved the way his mind worked. Most importantly, when she was with him, things felt effortless.

"So you're Sistine and your sister's name is Juliet. Are you Italian?" His eyes were touched by candle light, and maybe it was the grass because the green seemed to pop now. It could have been his expression, touched with beer and easy conversation, that changed things up. Sistine had no idea, all she knew was she'd never been on a date like this before.

"No." Her answer felt like a whisper as the smell of delicious flavors filled their space and two more couples were seated. "My mom was going through an Italian phase when we were born. *The Godfather*, Michelangelo, fettuccini. She was all things Italian according to my dad."

"Romeo and Juliet?"

She nodded. "We started calling her Jules because she was teased so much as a kid."

"What about Drake?" he asked.

"The story goes that my mom wanted her only boy to have a pirate name. So, Sir..."

"Francis Drake. Oh, I need to meet your mom too. Those are all great names."

"Ya think? Try having your friends unable to pronounce your name in kindergarten and guys in high school and college asking, 'Are you as pure as the chapel?'"

"That's not even funny. Your name is beautiful."

She managed a cursory smile as her time with Cade slid from pleasant to trouble. Cade was physically spectacular, which she'd learned to handle, but everything underneath was stunning.

"I saw Hattie yesterday," she said, needing to change the subject.

"I heard. She's unbelievable, right? One minute Aspen's eating beef jerky and then boom, another person is in the world. I was young and... distracted when Mase was born, but now I'm all in. It's so obvious that I'm her favorite uncle already."

The beaming uncle layer was not helping steady Sistine. Not one bit.

"She did tell me you were her favorite."

"Did she? See, I knew."

Their gaze held and she wondered if their surroundings had the same effect on him as they were having on her. Were all of his details so vivid? Dinner was delivered and Sistine reached into her bag. She slid the box she'd wrapped in butcher paper and tied with a bundle of Oasis 5222 across the table.

Cade grinned and as the sun slipped through the trees behind him, he looked younger, like a kid asking for five more minutes when his mom called him home. She'd never realized how happy he appeared until that moment. People likely took him for irresponsible or even charming. He was happy, joyful in a way she'd never considered.

"Aspen told you."

Sistine nodded, not confident she could speak without showing her nerves.

Cade unfastened the yarn. "Beautiful color."

Tell me about it, she wanted to say, as he set it aside as if he might save the yarn in some keepsake box under his bed. Did guys have those?

He lifted the sweater from its wrapping and her heart was pounding at the sheer joy in his expression as he held it across his chest and then grinned when he noticed the patches.

"Leather and a cardigan. I love it." He leaned over the table and brushed his lips over hers so gently it could have been a breeze. Except her heart was now clamoring to be heard.

Their dinners were served and their beers refilled.

Sunset was her second favorite time of day. The thought made her smile. She used to tell her dad that on the evenings when they all sat out on the back porch and played Sorry. She'd been little when she'd informed him that sunset was her second favorite. Drake had blabbed that there were only two times of day, sunset and sunrise. She'd tried to explain to him the path the sun and moon took and that there were several times of day. He told her she was making things too complicated. She tended to do that. As if knowing she needed to calm down, a four-piece band complete with banjo and a standing bass began playing. The air was clean and Cade was looking at her.

"This is the best date I have ever been on."

His face softened and Sistine's heart tapped on her chest again. "Are you sure? Maybe we should taste the food first." He handed her a cracker with cheese.

"I don't need to try the food. Well, maybe." She bit into the cracker and chewed. Crunchy with cranberries or cherries and nuts. Her taste buds were as delighted as the rest of her. "I love it here and you knew I would love it here. You are an excellent date. Has anyone ever told you that?"

"I don't remember anything before this date."

She nodded, still chewing. "Oh, now that is an outstanding line."

She smiled, a stirring in her chest that she both remembered and somehow forgot at the same time.

"You're my best date too. Can I ask you a question?" he said.

"Ask anything." She glanced up at the lanterns hanging in the tree above and knew in that moment she meant anything. She would certainly not tell him so, not right now anyway, but if he asked the right question, she would spill all her secrets.

The sun set, and oil lamps were placed in the center of each table, casting a glow over the wood that highlighted its story, the story of this place.

"Where did you go to college?"

"The University of San Francisco."

"Knitting major?"

She laughed. "No. I majored in marketing. Branding and promotion to be boringly specific."

"Did you work in branding before you moved to Petaluma?"

"I did. Well, while I was in college, I worked a lot on my parents' place. They own the Crab Shack in Bodega Bay and a couple of fishing boats. I helped them with their logo, social media, and put together some events for them."

"Nice. Did you do your brother's logo too? I saw it on his boxes. It's great."

"I did."

"So why knitting now?"

"So many reasons. I wanted something tangible, something all my own. It seemed like I spent a lot of time creating spaces for other people to be creative. Then when my brother lost his arm, I moved closer to home and helped my family. The pull of their life, their business, tends to take priority, so I moved to Petaluma hoping to be the priority in my life for once."

"So you must be an Instagram expert. Do you have other social media?"

"I have a strategy for my shop that involves keeping it simple. Knitting is about textures, color, and rhythm. I prefer visual platforms."

The last date Sistine had been on was with her accountant. The guy who set up her books for Knitterly. That was not something she was prepared to admit to anyone. They'd had one date, a few awkward text exchanges, one where he asked her how she felt about sexting, and that was that. Before that, she dated Harrison, her brother's friend and business partner. She was on and off with him for about four months before they both decided they worked better as friends.

Not exactly a stellar recent dating history for comparison, but it was still the best date she'd ever been on. Aside from the obvious five-star that Cade had chosen a sheep farm, she was so comfortable with him, so herself. That was the only way to explain how being with him filled her with sunshine and the luxury of her favorite socks. She had not once since he'd shown up at her door felt the need to be anything other than one hundred percent Sistine Branch.

As delightful as the sheep farm was and as delicious as the food and beer were, they could have been anywhere. She wasn't going to tell Cade that, but it was the truth. It wasn't the candles or the gentle breeze. It was him and the way he seemed right at home with her too. First dates were usually odd, even the decent ones. She wasn't putting on a show for him. She was relaxed, laughing, toasting under the night sky, and freely discussing whether they used olive oil or butter on the grilled vegetables.

One year, her dad informed everyone that they would be getting winter school clothes for Christmas because it was a tight year for the Crab Shack. That was the year he surprised her with a pink bike that had a basket and a bell. She wore out that bell until it went silent when she was a kid. But this, this man, laugh lines at his stunning eyes and more goofy faces than she had in her arsenal, took unexpected to a whole new level.

Part of her knew she had no business getting involved with someone now that she was Melissa's beck-and-call girl. She should hold back, thank him for dinner, point out her commitments again, and back off. It would make things easy for them both. But they ordered apple cobbler to split, the stars became even more brilliant in the endless night sky, and Sistine forgot to worry, forgot everything except the intoxicating way he seemed to see the person she'd always meant to be.

Chapter Sixteen

*C*ade forgot how to be cool and casual. Before their dinner arrived, he'd morphed into some dorkier version of himself. Now that they'd finished dessert, he was one of those cartoon characters with the heart pulsing from his chest. There was no way everything Sistine said was that interesting, but it damn sure felt that way. She'd told him it was her favorite date before they'd even gotten started. Like she saw some inherent value in things immediately. She didn't need to be taught or shown how great things could be; she knew already. Sistine was this complete person and he wanted to be good enough for her so badly that it taunted his normally healthy ego.

After paying the bill, they were invited to the barn to visit with the sheep and other animals. There, she asked questions about the wool process and they gave her samples of yarn and their website information. Gracious and kind, Sistine chatted with the owner about her last vacation to Washington. They commiserated that working for oneself was not always what it was cracked up to be but settled that the freedom far outweighed the long hours. Cade held back, watched her with the sheep, and took a couple of pictures. She didn't take one picture; she seemed to soak up the experience. He held her hand as they returned to the truck and after a brief kiss in the moonlight, they were back to animated conversation on the way home.

"Anyway, June comes into the shop for Blue Group."

"That's their name?" Cade glanced over.

She nodded, tucking one leg under and setting the yarn between them. "They're the Blue Hairs, technically, but I've taken to calling them Blue Group. So June comes in with her normally well-coiffed hairdo all over the place and bits of mascara smeared under her eyes."

"Did she oversleep?"

"She did, at Bernie from the hardware store's house."

His eyes went wide. "The guy who comes out from the back when you need keys made?"

"Yup. According to June, he is a stallion." She held up her hands. "Her words, not mine."

"Holy crap. He's like eighty."

"So is June. Well, she'll be eighty next year."

There were no pretenses, nothing he had to prove to her. He was being himself, not the guy behind the bar, but who he was when he sang in the shower or talked to Henny and Penny while he fed them. It was effortless and fun to be with her. He was surrounded by people having fun all the time and it felt incredible to be in the mix for a change.

"What's up with the hardware store? Graham's wearing leather and now his back room guy is hooking up with June. I wonder if Bernie has to… use something."

Sistine's face flushed and she shook her head. "I can't even…" She was laughing again, the light from the dashboard reflecting off her eyes. Cade didn't want the date to end. He wanted to take her back to his house and wake up with her the next morning. Not because he was buzzed or needed to get laid, but because he wanted more of her.

It reminded him of the times Javier added things to the menu and wanted Cade to pick one of his variations. Dipping sauce, no sauce, fresh garlic, or garlic spread. He was never any help because he loved all the different ways he made a dish.

"Let's rotate them on the menu. I like them all," he'd say, much to Javier's frustration.

Cade wanted every variation with Sistine too. He'd had early-morning, late-night coffee shop, even lunchtime Sistine, but now he needed to try after-hours-in-her-shop or even playful-on-vacation. He wanted, needed, more. But no matter how strong his attraction, he was not starting with naked beneath him or on top of him, although the thought of that variation had his blood racing. He was doing things differently. This time the relationship would build and grow, he thought as she bit her bottom lip to keep from laughing. Cade had never been one for patience, but he was going to give Sistine his best effort.

Once they arrived at her shop, she kissed him under the same street lamps she'd watched flicker on every night from her shop window. It was a new kiss full of their date and the lower walls of knowing each other a bit more. It was delicious and she could taste the beer on his tongue, the sweet apple of their shared dessert. They made their way into her apartment and the scenarios of telling Cade everything began playing in her mind until he kissed her again and all thought stepped back to make room. His lips played along her jaw and down the column of her neck. She'd intended one date, a good date even, but she wasn't going to find her way back from this. There would be no polite smiling at Cade the next time she ran into him, a pleasant acknowledgment that they were better as friends.

Nope. This kind of attraction had legs and stamina to go all the way. It didn't matter if it was their first date or their second year. Sistine knew there was no going back without someone getting hurt. Right as she was about to again surrender thought to sensation, Cade stopped kissing her and gently held her back. She opened her eyes.

"Hey." His lips were raw, his smile wicked.

She wanted him with an intensity she'd figured had gone to sleep long ago. "You're thinking I'm not a get-naked-on-the-first-date kind of woman, right?"

He broke eye contact and his smile deepened. "This is new."

"Well, of course. We left baby sheep a little while ago and now we're... not playing with sheep."

"I don't know how to do this with you."

She tried to keep her expression from falling in disappointment, but she didn't have the best poker face and Cade now looked like a guy who had said something wrong.

"Not that. That's not what I meant." He took her hands in his. "I know this sounds typical male, but sex isn't—it's not this. This is something I have never done."

"You've never had sex?" She smirked. "Oh, I understand. We can take it slow, and I'm happy to add some pointers along the way."

He laughed, deep and rumbling in the lovely chest of his, and then gathered her close. "The pointers sound intriguing, but I'm going to kiss you one more time and go home."

"Suit yourself. You asked me out. I was perfectly happy learning backgammon."

His mouth curved in between kissing her. "You're killing me."

"So, we're waiting? Don't you think that's a bit archaic?"

He raised a brow.

"NPR. Do you ever notice they use that word a lot?"

He shook his head, clearly wrestling with something, and brought her hands to his lips.

"Anyway," she continued. "If that's your hesitation, we already know each other. It's not like you're a stranger. I don't have sex with people I don't know."

"That is good news."

She put her head on his chest. "I had a nice time, a great time."

"Me too. Let's do this again on Wednesday." He lifted her chin and smiled, probably at the pure need she was unable to hide. "We need to keep our clothes on for now. It's important to me."

"Well, it's your birthday, so I suppose you get to choose. But you are clearly the one getting enough sex." She played with the front of his shirt.

"I'm serious, Sistine."

"You need clothes on more than—" She kissed his neck and decided they could leave their clothes on if she could spend a couple more hours simply kissing him.

He groaned. "Right this minute, both sound great, but tomorrow, when everything about us turns to the physical us, things will get weird and ruin the... nonphysical. Holy shit, I'm not making sense."

She touched the side of his face and he stilled.

"I had a great time. You are a convincing 'we.'"

He chuckled and she was glad to see his expression ease. "What does that mean?"

"Remember when my electrical blew and I was trying to figure things out?"

"At the Tap House? I remember."

"You said not to worry, that 'we'd' figure it out."

He nodded. "Right."

She brushed her lips across his. "I'm used to me. Running my shop, fixing my problems. It's always been a me. You offered a 'we' and so, I would love to go out with you again on Wednesday. And if you're ready to get naked then, I promise not to treat you any differently once you've kissed every inch of me."

"Every inch, huh."

"Oh, yes. You should not have taken me to a sheep farm on our first date. The bar is high."

"I'll try not to let you down."

"I don't see that happening." She kissed him but leaned back and held a hand to his chest. "I guess I should ask if you have any hang-ups first. Are you that guy who needs to leave after sex, or the type who has to sleep with his shoes by the bed?"

"Who have you been dating?"

"Not dating, but you know, a girl hears stories."

"I do not have any of those issues." He took her hand off his chest and brought it to his mouth.

"Are you into tying me up or asking me to call you Daddy? Those are both deal breakers too."

His lips curved and he stopped kissing her hand. "I do not need to tie you up, although I'd like to reserve the right to revisit that option later once we've spent some more time together. And please do not call me Daddy. Ever."

"Huh, so you like the whole *Fifty Shades* trend."

"No. I don't have toys or a room, but I do like to play."

She felt her face flush. Lord, the man did things to her, and something in the way he said the simple word, play, made it a bit difficult to breathe.

"Sistine." He ran his hand along the column of her neck and kissed her so gently it was barely there. "Thanks for going out with me."

"Thanks for lying on my floor and convincing me."

"Is that what did it?"

She nodded and held open the door.

He grinned. "Good night." As he walked past her, he kissed her one last time as if she were the last sip of beer. She hoped she had "we" potential and that she could get her life back before her college roommate screwed up yet another part of her life.

"Good night and happy birthday," she said before closing the door. Leaning against the wall, her entire body alive, she realized clothes on or off, she was already falling. He was knocking at her heart, offering a "we" she'd never imagined for herself. Nothing could touch that, taint it. Could it? Not Melissa, or Sistine's own stupidity, could change their evening. Lights on or off, money or no money, she wanted Cade. She knew it wasn't fair given her current situation, but she allowed herself a moment of rapid pulse and the excitement of something new. She'd meant what she'd told Cade earlier. Best. Date. Ever.

Chapter Seventeen

*C*ade and Sistine had takeout at his house the following Wednesday, which was a dangerous date considering his clothes-on stance, but there was so much to learn about Sistine that he hadn't needed anything else.

He showed her around his place and took her out back to meet Henny, Penny, and Cocky. She'd asked questions and was again fascinated and engaged. He gave her some eggs to take home and she texted him the next day inviting him to the county livestock show. They had a blast and he laughed until his sides hurt when she tried to convince him his backyard also needed a cow and a lamb.

"The chickens need friends," she'd said, wide-eyed and eating cotton candy. She was downright youthful and the lines between her eyes softened. Cade would admit that he was proud to be part of anything that eased her stress. Despite her best efforts, he'd argued lambs and cows were way too much work.

"The chickens have me. I'm their friend," he'd said and taken her on the Ferris wheel instead.

For the next sixteen days, she was either at the end of his bar, or he was at one of her lesson tables in the shop, occasionally with his sisters-in-law or the Blue Hairs. He tried to avoid the Knit and Chop crowd now that he knew Lauren's sister was in that class.

Sixteen days of dating. Movies, dinners after work, proper and more fun than Cade could remember having. Sixteen days. He knew that because every single time he dropped her off or saw her for the first time on any one of those sixteen days, he wanted to strip off whatever confection of an outfit she was wearing and not come up for air for at least twenty-four hours.

"So how are things?" his mom asked as she set the table for dinner.

Cade was the first one to arrive and his dad was out in the garage talking to one of their neighbors. When his mom turned to him, he thought about downplaying all of it and keeping what he and Sistine had to himself for a while longer, but he was reminded of where they lived and how quickly news traveled.

"Things are great. Perfect."

"Perfect, okay then. That's wonderful. I like Sistine."

"I know you do. What's not to like? She's great."

"But not perfect."

"What's that supposed to mean?"

"Well, no one is perfect, sweetie. Perfect is a pretty tight pair of pants, don't you think?"

Cade stared in amazement. "Where do you come up with these things?"

"Who knows?" She set the lasagna on the kitchen counter. "The genius just flows through me. I'm thinking we'll do buffet style, like grab a plate, some salad, and I'll stick this spatula right in there." She was talking her thoughts. That's what she called it. Cade listened and chose to ignore the perfect comment. He wasn't saying Sistine was perfect, was he?

Before he had a chance to think things into the ground, everyone arrived and they were out on the back patio eating and talking about the upcoming Fourth of July party. After dinner, Cade bounced Hattie in his arms, adjusting her sunhat and showing her their mom's flower beds in an effort to save her from the "barbecue logistics" conversation. She was getting so big and when she smiled, all pink lips and bubbled spit, his heart squeezed even tighter. He had no idea how Patrick spent so much time with his daughter without his heart exploding.

"Mom has informed everyone that you are having a great time with Sistine and she's concerned that you think she's perfect."

Cade closed his eyes. He couldn't say "Holy shit," with Hattie's perfect little ears right there, so he handed the sweet bundle back to Aspen.

"Thanks, Mom. Thanks a lot." He kissed his mom and hoped she caught the sarcasm before he accepted a beer from Boyd and walked out toward the barn. Patrick caught up a few minutes later in time for Cade's attempt at a shutdown of the entire topic.

"Of course I know no one is perfect, but all I'm saying—and then we're done—is that she's pretty damn close. She's smart and funny. She's beautiful in that way that's—"

"Beautiful?" Patrick said before sipping his beer. "Jesus, was I this bad?"

"Yes," Boyd said at the same time Cade said, "Worse." He met his older brother's eyes. "Worse, he was worse."

Boyd sipped and said nothing. "I think what we're trying to say is no one wants to be perfect, Cade. Don't put that out there. It doesn't give her room to screw up or mess things up."

"How? Why are we assuming she's going to mess things up? She runs a knitting store. Is this some weird gang-up because I'm looking for happiness? What, things only make sense in the McNaughton family if we're teasing Cade about his hair and his shallow girlfriends?"

Patrick and Boyd were suddenly interested in looking toward the river at their dad's new tractor. "That's not it."

"At all," Boyd said for emphasis.

"Then what's the problem. I'm happy. I think she is and we're getting to know each other."

"I've got no problem," Patrick said. "I"—he bumped Boyd's shoulder—"we thought maybe you wanted to talk. Everything has gone pretty quick and she's friends with everyone else so..."

"Is that what this is about? The book club sent you to confirm I wasn't going to hurt one of their own? My own mother thinks I'm going to hurt Sistine?"

Boyd cleared his throat. "Makes us sound like we're—"

"Two little errand boys for your wives?"

"Watch it." Boyd tossed his bottle into the bin outside the barn.

"Ella and Aspen, and yes Mom and Vienna have been talking. Sistine has been stress knitting again."

"What?"

"Apparently she knits random things when she's stressed, and she's been knitting a lot. They think it's her shop and all the work she had done and they're concerned that you will—"

"I haven't even slept with her yet."

"Are you for real?"

Cade nodded, eyes wide and hoping he was projecting "take that, assholes."

"Wow. That is different."

"I told you. I am doing things differently this time. I can't believe this. Aren't you guys supposed to be on my side?"

"We are," Patrick said. "It's the women. They're so dramatic."

"Yeah," Boyd added as they started back toward the house.

Cade laughed and tried not to take offense. He wasn't exactly the poster child for commitment, so it wasn't far off for Sistine's friends to question his motives. His brothers and his mother, on the other hand, were a different story. It was rough being the last single McNaughton. Suddenly everyone was an expert, but he'd given out plenty of advice when they were making their way through love, so turnabout was fair. Not that he was in love with Sistine... that would be way too fast. Love took time, didn't it?

Sistine was watching some true crime drama when a knock hit the side door of her apartment and she jumped. Scrambling across her bed, she looked through the peephole and saw Cade with something wrapped in tinfoil. Her stomach, still complaining from her earlier jelly bean dinner, perked right up at the idea of real food. She opened the door, accepting that she was in deep now. That this was not a couple of dates or one night. This wasn't one of anything. It was a "we" she didn't want to be without.

"Lasagna delivery from my—What the hell are those?" Cade set the lasagna on the bookcase and appeared mesmerized by her legs.

Sistine looked down, realizing her pajama shorts were the closest to naked she'd ever been in front of him, but he wasn't looking at her shorts.

"My socks?" she asked.

"Those are not socks. I have seen socks. I own socks and none of them go up to my thighs." He closed the door and locked it.

It had been awhile since what Bri now called her "fateful fall" at the Tap House and the kiss that followed. She was enjoying Cade, but they didn't seem to be progressing in the naked department. At first, she wondered if he assumed she wasn't the type to rush things, but she'd made it more than clear after their first date that she wanted him. She thought he wanted her too, but while they'd ventured painfully close to sex, he'd held back.

She'd entertained that he might be afraid of commitment, but he didn't seem like that guy. Sistine had no idea what was holding him back from taking her to his bed, her bed, the couch. At this point, the floor would be fine.

Feeling playful, she tugged at the fringe of the rainbow socks she'd knitted years ago. Even in July, her old building was cold at night, so she'd put them on. It was probably some issue with insulation or she needed to replace the windows. Sistine would wear socks all year if it meant keeping the original windows she loved the minute she saw the building.

She had not intended practicality to be sexy, but Cade's eyes flickered with heat and she had a feeling tonight was their night.

"So, you're a sock guy, huh?"

"Apparently. Those are—" He drew her into a starving kiss, full of passion she suspected he had held on to for far too long. Cade was potent at full strength. He roamed her body until she backed toward the bed she'd thankfully not put up before work.

Ready and more than willing as he settled his hands under her shorts, Sistine closed her eyes and his name fell from her lips. Dear Lord, a few more steps and they would be—

Cade stilled inches from her flowery quilt and Sistine thought she might explode if he said one word. Condom, that word was allowed, but nothing else. Please, nothing else. She wanted him, all of him, and she wasn't prepared to wait even one more minute.

"Here's the thing," he managed on a ragged breath as his lips left her neck. Doing her best not to rip the shirt off his back and push him onto her bed, she opened her eyes to his pained expression.

"I'm trying something new."

"Okay. I like new," she said.

"Less physical."

Dear. Lord. She knocked her head on his chest. "Cade, physical is good. It's so so good. Please reconsider."

"Your friends and my mom, my brothers. I came from there and they said—"

She reached up and put her hand over his mouth, her brow pinched at the mention of things, people a woman did not want to think about when she was about to get naked. His mother, did he actually have his hands on her body and want to chat about his family?

She was shaking her head when she found her words. "I don't care. I'm not interested in opinions or theories. I don't care if they're telling you not to hurt me."

He grunted, and she held her hand tighter to his lips.

"No. You don't understand. I can't hear one more word unless it's dirty and you're taking my clothes off. It's been seventeen days, Cade. Seventeen nights since you seduced me with the lambs and then left me... frustrated."

His hands gripped her tighter and he practically growled. Growling was good.

"Short of you telling me your family strapped an explosive device to your body, we are having sex. Long, hot, all-night sex, Cade. Are you listening to me?"

His lips curved against her palm as he nodded. His eyes were wicked and still filled with humor as he gently removed her hand from his mouth.

"A woman has needs. Please." She gripped his shirt and might have pounded on his chest.

He laughed, backing her up until the bed hit the back of her legs. "I didn't realize the urgency of the situation. I'm so sorry to have kept you waiting." His voice alone tickled every sense she possessed. When he pulled her Curious George T-shirt over her head, slowly trailing his fingers along parts of her body that had never felt his touch, she softened her knees to keep from falling over. Meg once mentioned that was the key to not passing out and Sistine was putting that theory to the test. She yanked his T-shirt off and while she tried to play it cool and *Cosmopolitan*, her need took over.

"Sweet Jesus," slipped from her mouth as she ran her hands over his warm skin, down his arm colorful with twining green, and along the dusting of hair at his stomach. When she met his eyes, it seemed important that he know she wanted him with or without his ridges. All of him, the whole man, the "we" he offered months ago.

"Your eyes are Oasis 5222. I figured that out long before you took your clothes off."

His lips curved and she rested her cheek against the hand he brought to her face. What started as hot and frantic turned tender. She forgot the urgency and it didn't matter that her bed was creaky or that she'd adopted candy as a food group. Trembling for him, she couldn't remember what she was racing toward or hiding from anymore. All that mattered was the two of them and this bond that had come out of nowhere. She hadn't been looking for Cade, but when he lay her on the bed and moved across her body, she was so grateful he'd found her.

Chapter Eighteen

The minute Sistine's hair fanned out on the pillow and she reached for him, Cade realized he was holding his breath. On a slow exhale, he found sex became less about expectation and more about pleasure. He peppered kisses up one side of her body and came to lean on his forearms over her flushed and beautiful face. Her eyes were lit with playful heat as her hands traveled over his back and came to rest on his waist.

"Am I allowed to speak now?"

"Yes." Her voice was thick with lust. Cade assumed it was lust because Sistine didn't seem like the kind of woman to fall in love easily. "But only sexy words, remember."

Resting on one arm, he let his hand graze along her neck and was rewarded when her pulse jumped.

"You're so soft." He'd meant to say she was gorgeous or he wanted her so badly he was losing his mind. Christ, he knew sexy, but her satin skin against his drowned out his ability to come up with anything.

"Thank you." She reached for him. "You are not."

A smile teased both of their lips before his mouth lowered, taking hers in a deep, slow pull. This wasn't going to be up against the wall, hot and dirty. There would be time for that later. Right now, he wanted to take his time. Sistine had once invited him to kiss every inch of her body, and he wanted to oblige.

Sex, while always a good idea, had become a routine for him, sort of like making a drink. The hot start, the up and down, some dirty talk or no talk at all, the build to climax, and then pleasure for them both. That was the recipe, the way a guy delivered great sex. He'd never questioned his abilities before or thought about his weaknesses. Occasionally his partner would mix it up. In a car or bathroom, even a little rough. Cade could do rough, but no matter what the extras were, the formula was the same. Not with Sistine. There was no recipe for this, no formula to guarantee she was not only panting his name, but still playing backgammon with him once their clothes were back on.

Everything was on instinct with her. He traveled her body, kissing and licking her until her hands went to what little hair he had and tugged, not up, but closer. The texture of her, the colors and taste of her body tested every restraint he'd taken for granted. He wanted to sink into her over and over again until there was nothing left of either of them. Until there were no friends and family to figure out, the crease that crept onto her face was gone, no blogs or business, no past or worries about the future. Only the two of them and the exploding need to please the woman he was falling in—

Holy shit!

Cade stilled, poised over her writhing body, his own drawn tighter than he ever thought possible. He was falling in love with her already? He was supposed to be pacing himself, like a damn responsible adult. Sistine wasn't a fall-fast kind of woman, was she?

At the stillness, she opened her eyes, and had he been able to speak, Cade would have told her that she was beautiful and everything he'd ever wanted in a woman. That he loved her and would do whatever was necessary to keep them both right where they were. That included fixing any other problems she had with her building. Hell, if she agreed to stay with him, he'd learn to knit. If her brother could knit, Cade was willing to try.

She pushed against his shoulder and he went onto his back. She straddled him, her hands resting at the center of his chest, right over his immature heart. She sat up, touching herself, and knitting never entered his mind. Her hands slid from her body before they found his in steady strokes. Cade closed his eyes and started counting to keep from losing complete control. By the time he made it to twenty, she'd reached into her nightstand, protected them, and drew him into the dizzying heat of her body.

Opening his eyes at all the sensations of her, he found her moving over him with a desire-filled expression that stole what little breath he had left. She somehow knew exactly what his body needed. She kissed him and continued her slow and penetrating pace until Cade thought he might lose his mind. He gripped her hips and when she closed her eyes on a sigh, he gathered her in his arms and flipped her beneath him.

Unsure how long he could maintain the mix of need and control, Cade moved slowly, taking her breast into his mouth and teasing her into another crest of pleasure.

"Cade, please," she moaned as if she felt him in every part of her body. He hoped she knew what she was asking for because when her lips parted on an "Oh, yes. Right. There," he flat out lost his mind. No longer able to manage his body or whatever plan he had for their relationship, Cade accepted that love had him by the throat. His heart raged in his chest as he drove them both toward a wave that left them clinging to one another before crashing into complete ecstasy.

Sistine didn't exactly wear her appreciation or even need for sex on her cardigan sleeve. She wasn't the walking pleasure poster that Cade was, but she knew how to work her body for her own and a man's pleasure. There had never been a doubt that sex with Cade would be spectacular, but what had happened between them was more than sex. She felt him everywhere, including her heart. When she'd been satisfied with fast and heated, he'd slowed down and revealed new pieces of himself, as if he was discovering his feelings as they went along. He held her face, kissed her long and lingering, and moved inside her like his next breath depended on her.

When she finally steadied her own breathing and he shifted to her side, a wave of guilt threatened to swallow her whole. Tears filled her eyes and she rolled over to face him, to tell him.

"And here I thought sex would ruin things." He smiled, warm and satiated.

Sistine kissed him, letting her hand travel the warm and well-loved planes of his body. Maybe he would forgive her, maybe they'd laugh about her past and present with Melissa and get on with the business of making those towheaded babies to play with Henny and Penny. Or maybe there was no reason to tell him. She was certain there were things he did for Foghorn that she didn't know about. Her side job was business, wasn't it? Cade shifted and brought her closer until their noses were almost touching.

"What's on your mind?"

Sistine shook her head and closed her eyes. The words were right there. She should sit up, put her clothes back on, and begin with, "Cade, I need to tell you something." She would then explain about the expo and how she knew it wasn't going to work out when she texted Melissa, which was true because Sistine received the thanks-but-no-thanks email from the committee last week. She'd meant to be devastated, but she was too busy being happy. Her shop was thriving and she had Cade now. She had Cade—what did that mean? He certainly wasn't inventory or something she had any control over.

She was falling in love with him, if she wasn't there already, and it was time to tell him. Not that she loved him, no one did that after sex, but it was time to tell him about Melissa and what Sistine had done in the name of friendship and money. Mostly money.

Opening her eyes, intent on saying something, she found Cade sound asleep. She swiped a tear from her cheek and watched him. Relaxed and vulnerable like he was in the picture, but this time in her bed. The weight of that parallel sat solid in her chest. He was a beautiful man in a way that had little to do with his body. No matter how hard she tried to explain herself, she'd break his heart or at the least, she would break her own.

Cade woke up in the middle of the night alone in Sistine's bed. The door to her apartment was barely open, allowing a rim of light to creep into the darkness. Throwing on his jeans, he pushed the door open farther and went into her shop. He stopped short at the sight of her at one of the lesson tables. Cade had seen women knitting. Hell, he'd seen her knitting at the hospital and before that his grandmother used to knit dish towels and gave them to his mom every year for Christmas. What was happening in front of him now, under the soft overhead light, was not his grandmother's knitting.

Sistine's bare legs, clad in those socks, were tucked under her, and she was knitting in nothing but a T-shirt. The large blanket she was working on sat half on the table and half in the bag at her side. Who knew knitting was so stimulating? There, in the middle of the night, her hair every which way, she was sexier than any fantasy he'd experienced or conjured up in his far-reaching imagination.

Stepping closer, the floor creaked beneath his bare feet and she looked up. Even from a distance, he noticed the crease between her brows and the weight of her expression.

"Stressed?" he asked, crouching down in front of her.

"No. I'm great." Her needles stopped as she leaned forward to kiss him. She eased back, started knitting again as if she needed to continue, and Cade knew something was wrong.

"Why did you ask me if I was stressed?"

"I heard a rumor that you stress knit."

She let out a nervous laugh that seemingly stuck in her chest. "That makes me sound like a weirdo. Knitting calms me and helps me think, that's all."

"What are you thinking about at"—he stood and glanced at the clock on the wall—"two o'clock in the morning?"

"I couldn't sleep, and I have this order on Etsy that I'm about twenty-five rows behind schedule on, so I thought I would catch up." She wasn't looking at him, so he crouched down again.

She was intent on her needles, but when Cade placed a hand over hers, she looked up. Her normally vibrant eyes were lackluster and burdened with something that gripped at his chest.

"What's wrong?"

"Nothing. I'm dealing with some stuff and—" She shook her head and set her work down on the table. "Forget it. I'm great."

"You're a lousy liar," he said, touching her chin.

"If only that were true."

Cade went to stand back up, but her eyes welled and her face looked about to crumble. He dropped to his knees and took her hands. "Sistine, you're making me nervous. What's going on?"

"I thought we'd go on one date. You know? And then we would go back to you being the hot bartender and me being, well, whatever it is I am."

She seemed to be pleading with him to back up or pull her closer, he couldn't figure out which, so he stayed put and hoped he could talk her through it.

"I've always had a hard time staying in my spot," he said. "Remember when you used to have to line up in school? I was always the terror who ruined it for everyone."

"Class clown?"

"Something like that."

Her expression eased, so he stood. "Are you hungry?"

She shook her head.

"Do you want me to go?" In the past, he'd asked the question after sex, but now, with her, it sounded a little cheap.

"No. I want you to stay." She stood, shoving the blanket and yarn into her big bag.

"And that's the problem?"

"It's not a problem. I'm simply trying to keep things—" She turned to face him. "You know how when you first have great sex with someone."

He tilted his head with a grin.

"Fine. You know how when you first have incredible, mind-blowing, multiple orgasm, the best of your entire life sex with someone."

"Better."

She smiled for the first time since he'd found her knitting.

"And you're so intimate, but there are still things you want to keep for yourself or hold back because you don't want to be an idiot and blabber all your deep dark thoughts and ruin the first sexy time."

"Is this a rule?"

"No. Well, sort of. People don't blabber after first sex."

"Okay. You don't need to blabber. I'm hoping there will be a lot more sex, so maybe you can share your deep darkness with me after ten or fifty."

"That's my problem. I'm having a tough time waiting. One time with you and the feelings are bursting out of me. I want to climb right inside of you and stay there. See, like that stuff. I'm supposed to hang on to that for a long time, at least for a few months."

"Are you reading sex advice columns or something? You can make your own rules."

At that, she laughed and then cried. Cade knew exactly how she felt. He was close to blabbing how he felt about her, but she threaded her arms through his and he was no longer able to speak. He wondered if she could hear his heart, if it was telling her everything she seemed reluctant to share herself.

"What if," she said, the middle-of-the-night quiet making every word sound like a secret. "What if I blabber and you don't like what I have to say? What if it changes things and then I lose this." She squeezed him. "How do I blabber, Cade, and still stay right where I am?"

He couldn't imagine anything she could tell him at that moment, save the standard body in the trunk or secret husband, that would ever make him back away, but the fear was real for her, so he held tight and gave her space to share.

She kissed his chest and stepped back. "I am completely ruining the post mind-blowing sex moment. Did you say you were hungry?"

"Sistine." He touched her arm, but she'd already reined in the blabbering. He was equal parts curious and concerned, but he knew two things: he was hungry, which normally took precedence, but he freaking loved her. An everyday, never enough, and no-matter-what kind of love thumped comfortably in his heart. He hoped she felt the same because he was gone and even the thought of losing her had him back to holding his breath.

Sistine had practiced every scenario, some even in the mirror while she was drying her hair in the morning, but none of them ended without Cade feeling betrayed in the worst way because he believed her to be...

What exactly did he believe her to be? Maybe she should ask him or not care. It had been a few months since she'd literally fallen into his arms. They weren't married, they'd only been dating for seventeen days.

That casual no-strings-sex scenario worked until, like all the other scenarios where she might come clean, he tells her what she already knows—a lie is a lie.

They sat on the bed eating his mom's delicious lasagna and talking about growing up. Every time he shared a part of himself, she felt worse. This was not how relationships worked. She needed to share too, and not some stupid story about her Halloween costume. She'd never considered herself a selfish person, but this was selfish. She was pretending that if she wanted him enough, the one detail she couldn't manage to tell him would vaporize into thin air. What if she came right out and said it? "Hey, you know how hard it can be to make ends meet when you're a small business, right? Well, I've been messing around on the side to—"

Messing around, that didn't sound right. Nothing would ever sound right, so she let it go again.

She snaked around him until she was lying across his lap and looking at his back. She ran a hand under his shirt. "Did you know that you have a little cluster of freckles on your back?"

"I do know that." He looped her with his arm and rolled her onto the bed. He was braced over her, and while she knew she loved the man inside more, sometimes it was a simple pleasure to lie back and enjoy his packaging.

"Don't guys like you normally have scars?" She laughed and he kissed her before lifting a brow.

"Guys like me, huh?"

"Yes, big, brawny, sexy bartender types."

"Oh, you're hysterical when you're naked."

"Speaking of which"—she took off her shirt and rolled down her socks—"you are entirely too clothed." She yanked at his clothes until he was gloriously naked again.

"Do you have any scars? I'll bet women like you have scars."

Oh, if that wasn't a loaded question, she didn't know what was, but lying there being silly, she was a woman like any other woman. Naked and willing to give at least some of herself to a man.

"Let's see." He started kissing her shoulders, and Sistine needed to speak fast while she was still able.

"I almost cut my finger off with a cat food can." She held up her left hand and looked for the now-faded silvery scar.

"Oh, I need this story." He took her hand and rested on his forearms.

"We used to have these cats that would hang out behind the Crab Shack when we were little. Seafood. Strays. You know?"

He nodded, kissed her finger.

"One of the cats had kittens and I wanted them to be safe. So, I put the mom and her babies in a box and asked my parents to buy some wet cat food. I ran out before school one day, so excited to get them some food and—why are those cans so sharp?" Cade flinched when she made the movement across her finger.

"That's an impressive scar."

"Not bad for a knitter, huh? Oh, and I fell off a swing in third grade, well, Brett Blanch pushed me. I scraped up the side of my leg." She rolled a little to see if she could find it, but Cade held her to the bed.

"That one sounds even more interesting. I think I'll go look for it." With a grin that was pure mischief, he kissed down her body until Sistine's hands were fisted in the sheets and she forgot about everything.

"Did you know I was chubby when I was a kid? A bit of a cliché, but I was," Cade said after they'd caught their breaths a second time.

"I'd go through these growth spurts and get wide before I sprouted up. Boyd and Patrick are tall, and they were lanky before they filled out. West has always been annoyingly perfect, so that was annoying. I was the husky kid. So right out of the gate things were always about my body. School clothes shopping, who picked me for sports teams... Shit, my mom called me Big Guy until after one shitty basketball practice, I told her to stop."

"It seems like things have worked out for you." She smiled and the lump grew in her chest.

"I guess. You know what's weird though? Once I stopped being chubby, things were still physical."

"Beauty can be a trap," she said, a little sick to her stomach now. It was one thing to share scars and silly stories, but he was giving her a piece of himself she did not deserve, and this had to end. If she couldn't get out of her contract with Melissa, she needed to end things with Cade.

She sat up and put on her T-shirt and a pair of leggings. It would take a hell of a lot more than flirty socks to survive this. Cade leaned up like he was about to say something, but she beat him to it.

"I have an early class tomorrow, and this was fun, but it's probably best if you go."

"It's almost morning anyway. You don't want to—"

Sistine shook her head and willed herself not to cry. She had no business crying. This was all her fault.

"Okay." Cade rolled out of bed and got dressed faster than she'd ever seen anyone dress. For an instant, before he was able to shift from vulnerable to charming, she saw him flinch, rendering one more crack in her heart before he was at the door to her apartment.

"Thanks for coming over."

"Don't do that."

"Do what? I'm—"

"Done with me. I get it, but don't be fake. Thanks for coming over? You're better than that, Sistine."

She could practically see him locking up like a person who was well versed in being dismissed. The ache in her chest was unbearable. If he kept looking at her the way he was, she was going to drop dead right on the spot.

"Cade, I'm not done with you. I have stuff and you have stuff. I'll see you tomorrow."

"I don't know what's going on with you or why when I chose to reveal something about myself you decided it was time for me to go, but whatever it is, I can take it. Be straight."

Her eyes were scratchy and if she didn't do this quickly, she would lose her nerve and be sucked right back into the cycle of guilt.

He met her gaze and it was like he could see right inside. She found herself wishing it was that easy.

"You're right." She let out a slow breath. "This has been fun, Cade. I like you, but I think we've run our course. You know?"

He shook his head. "No, I don't know. We've run our course?" he said slowly and nodded. A mixture of pain and anger crossed his expression, but he smirked. Arms overhead on the doorframe, he bent to find her eyes as she stared at the wall, hoping he'd walk away.

"You care about me." He touched her chin when she tried to look away. "I know you do. I appreciate your effort at trying to make what we have a hookup to protect whatever it is you're not ready to share, but you forget I'm an expert on the hookup. I know what that is and that's not what we have here."

At that moment, Sistine begged for a poker face. "We're too different, Cade. There's no reason we can't be friends."

He rubbed a hand over his face. They were both exhausted. Why didn't he give up and leave?

"Yeah, there's a big reason we can't be friends. I'm not in love with my friends. Goodnight, Sistine."

Cade walked out and when she heard the roar of his bike, she collapsed onto her bed and cried.

Chapter Nineteen

*C*ade had never loved anyone, save his family. He'd said he loved two of his girlfriends in the past, but he'd been wrong. This, this woman and the way she made him feel was love. As sure as he knew his heart was thundering in his chest when she'd told him to leave, he knew she was the one for him. And while that should have scared the hell out of him, especially since she was pretending to reject him, it didn't.

He was ready to be loved and Sistine loved him. It was all over her face, but if she didn't see it, didn't want to want him, he wasn't going to beg. He'd tried to call her two days after she'd dumped him, but she didn't answer. She didn't show up for backgammon on Wednesday, so he stopped calling. He felt like he'd been hit by a truck and for the first time since they'd opened the Tap House, he wasn't looking forward to his shift.

At the sound of the side door opening, Cade looked up to find Mason taking a seat at the bar, followed by Boyd, who continued on to the back office. Mason obviously took in Cade's surly expression—the kid missed nothing—and remained quiet. Cade dug deep for his fun-uncle routine.

"Can I see some ID?" he asked, raising a brow at his nephew.

"Very funny. Can I have a cup of coffee?"

"No."

"Why not?

"Because it shrinks your balls and you're still developing."

Mason huffed, and Cade slid him a glass of orange juice.

"I thought you were a driving man these days."

."I am, but it's only my permit, so I need a driver with me, which is stupid because I passed my test and I know how to drive. It's a big pain in the—"

Boyd cleared his throat.

"Pa-toot, that's what it is, a pain in the pa-toot, Uncle Cade."

"He tell you that he almost killed us making a left out of the school yesterday?" Boyd jumped in.

Mason shook his head. "I did not almost kill us. You told me to make a decision and execute. All I was doing was executing."

"Yeah, you're right. That's why I almost had a heart attack." Boyd set the box he carried from the back on one of the stools and then feigned grabbing his chest before sitting next to his son.

"You're so dramatic."

Mason was getting taller. His face was different every time Cade saw him. More mature, eyes deeper, more like his father with hints of his mother who was now raising an adopted son with her new husband in the city, maybe. Cade couldn't keep it all straight.

"So, how's it going?"

"Fine. Great. How are you?"

Boyd's expression narrowed, and Cade knew he was screwed.

"Who told you?"

"Told me what? I'm taking my kid to school and thought I'd drop by to say hello to my brother."

Mason and Cade both laughed.

"Fine. You know who told me. Word travels fast in the book club."

That's right. Cade had forgotten that the book club was supposed to meet last night. "Did they cancel their meeting?"

"No, it was at Mom and Dad's."

"So, they know I was dumped after the best sex—" He stopped, remembering Mason was with them. He met Boyd's eyes. "Sorry. I'm fine. Tell all inquiring minds I am great."

Mason rolled his eyes. "Please. I'm going to be a junior."

"In like six months. Let's not rush it," Boyd said.

"Still, it's not like I don't know about sex. Look around. Sex is everywhere. Chloe from eighth grade. Remember her?"

"I thought we weren't allowed to say her name out loud," Cade said.

Mason simply stared at him.

"What?" Cade asked Boyd.

"That was so junior high, man," Boyd mocked a dude voice.

"I don't know what that even was, but anyway." Mason flipped his hair out of his eyes. "Yeah, Chloe who ended up not being the love of my life. Big shock." He thumbed his phone and then turned the screen and showed it to both Boyd and Cade. The picture was a young woman's back. It looked like she was in Hawaii and wearing a thong. Cade couldn't see her face, but he was familiar with the bare-butt vacation pictures. They were all the rage. Shit, he was starting to sound like their dad.

"Why is that on your phone?" Boyd said.

Mason shook his head. "It's not. It's on her Finsta. That's Chloe."

Boyd took the phone, evidently shocked that Mason's first big crush had grown up and ditched the overalls. He shut the screen off and handed it back. "She's obviously looking for attention. And it's Insta, Mase. You said Finsta."

Mason laughed and put his phone on the bar. "Finsta is like a DL Insta, Dad."

Boyd stared at him.

"Down low," Cade offered as he entered three breakfast burritos into the register. He didn't bother asking if Mason and Boyd wanted one. If either passed, Cade would eat theirs. In addition to double workouts, he was eating his feelings lately.

"Thank you. But I'm still confused."

"Pictures people want to post but don't want everyone to see."

Boyd looked at Cade. He shrugged. He'd heard of Finsta, but like many things over the last twenty-four hours, he was again enlightened.

"Do you have one?" Boyd asked.

Cade cringed for his nephew. "Dude, you walked right into that one."

"Yeah. But I'm not posting bare-butt or giving away the D, Dad."

"Making it worse," Cade said, putting a box of oranges on the bar and starting his prep while Boyd tried to figure out how his son had grown up.

"And by the D, you mean?" He hesitated, glancing at Cade, who nodded.

"Holy crap. Hand it over," Boyd said.

Mason slapped his hand over his phone. "First of all, language."

Boyd wiggled his fingers, palm up, still waiting like a fool for his teenager to hand over his phone.

"I thought we had trust," Mason said. "Besides, it's private."

Boyd shook his head. "When you pay the bill, you can have all the privacy you want." His hand was still out, and Mason huffed. Cade realized he did a lot more of that lately as he watched him put in his password, swipe, and hand his phone over to his dad.

Cade kept making orange slices, and for the first time since Sistine dumped him, he laughed. The confused expression on Boyd's face as he swiped through what his teenager considered private was entertaining. "These are dumb."

"That's the point. It's not all sexual. But some people, mostly girls, use their Finsta for ass shots. Or Hartley Blake likes to post her boobs and—"

Boyd held up his hand. "I've had enough social media training for the morning."

"I wasn't trying to freak you out. I'm only saying that people from your... older people are weirded out by sex, but we're not."

Cade looked at Boyd, and they both glanced at Mason. "Old?"

"Er, I said old-er."

"I have no problem with sex." Boyd accepted the burrito. So did Mason, but he doused his with hot sauce.

"Yeah, you do. Well, maybe not sex," he said, his mouth still chewing. "But pictures of how fast we're all growing up freaks you out."

"First of all, I have no problem with pictures. I like pictures." Boyd wiped his mouth.

Cade swallowed a bite of his own breakfast. "That sounds wrong. Back it up, man."

Boyd tried again. "I think there's plenty of time for that stuff. You're a kid and so is Chloe. Just because I don't think people should share... everything with the world or their Finsta world, doesn't mean I'm against sexy or sex. Believe me, I like sex."

Cade almost choked on a laugh, and by the time Mason had joined him and they were both almost in tears, Boyd had balled his napkin onto his plate. He stood and jingled the keys at his son. "Party time is over. You're going to be late."

Mason popped the last bite of his burrito into his mouth before sliding on his backpack.

Boyd looked at Cade. "You said you were fine."

"I am." Cade returned to his orange slices.

"You also told me once that fine was barely living."

Cade nodded. "Like I said, I'm fine."

"Fair enough." Boyd went to leave and turned back. "She's going home for the weekend. I guess the Fourth is her favorite holiday."

Cade had accepted Sistine's brush-off, but that didn't mean he was ready to talk about her or know what she was doing. He held on to the bar and shrugged. "I didn't know that, but she's not on my radar anymore."

"Maybe you should show up and work it out. Ella said she looked awful at book club."

"Did she? Are you part of the book club now too, Boyd?"

Mason laughed and high-fived Cade. The kid was too young to realize his uncle was trying his damnedest to deflect so he didn't say, "Do you think she misses me too?" Boyd was smarter than his son.

"Don't be a dick. I'm trying to help you. Something's up with Sistine and if you care about her, you'll go find out what it is."

"Sorry. I'll think about it."

"Good." He grabbed Mason by the backpack. "Let's go."

"Later, Uncle. Remember what Grandma says. 'Mind your Ps and Qs.'"

"Any idea what that means, younger generation?"

"No clue." He stole an orange slice and ran out the door behind his dad.

Something's up with Sistine, he heard his brother's voice echo in his head during the dinner rush. No kidding, something was up with her, but she'd shut things down twice now. As much as Cade wanted to believe she needed him, he wasn't willing to risk his heart if Sistine, like most women in his life, only wanted what was most obvious.

Sistine's phone vibrated with a voicemail when she went back into her apartment after closing up the shop for the holiday weekend. She knew it wasn't from Cade. He'd given up earlier in the week and while she still had two of his voicemails on her phone, she would admit to no one that she replayed them to hear his voice. She'd made the right choice, but that didn't mean her heart wasn't still pissed at her every time she thought about him.

The voicemail was from Melissa. Sistine tapped her phone and the saccharine-sick tone spoke from the speaker.

"Tiny. Listen, give me a ring as soon as you get this. We need to talk. Ta."

A silver hatchback Uber stopped in front of her shop and Sistine grabbed her bag. It would take less than an hour to get to her parents' house, even with beach traffic. Locking her apartment door, she walked out through the front of her shop. Should she call Melissa now and get it over with? What would waiting do other than postpone the something that might have to play out under the prying eyes of her family? She closed the front door of her shop, strangely aware of the little bell and the muted brass of the doorknob as if she were looking at them for the first time. Or the last, she thought as she put her bag in the trunk of the Uber and patted her shorts to confirm her phone, and Melissa's message, were safely in her pocket.

Up until recently, things had made sense to Sistine, which she knew was a luxury because a lot of people seemed pretty confused most of the time. She'd spent most of her life firmly planted in reality. Her parents often said things like, "You play the cards you're dealt," and "No one owes you anything." They were business owners, hard workers, and they'd raised her to be the same. Based on that reality, she had come up with certain truths for herself. And while she'd spent plenty of time in lacy thongs and push-up bras, she was always going to prefer socks and scarves. All of that changed her freshman year when she met Melissa Dunn. Nothing in Melissa's world was real, and like a glitter vortex, Sistine was sucked in.

Mel, as she used to affectionately call her friend, was one of her three roommates at the University of San Francisco. Sistine's first memory of that afternoon was being mesmerized by the shine and brilliance of Melissa's hair. As her own parents shook hands with Melissa's parents, Sistine tried to see how someone inherited such gorgeous hair. Melissa's mom's hair was equally dark and cropped short. She had an enormous necklace and bright red lips. Her father was less ostentatious, but still had an air of money and power. Sistine still remembered his shiny bald head and that he smelled like apple cider. At the time she wondered if it was the candies. She'd never seen the man without hard candy in his mouth.

Both of Melissa's parents were as shiny and fluid as she was, and Sistine was captivated. Melissa grew up in San Rafael. She "lunched" in the city with friends during high school and once spent an entire weekend at the Ritz for "girl time." Sistine had never been out of Bodega Bay save several road trips with her parents and one weekend when her brother took her to Seattle before his "dark period," as their mother liked to call it. Sistine had chores, had read, actually read, every Jane Austen book, and realized her hair was somehow frizzier in the city. Melissa had a nanny, her daddy's credit card, and read fashion magazines. They could not have been more different and yet they were instant friends. It would take Sistine years to realize that she was Melissa's assistant and sidekick, and that was not the same as friend.

Having still not mustered up the courage to return the call, Sistine rested her head on the warm glass of the back window and felt a relief, which she knew like everything else was temporary. Yet as the small town she grew up in approached, she felt protected, a bit like the cove. Nothing bad happened in Bodega Bay.

She could smell the ocean before the Uber driver came around the bend near Salty's Taffy. The small town of Bodega Bay began filling up as early as July 2. The five hotels and motels they had were booked months in advance. Sistine came home every year. By July, she usually missed her family, and the Fourth of July was her favorite holiday.

When they were little, her brother and sister used to tease her that Independence Day was a lame favorite holiday.

"You like Fourth of July more than your birthday?" Jules had exclaimed one year as they walked in the parade.

Sistine remembered nodding, chewing on her red, white, and blue taffy from the same Salty's she'd passed a minute ago.

"People shoot fire into the sky, Jules. Nothing's better than that."

Her sister had laughed at her, would probably still laugh at her once she arrived at their parents' place, but that was all right. She loved everything about the day and never apologized for it. When she was younger, she had red jelly shoes before graduating to flip-flops with glitter straps and flags on the soles in her teens. In college, she wore cutoffs and tank tops that made her father roll his eyes and ask if she was cold in such "itty bitty shorts." Now in her thirties, her shorts were longer but her spirit the same, even with Melissa's message. Sistine had packed longer jean cutoffs and a knit tank top she loved so much she'd worn it three years in a row now. Tomorrow she'd pin her hair back with little flag clips she found in one of the stores on her street and her shoes, red Converse, had blue curly laces and glitter stars.

The Crab Shack stood in the foreground of her parents' property. Blue and white in the distinct coastal way, they welcomed locals and visitors alike. Sistine remembered when her parents bought the place. Back when they lived in a smaller house than the one behind their restaurant and her father was a crabber with a dream. The small one-room building with a large front patio that looked out over the bay was brown when they bought it and served as a bait shop for visiting fishermen. Tate Cooper's dad owned it, and when his wife Emma passed away, he sold everything to Sistine's parents. Tate now lived on a tugboat in Long Beach.

"There she is. The patriotic princess of Bodega Bay," her father said, coming down the walk of their home and offering to pay the Uber driver until Sistine explained it was all done through her app.

"Huh. Technology is stealing a dad's ability to help his daughter out too. What's next?" He kissed her forehead and took her bag. Chuck Branch smelled like the bay. Sistine never realized that until she left home and returned. It was as if her nose and every other part needed to clear itself of home before she noticed the details.

"That kiss helped me enough." She kissed him back and when he looped his arm, she threaded hers through it as she had done as far back as she could remember. "Good to see you, Dad."

"You too. I bought extra sparklers for you this year, and your mother made two flag cakes."

"Really?"

He nodded and held open the screen door with his foot to let her walk into the home she grew up in.

"We spiffed up your room a little now that your mom is getting back into painting. Yours has the best view, so she works up there sometimes."

Sistine looked around the living room as her dad tromped up the staircase to put her bag in the back bedroom. There was no point in telling him she could get it, or he didn't need to bother because he always bothered. He was the kind of man who found value in doing. Their mother explained that to Sistine one time when she'd been upset that her dad had done something without asking her opinion. She didn't even remember what it was anymore, but the inside information on her dad stuck and with that knowledge, she tried to go a little easier on him when he insisted on taking charge.

"Hello, my darling." Her mom came from the kitchen drying her hands and offered her cheek to Sistine. She kissed and handed her mom flowers she'd bought from the new florist three shops down from her before she left Petaluma.

"Oh." Her mother threw her towel over her shoulder and brought the paper-wrapped bundle to her nose with both hands. "These are gorgeous. Peonies?"

"And lilacs."

"Not a carnation in sight." Her mom hated carnations, had made that known from the time they were little and still mentioned it every time someone brought her flowers. One year for Mother's Day, Sistine's brother Drake sent their mom a giant vase of carnations and then showed up at their house for dinner and laughed himself stupid. He brought her "real flowers" to make amends, but it was a great joke. Before his accident, Drake used to be silly like that. Now, he still had his sense of humor, but it was dry with more edge.

"I love them," her mom said, breaking Sistine from her memories. "Now, come into the kitchen so I can show you the new microwave. Your father says it spins the right way, but something is wrong with it."

Sistine tried not to smile, but as soon as her mother turned toward the kitchen, she couldn't help it.

"Jules is still on the boat and your brother is coming over later, but we can have tea. Do you want some tea?"

"I would love some tea."

"Great. Look at that microwave while I put these in some water."

"She doesn't need to look at the microwave. It works beautifully," her father said, walking past the kitchen, carrying lawn chairs through the front door.

While her mom made tea and argued a bit more with her father over where exactly the lawn chairs should go, Sistine called Melissa. She was sent straight to voicemail and while she was curious, part of her didn't care what Melissa wanted. It's not like she was her friend anymore. Sistine was under contract. Trapped in a weak moment of desperation and resolved to serve, but she didn't have to like it.

Later that night when her parents were settled on the couch for one of their CSI shows, Sistine went to bed early and lay there trying not to think about Cade or what his plans were for the holiday. It would be so easy to blame Melissa for all of this, but Sistine was never one for blame. She'd taken the money, chosen her shop over everything.

At least now, she'd managed to push Cade out of the way of the runaway train that was her life. He would move on and she would find a way to live with the pain of that thought.

Chapter Twenty

The next morning, Cade woke to Cocky singing his lungs out. After feeding the chickens and a quick shower, he ran by the Tap House to check on supplies for the holiday weekend. Max and Tina were working the bar, but Cade liked to double check. He also wanted to get a few pictures of the beer garden for a blog post he was submitting about summer brews and outside spaces. He was getting the hang of the blog and was actually having fun with Henny and Penny's Instagram.

Comfortable everything was set, he stopped by his parents' house. They had a cookout every year and then they all watched fireworks on the back patio, but he wasn't in the mood for fireworks.

"What the hell are you doing here?" Patrick was wearing one of their mother's aprons around his waist and making hamburgers.

"What the hell are you wearing? Forget that, where is my beautiful niece?"

"Home with her beautiful mother. They'll be over later. I thought you were going up to Bodega?"

"What made you think that?" Cade opened his parents' refrigerator and grabbed a handful of mini carrots.

"Sistine is there. Boyd told you she was going through stuff. I thought you'd be with her."

"Sistine and I are not together. To recap one more time, we were together, we slept together, and she kicked me out. Are there any questions?" Cade crunched his carrots and hoped like hell he sounded aloof.

"So, you're giving up?"

"Don't start. I am not in the mood for some big brother speech. Mind your own fucking business."

Patrick's expression grew serious.

They told each other practically everything. Some things Cade didn't need to hear and tried to forget, but he'd given out plenty of advice over the years. Maybe it was his turn to shut up and take it.

"Can I say one thing?"

"Sure. What?" Cade popped the last carrot into his mouth and folded his arms.

"I'll make it quick. The illusion is easier than the reality." His brother finished making the last burger, set it on the plate, and washed his hands.

"That's it?"

Patrick nodded.

"Okay. Thanks."

"Aren't you going to ask me to elaborate?"

"I... okay. Elaborate away."

"You see the three of us—you watched Aspen and me get married and have a baby. Boyd found love with Ella, and we all know if Meg can love West, anything is possible. You want that for yourself. You told West, and even if you hadn't, I can tell. What I'm trying to tell you is wanting it and having the balls to be in it are two different choices."

"I know and when I meet the right person, I'll put in the work."

"No, you won't. You've met the right person and she's not that easy, so you're giving up? What the hell is that? We don't give up."

"How many different ways can I say this: she stepped back. I was right there, ready to dive in, and she didn't want me."

"And you're using that as an excuse not to love her. Because what if she doesn't love you back."

"Oh, no. I'm not paying for therapy. Listen, as helpful as this chat has been, Sistine and I are friends again, or we will be. It's fine. So, having quadrupled our social media following and making our blog kickass will have to be proof enough that I am all about effort. In fact, I'm off to the gym right now." He patted Trick on the shoulder. "More effort."

"Don't do this, Cade. It doesn't work."

"I'm not you, Trick."

"No, but you come from the same stuff. We're lovers, us McNaughtons. Fight for it or you will regret it for the rest of your life."

"You know that how?"

"If I could go back to when Aspen and I were twenty-five, I would have had ten more years with her. Ten more years of mornings and watching her with our daughter. We could have gotten started sooner."

"Maybe neither of you were ready."

"Maybe, but I'll never know. You can't simply want it and then bam, it falls into your lap. It's work, man. Harder than a blog."

"Hey, don't knock the blog."

"I'm not, but loving someone is every damn day. It's getting up and hoping like hell you don't screw it up. Sulking that it didn't work out, wanting is easier than doing. If you work things out with Sistine and love her, you give her the power to destroy you. What if she changes her mind and doesn't love you anymore?"

"Exactly. Like, figure out who you are, so I know the game."

"But that's it. No game. No rules. She gets to change. So do you. It's how loving someone works."

"When did I say I loved her?"

Patrick shook his head. "Get the hell out of here or you're going to be buried in traffic heading toward Bodega."

"I'm not going to Bodega. I'm going to the gym. I never..." Cade ran a hand over his face. "I don't even know where her family lives."

"Call Drake. You should still have his number."

Cade did. He tossed his phone from one hand to the other and glared at his brother.

"You don't know everything."

"Agreed."

Cade walked outside to say hello to his parents before leaving.

"Tell Sistine I said Happy Fourth." Trick grinned.

"You're an idiot," Cade said as the screen door slammed behind him.

"But I'm your idiot," he called out from the kitchen. "Drive safe."

He went to the gym, but called Drake on his way home and was on the road an hour later.

Crap, he was not looking forward to Patrick's gloating.

Sistine woke to find her laptop charger chewed up and spit out at the foot of her bed. Her parents had a new puppy that obviously had free roam of the house.

Shaking off the drowsiness of another night spent tossing and turning, her brain registered what a laptop without a charger meant. Grabbing her laptop, she ran down to the kitchen hoping her mom still had a Mac. She set her laptop on the kitchen table and noticed the new Toshiba laptop in the built-in desk by the window. Why was her mother always switching laptops? Damn it.

She sat staring at the 5 percent battery icon on her screen before slamming the laptop closed. Right as she was about to scream, her brother walked in pulling a T-shirt over his unruly head of dark hair.

"Macs, can't live with 'em. Can't live without 'em," he said.

Sistine was so happy to see her brother she forgot for a minute that she had mere minutes to charge her laptop or Melissa and a whole lot of other people she didn't know would be all over her before the first firework lit up the sky.

"Drake Branch. The elusive one-armed brother."

"At your service." He kissed the top of her head and grabbed a coffee cup.

Sistine grabbed the edge of the table so hard her knuckles turned white. She wanted to grab her big brother and yell, "Please help me. And when Melissa calls again, could you talk to her?"

Drake stuck a bagel in his mouth and sat across from her with his coffee in a mug that read Branch Crab Shack in red lettering. "Problem?"

Sistine shook her head and put the laptop back in her bag.

"Honey, can you help me with these tablecloths?" her mom yelled from the top of the stairs.

"Nope, no problems." She stood. "Not yet anyway," she said under her breath before calling to her mom that she'd be right up.

"I'll be back. Don't move. I want to hear about your new glass designs. Dad showed me some pictures at dinner last night."

Drake ripped a hunk of bagel and set the rest on the table, toasting her with his coffee cup as she left.

She stood in the kitchen entrance debating if she should grab her bag. She'd been hiding for so long she second-guessed her own family. Drake lowered the newspaper he'd started reading and flashed her his signature you're-an-idiot look. Sistine walked out before her mom fell down the stairs in the name of perfectly ironed tablecloths.

When she finally finished draping all of the outside tables in red, white, and blue, Sistine went back to the kitchen. She still had fifteen minutes. Maybe she could figure out a way to download the software onto her mother's laptop in time. That wasn't going to work. She needed to come up with some way to use her own laptop by nine. Or for the first time since Melissa had sold their brilliant idea out from under Sistine's nose, *Cosmopolitan* would go to print without an Ask Amy column. There would still be time to get something up on the blog and the electronic edition, but most readers loved the print copy. She had no idea what the financial penalties were if she missed a deadline. She did not need any more financial penalties.

Her brother was no longer in the kitchen, but her laptop was on the table with one of her sticky notes on top that read simply, "Learn to ask for fuck's sake," in Drake's familiar scrawl.

Sistine's heart banged against her ribs as she noticed the charger and opened her laptop. The column she'd worked on last night was still minimized at the bottom of the screen. Having no idea if her brother had read anything or had time to care, Sistine proofed her copy one more time and submitted the file.

She received confirmation that the file was received and rested her face in her hands. After her pulse settled back to its normal rhythm, she noticed and clicked on an unopened email.

Dear Sistine-

I hope this email finds you well. It turns out we have a mutual acquaintance. Mrs. Platt, who sits on our board, is the mother of your good friend Vienna Platt. After discussion with Mrs. Platt and her glowing recommendation, despite the age of your building, we have reconsidered and are hoping you will agree to host our expo next July. It is our understanding your shop has had a complete electrical overhaul and we are excited to host in a place with both charm and technology. Please let us know as soon as possible and we will send over a contract and holding deposit.

Sincerely,

Deidra Welch

Sistine swallowed the lump in her throat. She was so tired of going at full speed all the time. Vienna must have called in a favor with her mom and gotten the expo. Sistine texted her dear friend to thank her and received a winking emoji, followed by a kissing emoji and Happy Fourth. She sat back in her chair and thought about Drake's Post-it. Maybe if she'd asked for help, she could have avoided Melissa and she'd still have Cade.

Sistine rarely dwelled on the fallout from Melissa's betrayal, but that was probably the reason she did most things on her own. Weird how she'd returned to the woman who had caused so much damage rather than risk asking her true friends for help.

"Oh, beautiful for spacious skies," Jules sang as she approached the kitchen. Sistine smiled before she even turned around. Her big sister did that to her. "Statue of Liberty, oh, Statue of Liberty." Jules tromped into the kitchen, still in her bright orange bib overalls and black waterproof boots. The outfit never changed; neither did the smell.

"There you are. Happy Favorite Holiday," she said, pulling Sistine in for a hug, not caring that she smelled like fish.

"Can you smell that anymore?"

Jules shrugged. "Occupational hazard. Keeps the men away."

Sistine laughed. "You work with men all day."

"Right, but I get to order those men around, so it's different. It's good to see you."

Sistine felt that same urge to say, "Please help me clean up this mess," but instead smiled. "Me too. Are you showering before the parade?"

Jules chomped into an apple she grabbed from the bowl on the kitchen table. "I was thinking about it."

"Probably a good idea, but you need to hurry up. I don't want to be late."

Snapping off her elastic suspenders until they hung at her waist, Jules took another bite and with the apple stuck in her mouth, yanked the elastic from her hair. What looked like yards of dark hair fell to her shoulders and her sister instantly looked younger.

"Oh, yeah, it would be a shame to miss Old Man Frazier's twin bulldogs taking a crap right as the parade gets started."

"He never picks it up. Does that bug you too?"

"The whole event bugs me. Ten minutes," she said over her shoulder as she went up the stairs for a much-needed shower.

Their dad liked to say that Juliet "Jules" Branch was the middle branch on the tree. "The one who held the thing together." Drake only had one year on her, but Sistine was three years below. She supposed that made her the bottom branch. Huh, she'd never thought of it that way.

Jules had been married and living in Portland when Drake wrecked his bike, which looking at her sister now, seemed like a lifetime ago. Up until they learned Drake would lose his arm at the elbow, he'd been their father's right-hand man. He ran both fishing boats, up at three a.m. every morning, and once everything was cleaned up, home after eight. The life of a crabber was hard work. Work Drake could no longer do. Their dad had started looking for other captains while Drake was still in the hospital. The business never rested, not for one day.

Jules stepped in and took over. She now ran both boats and enjoyed arguing with Drake over which one of them was the better captain. She really did hold them all together.

Now that Drake was used to his RoboCop arm, he could have returned to the boat, but as part of his therapy, he'd learned glassblowing. He'd found his passion, and his business was thriving. All Sistine wanted was the same chance to make her passion work.

Before she had a chance to rationalize her choices for the hundredth time, Jules returned, less fishy in cutoff shorts and a red tank top. Her sister was beautiful. Some people may add, "in an athletic and badass way," but Sistine didn't like qualifiers. Her sister was beautiful, period.

Chapter Twenty-One

The parade was in full swing when Drake fell into step with Sistine as they walked along Main Street. He wore a gray T-shirt, the same one she'd seen on him earlier, probably the same one he'd worn the day before, and dark green cargo pants.

"Feeling patriotic?" she asked him, all while smiling and waving at a cluster of kids watching the parade with a plasterboard sign that read: "Wave for the Red, White, and Blue."

"Not particularly. Feeling like you want to tell me why you're answering to some random question about nipple piercing from a woman named Shy in Seattle?"

Sistine cursed her luck, kept smiling, but dropped her arm. Enough with the waving. "Not particularly." She looked at her brother. "Snooper." She was going for playful and then she remembered playful in her house often drew blood. "Please don't tell me you told Jules about—"

"The nipples." Her sister came out of nowhere and threw her arm around Sistine, waving with uncharacteristic gusto that would put a prom queen to shame. "Yeah, I'm in on the nipples. What'd I miss?" She looked at Drake, still walking with his hands in his pockets.

"She's going with the 'it's none of our business' approach."

"Oh." Jules tucked her tighter into the curve of her arm but kept smiling. "I'm sorry, but that one never works. Are your nipples pierced?"

Sistine slapped her away in as playful a gesture as was possible when slapping a sister. "No, mine are not pierced. I was only writing about nipple piercing."

"As one does." She looked to Drake, who shrugged and cracked a grin.

Bastard.

"Are you sure your nipples aren't pierced?" She tugged at Sistine's shirt. "Because that would be the perfect thing to send Mom and Dad into a Jules is our favorite daughter frenzy."

"My. Nipples," she whispered that part, "Are. Not. Pierced."

"Easy there, darling of the Branch family. Smile for the small-town folk," Drake said, taking one of Sistine's flags and waving it.

"That's not nice. *We* are small-town folk."

"Well, apparently you're not anymore, Nipples," Jules said, elevating her wave to royalty.

Sistine shook her head.

"Does Cade know?"

Sistine tripped over what appeared to be nothing, and her brother caught her by the arm.

"Who's Cade?" Jules asked.

"You haven't met him. He's part owner in the brewery I did all the glasses for last year. Sistine, does he know?"

"There's nothing to know."

"Yeah, right. Better add a toothy grin to that monster lie. He called me, and I gave him the address. He'll be at the house when we're done with this shitshow."

"It's not a monster lie. It's a Britney Spears lie, and why did he call you?"

Drake shrugged. "I guess because you're not speaking to him, Nipples."

"Not funny. What else did he say?" Sistine stopped walking while she tried to process why Cade would want anything to do with her.

"Keep moving. This is a parade." Jules dragged her along. "It only works if we are actually parading."

"That's Cade?" Jules asked Drake who, of course, nodded as the three of them approached the Crab Shack.

"Oh, I would totally pierce my nipples for him. Ho-ly cann-oli."

Cade was smiling and chatting with her parents as if they were still dating and he was popping by for a visit. Her heart sprinted in her chest, but her head still didn't understand. It had been over a week since she'd ended things. Why was he there, and how was he managing to keep from rolling over with laughter at her parents, who were both wearing crab-shaped hats, T-shirts with Branch Crab Shack scrawled across the front, and blue socks she'd knitted for them last year?

Sistine walked toward the counter as her mother was giving him a sample of their world-famous chowder.

"I can't believe I shared my mother's lasagna with you and you're holding out on me with this chowder." He kissed her cheek, and Sistine watched her mom's eyes light up.

"You can stop by for chowder anytime you want, Cade. What do you do for a living again?" her mom said.

"I run Foghorn Brewery with my brothers. I'm in charge of the Tap House."

"You're a bartender?" Her mother handed over another small cup of chowder and a crab sandwich.

"I am." Cade leaned against the wall and ate his chowder.

Sistine still couldn't believe he was there, talking with her family, eating chowder. She needed to talk with him, but her mom had begun what they all referred to as her "passive interrogation tactics," so it could be a while before Sistine got him alone.

"Interesting. Do you drink a lot?"

"Mom," Sistine said. "Cade, can I talk to you?"

He nodded, still eating chowder.

"What? I'm asking if he drinks. That's important if you two are dating."

"We're not... we are playing backgammon," Sistine said and flinched.

"Actually, we stopped playing backgammon, remember?" Cade quirked a brow.

"Aw, is that what you kids are calling it these days?" Jules asked as she and Drake entered the kitchen and kissed their mom on the cheek.

"Why backgammon? Wouldn't bunco be a better analogy?" Jules grabbed a cup of chowder and parked herself right next to Cade.

"Or Sorry," Drake added.

"What's that game where you smack the groundhogs?" Jules grabbed a piece of bread.

Why the hell were they all standing in the kitchen? There were perfectly good tables outside on the grass and a line was forming while her siblings tried to figure out the best game to describe the sex she was no longer having with Cade. Her entire body wanted to remember the sex, but Sistine didn't let it in. She'd ended things with Cade to protect both their hearts.

"Whack-a-Mole. That's an arcade game." Drake took the offered crab sandwich.

"Now that's a metaphor for sex. Whack-a-Mole." Jules chuckled and bumped Cade with her shoulder.

"When did we start talking about sex?" Sistine asked.

"I have no idea. Could you please grab some more napkins from the storage closet?" Her dad came out of nowhere and suddenly the impossible happened and things became more awkward.

"Dad, why don't you show Cade around the place." Sistine wanted him anywhere but trapped in a kitchen with her entire family.

"He doesn't want to know about that. I'd rather hear about the bar."

"Great. You take Cade and I'll restock the napkins."

"Cade?" her father said.

Tossing his trash in the basket, Cade said, "Lead the way. I'm happy to talk shop."

Sistine smiled in spite of her angst and Cade kissed her shoulder before leaving with her dad. She turned to find her brother, sister, and mother all staring at her.

"What?"

"He's cute," Jules said.

"Yes, he is."

"You always were better at Whack-a-Mole," Jules said.

Sistine went back to the storage closet and grabbed the napkins. "Are you ever not... like this?" she asked, grabbing the napkin dispenser off the counter.

"Probably not. Dear Lordy, what I wouldn't give for a little Whack-a-Mole."

"Never settle for a little Whack-a-Mole, sis," Sistine heard Drake say as she left to refill the napkins on the tables. She couldn't help herself and smiled. They were crazy.

She needed to find Cade before her father told him all her secrets. Not that he knew all of them, but the man had an arsenal of embarrassment.

Cade realized he'd never seen Sistine in a baseball hat as she yanked him away from her father and around the back of the house. When they were out of sight, she whipped around to face him.

"What is going on? Why would you subject yourself to my family without warning me first?"

"I thought I'd surprise you."

Her brow furrowed. "What are you up to, Cade?"

"I was craving the best chowder this side of the Mississippi?'"

"Don't let my parents hear that. Best chowder in all fifty states."

"I stand corrected."

They both laughed. It had been a little over a week, but God he'd missed her. "I'm not giving up," he said before he had a chance to change his mind. "I love you, Sistine. It's simple, right there in my chest." He took her hand and held it close. He had never considered himself all that romantic, but from the look on her face, he wasn't a complete failure.

"I know you're going through some things with your shop and I'm not minimizing that, but I'd like a chance to help you and—"

She turned her baseball hat backward and went up on her toes. Cade snapped and drew her into him, taking her mouth with his like a starving fool. Sistine kissed him back and drew him toward what looked like a shed. When they managed to get the door open, he noticed boxes and two giant freezers. There were fishing nets and crates everywhere, but that was the extent of his observations because she took off her top and was pulling at his. He didn't bother to think about anything other than the touch of her skin. All he wanted when he hoisted her up on one of the freezers and dragged her shorts down her legs was one more taste. At that moment, it didn't matter if it was the last or the first of many more. He needed her and when she opened to him, he knew she needed him too.

Later, as they lay on a blanket tangled in her parents' shed, they regained their breath and she turned to face him. He met her gaze, still holding her hand, caressing her wrist. She was still so soft.

She touched his face and closed her eyes as if she had lost some internal debate. "I love you too," she said, barely above a whisper as the outside sprinklers turned on and the water hit the wood of the shed. "I didn't mean to love you, and once you find out what a mess I am, you'll take your love back. But while we're safe in here, I want you to know that I love you too." She pushed up on her arms and was looking down on him now. He reached up to move her hair off her face and felt the moisture at the edges of her eyes.

"There is nothing you could tell me that would change this, Sistine. I love you, and it's not going anywhere."

"I know that it seems like I always want you naked, but I fell for you before you took your clothes off."

Cade smiled and knew she loved all of him, and he wasn't complaining that she liked him naked too. "Can you tell me what's bothering you? Is something up with your shop?"

Sistine rested her head back on his chest. "When I was in college, I had a friend. Remember I told you about the dancer who—"

"Walked around naked. Yeah, I remember."

"Okay, well, she and I were complete opposites, but we were in this class and the project was to create a—"

"If you two are playing Whack-a-Mole in there, you'd better finish up. Dad is on his way back."

Cade sprung to his feet, almost smacking his head into Sistine's as she reached for her shirt and got dressed.

"To be continued," he said, adjusting her baseball hat and kissing her one last time before the shed door opened and they pretended to be fascinated by the crabmeat stock in one of the freezers.

Sistine and Cade joined in to help serve the crowd at the Crab Shack and he was struck by how similar their families were. Not the surface stuff, but when it came to what mattered, he and Sistine both came from hardworking families committed to great products and even better service. He'd always thought of Petaluma as a tight-knit community, but Bodega was a small town in the true sense of the word. Everyone seemed to know everyone else as the sky faded from blue to black and they all sat on blankets to watch the fireworks. Sistine's hands were clasped in front of her, her eyes mesmerized by something most people took for granted.

She loved him. The thought would have knocked him over had he not been already sitting with his arms wrapped around her. After the grand fireworks finale, the crowd started packing up, patriotic music still playing from every direction on the grass. He kissed her before he lost the chance in the flurry of activity. They all went into her parents' house for her mom's famous flag cake.

"Is that a tree on your arm?" Jules asked, taking a seat across from him at the table. Cade knew the sibling game and was more than ready.

"A beanstalk," he said.

She snorted. "Should have stuck with a tree. What the hell, like Jack and the... beanstalk?"

"That's the one."

"Why?"

"Jules, tattoos are personal," Sistine said.

"I know. I'm asking a personal question. The guy wouldn't walk about with a beanstalk up his entire arm if he didn't want someone to notice it. Wasn't Jack an idiot?"

Cade laughed and Sistine's expression was pleading. He squeezed her hand.

"Jack believed in magic. He stole from the giant to buy back his cow, which was noble, but then he got greedy. He took the easy way out. I believe in magic, but I'm also leery of easy answers."

"Is that so." Jules ate her cake as Sistine's mom and dad excused themselves to talk with neighbors.

"And... it looks sick." Cade turned his arm, still admiring the work even years later.

"I'm not big on tattoos, or nipple piercing for that matter. Every time I see them, I picture the person old, shriveled on a slab in the morgue. You know?"

Sistine glared at her sister and Drake bumped her shoulder.

"Not cool," he said, sipping his coffee. Sistine's brother managed more with a look than most people did with a full speech. He wondered if Drake was that way before the accident but decided to deal with Jules first.

"No. Sounds like a perspective problem. Did you want to discuss your nipple piercing?"

Jules was screwing with him. She obviously didn't know how thick the McNaughton sarcasm ran.

"I don't have my nipples pierced, but I know people."

Drake bumped her shoulder harder this time. "Cut it out."

Cade didn't know what he was missing, but he'd never seen Sistine so tense. No way she'd had her nipples pierced, he'd recently seen them in a dark storage shed. That thought alone made him smile.

"My perspective is a problem, huh? Do you think I should have it looked at?" she asked, batting her eyes.

"Maybe. They might offer you a deal while they're fixing your attitude."

Jules stared at him and then burst out laughing. "You're okay, McNaughton." She carried her plate to the sink and walked out back.

"Thanks, I like you too, Jules," he called after her. "You didn't tell me your family was so friendly."

"Didn't I?" Sistine seemed deflated, and something passed between her and her brother before she stood and walked out toward the water.

"What just happened?"

Drake licked his fork and took both of their plates to the sink. "No idea," he said, leaning against the counter with his arms crossed. "You should probably go after her."

Shit. Drake made Boyd look downright chatty. Cade nodded and took off out the front door.

"I'm sorry about that. Jules can be... abrasive," Sistine said as he fell in step beside her.

"I am well trained in abrasive." He put his arm around her. At first, Sistine stiffened as if she wanted to be alone with whatever was causing that wrinkle between her eyes to deepen, but when he tried to remove his arm, she held on.

They walked along the rocky coast of the bay and he found that he loved the layers that being in her hometown brought. He didn't know what about her sister had pissed her off, but even with the family dynamic, there was something profound about Sistine outside of Petaluma. It was as if he'd loved all of her in the dim light of a bar, and now they'd stepped out into the afternoon light. He adored everything about her and hoped she'd share what was bothering her, but later that night they fell asleep in each other's arms on her parents' back patio.

Chapter Twenty-Two

*S*istine woke early the next morning to her phone vibrating on her nightstand. Cade had chosen to sleep in the guest bedroom out of respect for her parents, which wasn't necessary but scored major points with her mom.

Only one person had the audacity to call her at five thirty in the morning, so without even looking, she answered her phone.

Melissa didn't bother with a greeting—she never did. She believed there was something powerful in jolting a person into the middle of a conversation without niceties, she'd once said when they were still in school.

"So, I'm sure you don't keep up with Washington news, but one of the rag sheets ran this ridiculous piece on me and they called me outdated. Frumpy. Can you fucking believe that?" She was breathing heavily. "Me. I am the complete opposite of frumpy."

"Agreed. Are you running for your life or your health?"

"The first lady is a former model and it seems the men in Washington need to up their game. Fucking assholes." She ignored the part of Sistine's question she didn't want to answer, another Melissa trait that never changed. "Anyway, my publicist is totally feeling the reveal about our being the real Ask Amy, especially the 'two college girls make it big' angle. I can't wait to see these bastards when they find out we write a sex column for none other than Cosmo-fucking-politan. Ya know?"

The sounds of big city traffic and Melissa's labored breathing filled Sistine's space even in tiny Bodega Bay. Her head began to throb as she hoped to all things holy that Melissa wasn't heading down the path it appeared she was heading. Although, as she continued to ramble, it seemed that maybe she would simply take the Amy column back again.

Sistine no longer cared about the money. She'd contacted Deidra and accepted the expo next year. That deposit would go straight in the bank and Sistine would have a cushion for the first time since she opened Knitterly's doors. She didn't need Melissa.

"Hello? Are you there, Tiny?"

"I... yes, I'm here. So, you're taking Amy back now. I thought you had to keep this a secret, so it didn't tarnish James's reputation."

"Yeah, well, that was before some asshole with a camera called me outdated. James wants me to be happy."

Sistine closed her eyes, willing the conversation and her headache to go away.

"I told my publicist about our little college project and how I grew it into a *Cosmo* sensation. He thinks it's a fabulous plot twist. I don't know why I panicked."

"Your husband was running for the United States Senate in the state of Texas."

Sistine could almost see Melissa flipping her long, shiny ponytail in dismissal. She must have stopped running because her breathing was even again. "True, but things have changed, Tiny. Look who's in the White House. Trashy is so in these days, it's practically trending."

"Even Ask Amy isn't *that* kind of trash. Mel, I'm still in Bodega, so I'm going to let you go. Let me know when you're ready to transition things back. Things have changed a bit for me too and—"

"Oh, sorry, Tiny, hang on." Melissa started speaking Spanish. Someone let out a laugh that sent a familiar frustration straight up

Sistine's spine. It was the same laugh she remembered anytime they went to a party and Melissa had too much to drink or sat down in a parking lot or the middle of a frat house.

Sistine closed her eyes. Maybe she could hang up.

"Tiny. Are you still there?"

"Unfortunately."

"What? Sorry, I'm meeting some girls for breakfast at this kitchy little burrito shop. This town still has the best food. Let me step back outside." More laughing. More Spanish.

"I thought you were running. Where are you?"

"I was and now I'm getting breakfast. Keep up, Tiny. I'm in our favorite city, our old stomping grounds. Anyway, the news that I am one half of Amy will drop today and Kurt wants—"

"Who is Kurt?"

"My publicist. Kurt thinks we need to spin the fun into this, starting with an interview with the two of us. At your shop. I'll be in your village tomorrow afternoon."

"I do not live in a village." Sistine was going to throw up.

"It always reminds me of one of those snow globe towns or those quaint little villages they set up in store windows."

Sistine let out a slow breath. This was not happening. "Everything is in the cloud. You know the password. Amy is all yours again, but I am not doing an interview."

"Oh, no no. We can't do that. For this to work, Kurt says we need the back story. The puff—he calls it the puff."

"And how am I the puff?"

"Once the story drops in the *Times* and *People* magazine, we'll be trending, so it's important to do the interviews right away."

"What story?"

"You and me. Two college friends who launched a blog for their junior project that turned into a global phenomenon and now runs weekly and in the print magazine. It's the year of the woman, Tiny. Sex and ball-busting women. It'll be fun. I'm driving up with the crew tomorrow. We'll be to you by one o'clock."

"Tomorrow? Mel, what crew? Are you morning drinking again?"

"Always, Tiny." There was that damn laugh again. "The *Today Show* crew. Do you need me to bring you some things to wear?"

"You expect me to tell everyone I know and love that I write a sex advice column for *Cosmo* in less than twenty-four hours and then you want me to sit through interviews while you sell our, your, story?"

"Yes. I know it's short notice, but these things happen overnight. Do you need me to bring you a few things to wear? I can have my stylist—"

"No." Sistine may have raised her voice. "I do not know how things happen overnight. I do not want your stylist or your publicist. I am not doing this. Take Amy back. Prove to everyone that you are not a frump, but leave me out of it. I have a life, Mel. And it's not sitting on the sidelines waiting for your next whim. Are you listening to me?"

"Did that sound rude when I asked about your clothes? Is that why you're pissy? I'm certain you have cute things to wear, but this is national television, so go easy on the animals or barrettes. Oh, Tiny, please no barrettes."

Sistine said nothing—there was no point. Melissa was on her own custom-colored train and Sistine had two choices, get on or get plowed over.

Melissa prattled on, oblivious as always to anything she didn't want to hear. "Okay, I'm sure you'll look great. My bad. Kisses. I'll see you tomorrow. Ooh, I can't wait to see you. Weird how things keep bringing us together, isn't it?"

"Mel, please listen—"

"Gotta go. We'll catch up over drinks tomorrow. Ta."

The phone was dead. Sistine touched the screen and lay back in bed staring at the slow-moving blue bubbles of her phone wallpaper. There were so many things wrong with what was about to happen to her world. Tossing her phone away as if that would toss Melissa too, Sistine put a pillow over her face and screamed.

There was no easy answer for Cade. They were... involved. She loved him more than she'd ever expected, and he made her believe she had a soft place to land. That didn't happen every day and it definitely didn't happen on her timetable. If she could go back, she would have done everything differently, but there were no do-overs in life, certainly not her life.

By tomorrow afternoon, Melissa and her band of shiny people would once again eclipse Sistine's life, and she had no one to blame but herself. She'd sold her soul because as Drake had said, she couldn't simply "ask for fuck's sake." Sistine pulled on her jeans and began packing her bag. She needed to get home and think.

The *Today Show*? Had she said the *Today Show*? When Sistine had a store sale or a new product reveal on Etsy, she ran an ad, printed flyers, even did an email blitz to her mailing list subscribers. Melissa called the goddamn *Today Show*.

Sistine's life was turning into a real-life metaphor of Gracie's knotted mess when she tried to knit from a hank instead of a ball of yarn.

What was she going to say to Cade? Now that Melissa couldn't take Ask Amy and go away for good, now that there would be publicity and interviews, Sistine needed to explain. And she needed to do it today, prepare him for... For what? For everything he thought was real to appear fake? For the realization that even though he loved her, and she loved him back, she'd lied to him?

Shoving things now into her bag, Sistine debated the age-old question. Was withholding information the same as lying? Technically Cade never asked, "Hey, do you write an advice column for *Cosmo*?" or "Have you ever used our conversations, my experiences, because you panicked?"

She stepped into her shoes and threw her bag over her shoulder. There was no way any of this led to a happily-ever-after for anyone. He was going to feel used, no matter what she said. And her friends. Oh no, she could only deal with one mistake at a time, and before any of it, she needed to get home. She had until tomorrow at one before the she-devil of Washington arrived with her crew.

Maybe some revelation would come to her on the drive home, some great idea while she held onto the man she loved for one last time before he hated her for all eternity. Willing herself to breathe, Sistine went downstairs, hopeful and hopeless in equal measure.

Chapter Twenty-Three

After hasty goodbyes and less than half a cup of coffee, Cade was on his bike back to Petaluma, Sistine holding him tighter than usual from behind. According to a text from Boyd, she'd asked everyone to meet her at Knitterly for lunch. She had something she needed to explain.

Cade didn't ask her specifics, deciding he'd wait to hear whatever it was with everyone else. Maybe she needed help with the shop or money? He knew everyone would pitch in. There was no way any of them would allow Sistine to lose her shop. Wondering how far in debt she could be to cause so much stress, Cade turned down Main, but couldn't park because there were several huge trucks blocking her shop. Sistine grabbed hold of his jacket and Cade parked on the opposite side of the street.

She took off his helmet and handed it to him before getting off the bike and standing at his side. Cade watched people unloading equipment from the trucks as Boyd and Ella approached the store, followed by everyone else they knew and loved. What the hell was going on?

"Cade, look at me." She turned his head and held his face.

Her expression was pure panic and because he had no idea what was happening, he couldn't help her.

"This is not what it seems. Repeat that for me."

He began to laugh at the cryptic tone but stopped when tears filled her eyes. "Okay, okay. This is not what it seems."

"Right. Remember that in about five minutes." She kissed him, still holding his face. "Remember that I love you too." Wiping her tears, she crossed the street and fell right into talking with the woman who looked like a news anchor, politician maybe. Whoever she was, Sistine's hands were flailing. Cade got off his bike and walked across the street.

"You said you were coming tomorrow. I accepted that and now here you are messing with my life again," Sistine said, handing Cade the keys to her shop.

He opened Knitterly and flicked on the lights. Boyd and Ella, Trick and Aspen, along with Bri, Vienna, and Thad all filed into the shop, take-out bags in hand.

"Any idea what this is about?" Trick asked.

Cade shook his head and stepped back outside hoping for some answers.

"Fine. Don't believe me, but I tried," the woman with the long dark hair said through a clinched perfect smile. "I am merely a puppet and Kurt wants this now."

"We need to speak with the property owner," some guy in a V-neck sweater said.

"I am the property owner," Sistine said.

"Is there a problem?" Cade asked. He had no clue what he was walking into, but Sistine seemed trapped.

They all turned on him and the guy with the open folder said, "Great. Let's take this off the street."

Once they were in her shop, everyone was silent at the lesson table. He needed to know what the hell was going on, but Sistine was not looking at him anymore.

"We'd like to film one segment inside and the other maybe on that back patio, or we could even film a segment with the two of you walking down the cute little street. I can't gauge what kind of crowd we'll get. Kurt, thoughts?"

Kurt, who must have been the man talking with the dark-haired woman by the window, held up his hand.

"I don't understand," Cade said. "What are you filming?"

"Oh." The guy looked over his shoulder as his crew continued moving pieces around Knitterly's tiny space.

"Cade, let me—" Sistine was interrupted when the guy stepped between them.

"I was under the impression you already knew about the interview with Ms. Branch and Ms. Dunn. Are you a moving part in this? Do we need to go over the vision?" He snapped over his shoulder. "Kurt, we are not all on the same page here." Kurt, in the jeans and starched shirt, sauntered over from the window like they were all at a cocktail party. Sistine was frozen in the center of her shop as if she too was something these guys might pick up and move for better lighting.

What the hell was all of this?

"Keep setting up," Kurt said before gesturing for them to meet him at the lesson table. "Sorry about this, guys. So, here's the deal. Now that the news broke that Ms. Branch and Ms. Dunn write the Ask Amy column for *Cosmo*, we need this interview to follow quickly to spin things out. You know what I mean?"

Bri snorted and the rest of them laughed. Cade still had no clue. He glanced over at Sistine, who finally managed eye contact. She sighed and shook her head.

"They are not involved in this," she said in a practically catatonic state. Patrick and Boyd stood next to Cade in some automatic show of brotherly solidarity and Cade still had no idea what was happening. Who the hell was Amy, and why were they interviewing a knitting shop owner on the *Today Show*?

Sistine was whisked off again by the crowd of clipboard-carrying strangers. Cade turned to the people he knew.

"So, Sistine, our Sistine, writes a column for *Cosmo*?" Bri said.

"What does the senator have to do with this?" Trick held out a chair for Aspen, who was bouncing Hattie in her carrier.

"Could someone please explain?" Cade leaned on the back of a chair.

"Well, from what I overheard, Sistine and her friend Melissa, she's the dark-haired gorgeous woman over there"—Bri pointed—"write a sex advice, correction, *the* sex advice column for *Cosmo* magazine."

As the pieces came together and the discussion grew, Cade squeezed the back of the chair like his life depended on it.

"She lied?" he said before he realized he was speaking, instantly hating the bitter taste the words left in his mouth.

"Oh, bullshit," Bri said. "There's an explanation for this. We need to wait, and besides, what does it matter?"

"Do you read Ask Amy?" Ella asked.

"Every month. It's brilliant. I would have never guessed it was Sistine, but it's a great column."

"Why?" He walked toward Bri. "Why wouldn't you guess it was Sistine?"

She swallowed a sip of her soda. The lunch they were all supposed to enjoy after an awesome Fourth of July weekend still sat in the center of the table.

"Ask Amy isn't exactly... knit store owner material."

"Racy?"

She smiled. "You could say that. Cade, it's a sex advice column."

"Do you have one, a magazine?"

"Not on me, but you can pull it up online. She has a huge following."

He grabbed Patrick's iPad right out of his hands and gave it to Bri.

"Find one." His breath was ragged now. "Please."

"You know, I don't think this is a good idea," Boyd said. "Why does it matter what some sex column says?"

Cade held up his hand and for the first time in his life, his brother backed down.

"Pull it up, please."

Bri typed away, swiping her finger along the screen. "No, probably not that one."

He took the iPad even as Bri protested and went brows up at the illustration. A pair of long legs in heels poking out from a chair and crossed at the knees. There was no face on the figure, just legs and a

pink background with black swirls. Cade clicked on the post title—
"Dear Fetish Queen." The question was pretty straightforward, but
the answer was from a person Cade didn't recognize. Ask Amy was
not only knowledgeable, she was inventive. Hell, the answer made
him blush like a damn virgin. He tapped back and scanned the other
blog post titles. "Threesomes," "Can Guys Commit?" "Worst Pickup
Lines."

Holy shit!

At some point, his mouth must have fallen open.

Boyd stood. "That bad?"

"Oh, come on, there's nothing wrong with that blog," Bri said.
"It's an advice column. People write in with questions. She's simply
responding with informed and in my humble opinion as a nurse,
responsible answers."

Cade glanced up. "She's right. There's nothing wrong with any of
this." He closed the iPad and handed it back to Trick. "Other than
the fact that at least the last ten posts are taken almost directly from
what I thought were private conversations I had with Sistine." He
grabbed his helmet. "I've gotta get out of here." He leveled a stare at
Boyd and Patrick, who seemed almost as shocked as their wives, but
both of them managed a nod. Cade understood the gesture to mean
they were there for him if he needed anything.

After another moment of hesitation in which he thought he
might ask for advice, Cade realized there were no brotherly words of
wisdom to help him this time. He'd been screwed over again, simple
as that. Sistine obviously needed some Instagram ass man to help
with her secret project and she'd found him. Stereotypically not too
bright and stupid in love with her, he must have been an easy target.
He was going to pass out and he sure as hell wasn't going to do it in
front of her, so he left.

Sistine stood at the front window of her shop, arms wrapped tightly
around her middle as if with enough effort she could keep herself

from crumbling. All of her real friends left shortly after Cade walked out, which was better than having them around while she smiled for cameras and allowed Melissa, contract or no contract, to steal the last bits of her dignity.

The night was dark blue and even now that Melissa had "left to sleep somewhere suitable," and Sistine was finally alone surrounded by a space she loved more than most, she felt awful. When she was younger, her father used to tell her that there were all sorts of people, and liars were the most miserable of all. As it had been her whole life, he was right. Dunking her tea bag a few more times, she removed it from her cup and held her hand under it until she made her way to the trash.

Hearing a knock on her shop door, Sistine felt as though her heart had stopped. She knew it wasn't Cade. The anger when he left would take time to settle into disappointment and even then, he would never come to her again. Never offer a "we," and she couldn't blame him. Glancing at the window, her eyes burned at the sight of Bri, Ella, Vienna, and Aspen standing outside with two bottles of wine and bags of takeout.

She wiped the tear that escaped and opened the door.

"Aspen here has pumped her breasts down to gym socks, so she was hoping you'd have a glass of wine with us," Ella said, walking toward the back of the shop.

Aspen nodded as she passed. "And food. We brought spicy food."

"We're glad you're not dealing drugs." Vienna kissed her cheek. "Bri thought you were dealing."

Bri locked the door and put her arm around Sistine as they joined the others at the lesson table. "I did not. You did. I voted for rich dead relative. You were drugs."

"You voted?"

They all winced as they passed food and poured wine.

"Sort of," Aspen said, closing her eyes at her first sip of wine. "We all wondered how you came up with the money for the electric. You watch every cent and it didn't seem like there was much left over."

"There wasn't." Sistine sat, relieved that her friends didn't hate her.

"Then you added the fountain to the back patio and we knew something was up." Ella handed her a plate of Mexican food.

"To your credit, none of us saw the naughty knitter coming," Bri said and they all, including Sistine, laughed. "See what I did there?"

She had assumed everyone would turn on her once they knew. She should have trusted her friends would stick with her even when she wasn't quite worthy of their friendship. After apologies that they pushed aside and instead asked her how she was holding up, Sistine explained who Melissa was and how their seemingly timid knitting friend ended up writing a column for *Cosmo*.

"We were crazy popular. Everyone read us, magazines offered to buy us. It was insane. Women with no boundaries. There wasn't a topic we wouldn't touch. By the time we graduated, we had offers to work anywhere we wanted."

"Sounds incredible." Bri poured more wine. "What went wrong?"

"I came home one day, and Melissa was gone. She'd moved out and taken Ask Amy with her. She had lawyers and I received paperwork in the mail, copyrights in her name. I was completely cut out."

"Good God," Aspen said.

"That was the last time I partnered with anyone. Male or female. I was a different person back then. I ran with a crowd that would be right at home at Cade's bar." Her heart squeezed at the mention of his name, and Sistine lost interest in telling the rest of the story she'd held secret for too long. "Melissa turned me into one of those flirty women and then left me flat on my face with nothing. I started over. My brother lost his arm two years later and our family was thrown into chaos for a while. The bullshit I surrounded myself with in college no longer had a place in my life. I came face-to-face with who I was and what I wanted. That's when I came up with the plan for my shop. I worked and saved. I vowed to rebuild something that was all mine. No one could mess it up but me."

"Plans are easy. Doing something on your own is a lot harder, sis. I know firsthand you can't make it alone. Why didn't you ask us for help?"

Sistine wiped her eyes. "I don't know. I didn't want to give any of you something else to worry about. You'd just given birth," she said to

Aspen, who shook her head as if to say birthing a human being was no big deal.

"And you and Ella save lives for crying out loud."

Bri and Ella laughed. "You could have asked us for anything," Ella said.

"I know that now, but after I thought I lost the expo"—Sistine smiled at Vienna again, hoping her friend knew how grateful she was—"I got the quote from Keith and Mel seemed like my only option. I guess I saw it as a way for her to pay me back."

She finished sharing all the rest of the sad and sordid details of her history with Melissa and by the time both bottles of wine were gone and nothing but stale chips remained on the table, she felt strangely better, stronger.

"What a bitch," Bri said. They all agreed.

"She's not all bad. She brought me out of my small-town shell when I needed someone to do that because I was probably never going to do it on my own. There were good times."

"She could have included you," Vienna said.

"No, she couldn't have. I wanted to expand into other areas, have Amy address violence against women, the truth behind college frats, and dating. She didn't want that. No one wanted that. Orgasms are easier."

"Well, not always," Bri said.

And they all laughed until they were shedding tears of friendship and understanding. Sistine was so lucky to have each of them in her life and grateful they'd seen the Melissa thing for what it was—a means to an end to save her shop. None of them mentioned Cade or the fact that she'd used things they talked about for Ask Amy, and at the moment, she appreciated the gesture. Fixing things with Cade, if that was even possible, wasn't going to be nearly as easy, even with wine and beer.

"So, what are you going to do now?" Aspen asked.

"I'm going to smile for the cameras and let her take it back. Knitterly has everything it needs now and if I get into trouble again—"

"You'll ask your real friends," they all said at once.

Sistine nodded, tears threatening her eyes again as she walked them to the door. "Yes, I'll ask my real friends. Thank you." She hugged each woman and knew for the first time in a long time that being part of a "we" was possible with the right people. Now, she needed to finish with Melissa and see if anything could be salvaged with Cade. She would settle for friendship if he'd have her. She would never like it, but she couldn't blame him. She had always lived with her choices—owned them. This would be no different. She had her friends now. If she and Cade found any way forward, she would consider herself lucky.

Chapter Twenty-Four

Cade hadn't slept. Instead he spent most of the night reading Ask Amy blog posts and the rest of the time wondering if he was a complete fool. During his generous moments, he believed there was a logical explanation for why he knew Sistine had a scar on her hand from a cat food can but had no idea twenty million Twitter followers looked to her for sex advice.

During his darker moments, one striking right before he gave up the chance of sleep and jumped into the shower, a woman like Sistine would have never bothered with a bartender unless she was securing research. He wouldn't know the specifics until he talked to her. He wasn't ready to reply to any of her text messages yet. He had no idea what to say, but he was pretty clear that when he'd told her nothing could push him away, he had not imagined this punch to the heart.

There was no way she was the woman he'd fallen in love with and also Amy. Those two people did not exist in the same body, which meant she'd lied to him about more than *Cosmo*. Was any of it true? Leaning on the bar with his hands in his face, all thoughts of her were physically painful.

When he heard the door open, he knew it was her. Pulling his hands away from his face, he stood and busied himself on the back bar.

Sistine took her seat at the end of the bar. She was wearing her narwhal sweater and he wasn't sure whether to yell or cry. Was the narwhal the act or was it Ask Amy? Cade wiped the bar and told himself he didn't care. There was no going back. He had trusted her and she'd... Hell, he had no idea what she'd done, but whatever it was felt a whole lot worse than any Instagram picture.

Sistine had played this moment out since she'd roamed the grocery store the night Cade kissed her. She hadn't planned on loving him any more than she'd planned on Melissa showing up early in grand style or having to pay out thousands of dollars to save a building she also loved. There were so many things about her current situation that she had not planned, but she'd thought about telling Cade about her side job from the instant his lips touched hers.

Honesty was part of loving someone, sharing the good and the ugly. She knew that and yet there she was about to navigate Cade's deep chill. Everyone had different sides based on circumstances. She'd never seen Cade without his warmth, his charm, and it broke what was left of her heart that she was the reason he stood in front of her like an empty room. No worn couch or family pictures. He'd closed everything she knew him to be behind a generic door she more than deserved.

"Five tips for the best blow job, huh? I don't recall discussing that one. Personal experience maybe?" he said through a clenched jaw. "You know who you'll want to ask about blow jobs? Lauren." His stare was razor sharp and he raised a brow. "I know she's an expert in that area."

Sistine closed her eyes. He wanted to hurt her, and he'd succeeded. But, when she'd ended things hoping to avoid the very moment they were in, Cade came to Bodega for her. The least she could do was try to find him now.

"Google," she said.

"Your browser history must be epic." An almost imperceptible twitch at his jaw was the only indication of emotion.

"I clear my history."

"Yeah, I should have known that."

"What's that supposed to mean?"

Cade turned away and then turned back, arms crossed. "When were you going to tell me?"

"I was trying to figure that out, but then…"

"You thought you'd fall into bed with me first, test out a few theories? After all, sex is practically a college major for a guy like me, right?"

"One has nothing to do with the other." She swallowed. "I used experiences from my life to help inform the column. Loving you had nothing to do with Ask Amy."

"No? Seems like our entire relation—Shit, was it a relationship, Sistine, or research for some horny women's magazine?"

She held onto the sides of her stool. "Do you honestly need me to answer that question?"

"I do." He dropped his arms to his sides, no humorous T-shirt today. Probably her fault too. She took a deep breath.

She explained about the electrical and a bit of her history with Melissa. Cade listened but said nothing.

"And *Cosmo* is not a 'horny women's magazine.' That sounds obnoxious."

"Yeah, well I'm obnoxious. Why are you here?"

"I wanted to apologize for not telling you about—"

"Nipple clamps?"

She shrugged. "I was going to say the column, but if you want to get specific, okay, nipple clamps."

"Did we cover that one? The nipple piercing comments from Jules make sense now. She obviously knew about your little side job before I did, right?"

"Wrong. Drake helped me fix my computer. He saw—It's not important. What exactly bothers you about this? That I didn't tell you, or that I know more than you're comfortable with your little knit shop owner knowing?"

She returned his glare. There was no way she was shrinking under the clear judgment in his expression. Granted, she wasn't proud to have kept things from him or that she'd allowed Melissa to get her into this situation in the first place, but something in his expression suggested she should be ashamed. That pissed her off. She wasn't a child, and simply because she preferred sweaters to push-up bras didn't mean she would apologize. She'd never been anything but honest about her feelings in and out of bed.

Cade ran a hand over his face. "Don't make me sound like that guy. I have absolutely no problem with sex or you being—I love sex and sex with you is—Damn it, this is not what I thought was going on."

"Cade, this has nothing to do with you or with our relationship."

"No? What about your little demure knitting shop-owner routine? I read almost every post, and the woman writing all of that crap does not seem like the you I know, or thought I knew."

Her eyes widened, and she said nothing.

"Yeah, most of it was crap. Newsflash, it's not unheard of for a woman to climax three times in a row. I would know."

Her eyes narrowed.

"And not to be crass or offend your narwhal sweater there, but you're no stranger to three in a row either. Unless you were faking that too."

"That was an old post."

He snickered, anger radiating off his shoulders. "Great. What about the pickup lines post? That was our conversation, pretty much word for word."

"I did what I had to do to make my deadlines. I wrote from life experience."

"From my damn experiences," he yelled, and then he appeared to check himself with a deep breath. "Your deadline. Wow. This feels like bullshit, Sistine. Like this whole time has been a game."

"Oh, for crying out loud, enough." She threw her hands up. "You caught me. I was using you to gather intel for a column that I sold my soul to in order to keep my shop open. It was all a hoax. The being insanely in love with you part and the general melting in place when you walk into the room. All of it was part of my plan so I could write that Pulitzer Prize-winning piece about threesomes. Come on, Cade.

I should have told you. I feel awful and I don't blame you if you no longer trust me, but you're turning this into something it's not."

He stared through her for a beat and stuck his hands in his pockets. He looked young for an instant and hurt. Sistine had trouble breathing through the squeeze in her chest.

"You could have asked. I would have helped you with anything."

"I didn't think we were going to be... what we are."

"Were."

"Fine, were. It was right after the Instagram thing and I didn't want you to think that was the only reason I was interested in you. I didn't tell anyone, and maybe that was because I hadn't reconciled things with Melissa or why I'd gotten back into Amy. It's kind of complicated."

"So, you lied."

"I didn't lie. I mean sort of, but it was more a withholding of information that went on for far too long."

At that, he laughed.

"Like I said, Melissa was my friend in college. We started a blog as an assignment. Then it took off. She took it after college, but then she..."

Cade held up his hand. "Save it. I'll watch the interviews. Thanks for the apology. I'm sure you need to get back to your deadlines."

"So, that's it?" Sistine wiped her eyes, angry at herself for still caring. "You're going to shut me down. I don't think that's fair."

He turned on her so quickly she felt the force of him clear across the bar. "I know what I'm getting with other women. How to act. You let me believe you were—"

"Exactly who I am. I'm sorry I left this part of my life out, that I didn't tell you about my business decision."

He shook his head and leaned against the back wall of the bar, eyes to the floor.

She wished with all her wishes that there was something she could say that would lead him to a conclusion that made sense. More sense than truth, which was that she'd allowed her friend to hijack her life again. In the name of money and pride and not wanting to fail, she'd pretended that taking Amy back was no big deal. On some level she must have been embarrassed; otherwise she would have told him, told her friends and family, but the embarrassment stemmed more from the way Melissa had left things than anything she wrote as Amy. If she told the people close to her about the blog, she'd have to tell them about the humiliation, and she wanted them to see her as she was.

She'd wanted Cade to see her in the simple and lovely way his eyes seemed to capture, but now the veil had been lifted and she found it hard to breathe under the judgment.

"I did what I had to do to meet deadlines and run my shop. I'm exhausted all the time." Her eyes teared again, but she willed emotion from her voice. She wanted to push back yet didn't want his pity. "I will not apologize for knowing or writing about sex, Cade. For knowing about nipple clamps or anything else you read. I'm sorry you set your sights on me as your little demure settle-down woman now that you've screwed half of northern California, but I'm not that simple either."

"Who are you?"

"Oh, come on. Who are you? Which one are you, Cade? The guy who taught me backgammon and lies on the floor of my shop or the naked guy in Lauren's bed? Are you the charmer who winks at every set of boobs or the guy who took me to a sheep farm on a date?"

"This isn't about me, and I don't wink at boobs. Damn it, I'm not the one wrong here. You are. I didn't lie to you. I told you, showed you who I am and you... fuck, you were taking notes, Sistine. Can't you see this? I don't share myself with everyone and... You know what? I need to get ready to open. My show's about to start and you need to get back to yours. Again, thanks for the apology." He walked away and when she heard the door to the kitchen slam, she let herself cry. Wiping her eyes, she walked out too.

Much later, Cade was back in his zone. The band was loud, and he was flirting and pouring drinks. Giving the people what they want, he

told himself as a group of women sang, "It's getting hot in here. Cade take off your clothes."

He reached for the neck of his T-shirt. He'd barely tugged on it when a hand from behind held his in place. Boyd stood at his back.

"Get your shit together or these assholes win."

Cade looked over his shoulder and dropped his hand.

"Tina?"

"Yup, I'm on it."

Boyd took Cade to Patrick's back office.

"Don't ever touch me behind my bar again." Cade spun around and was chest to chest with his oldest brother. He no longer cared. In fact, he'd welcome someone beating the crap out of him at this point.

"Or what? You're gonna whip me with one of your snazzy T-shirts?" Boyd didn't back down. "You can thank me later for saving your last strand of dignity."

Cade had nothing left, so he collapsed into the chair and put his face in his hands.

"If I want to take my shirt off, I can. It's all part of the entertainment. That's what I'm doing back there. Patrick should appreciate that, right? I'm bringing in the money."

"Not like that you're not." Patrick walked in eating a sandwich. "Damn, these are good."

Patrick leaned against the wall, crossing one foot over the other and eating his sandwich like a man with all the answers. Cade wanted to steal his sandwich. "I gotta say, I'm not feeling your sad little story tonight."

"I'm not telling a sad story. I was doing my job."

"Ya think? Boyd, when did we add the male entertainment piece to the Tap House?"

"We didn't." Boyd sat at the edge of Patrick's desk.

"Right." Trick finished his sandwich and tossed the trash. "We don't have strippers and your blog post is late."

"I'm not doing those anymore. I'm sticking with what I'm good at. A guy like me needs to understand his limitations."

"Oh, boo-fucking-hoo. What does that even mean, a guy like you?" Boyd said.

"I'm a joke. A good time and no more than that. Even Sistine saw me as source material for *Cosmo*. Fucking *Cosmo*."

"Ella talks to me about cases at the hospital. I have her test some of my batches. Trick and Aspen, they talk work. West and—"

"Stop. Okay, just stop. You're not going to big brother this. She didn't tell me. I was not her partner. I was research. Lesson heard loud and clear this time."

"You need to forgive her, Cade. I know you're still pissed, and it might take some time, but she didn't mean to hurt you and somewhere beneath all of that unnecessary muscle, you know that."

Cade shook his head.

"Remember when you gave that girl the box of chocolates that year for Valentine's Day?"

"Don't. I am not walking down memory lane. Not tonight. Besides, Sistine doesn't eat chocolate. It gives her a headache."

"Then get out of here and find her chocolate equivalent."

"Ooh, great word," Boyd said, obviously mocking Cade.

"I managed that one for our little brother," Trick said.

"Thanks for the word and the talk, but I have a job to do." Cade stood.

"Tina is finishing your shift," Patrick said, glancing over his shoulder.

"I'm not leaving the bar to Tina. She's already taken over a few times for me and it's Thursday night."

"Finish one sentence for me. When I'm with Sistine, she..."

Cade laughed and struggled past the lump in his throat. Her name, the thought of her sent him spinning to a place he wanted to stay for the rest of his life.

"Waiting. When I'm with Sistine, she..."

"This is stupid."

"Answer the question or I'm going to tell this entire bar that you locked yourself in our bathroom when we were kids and ate a can of cat food." Boyd stood next to Trick.

"Jesus."

"And liked it. Finish the sentence, Cade."

He shoved his hands into his pockets. "Fine. When I'm with Sistine." He mocked like a grade schooler. "When I'm with her, she… she." He met his brother's eyes. "She's every damn color on that yarn wall in her shop. She's the best person and I—" Cade quickly wiped away the tear. "Shit. Are you happy now?"

Patrick let out a deep breath that seemed to clear the emotion from his throat and did what he always did. He handled things, so his brothers could have what they wanted. "Right. Well, go tell her that. Just like that. Go home, Cade."

"And don't come back until you're happy." Boyd patted him on the back. "Because we're all getting a little tired of seeing your naked body."

The vise grip that had been on his chest since the big *Cosmo* reveal eased a little. He was grateful for his stubborn brothers, but despite loving her, he didn't know if "fixing things" with Sistine was realistic.

Climbing onto his bike, he glanced down at his arm. He could use some magic these days. Maybe there was a way back to her, probably not back but forward. By the time he got home, he realized Sistine's chocolate. Not that he was ready to give her anything at the moment. He would admit that he still loved her and that he wanted to find a way, but that was all he was giving up. Right now, he needed to sleep, maybe all weekend.

Chapter Twenty-Five

By Sunday, Cade needed to get off the couch. It had been almost two days since Patrick sent him on an "extended weekend." He'd brought all of their social media up to date, including a blog post titled "Best Beers to Drink When Life Sucks." Not all that professional, but their most-liked blog post yet. Obviously Cade wasn't alone in his recent misery.

But that was yesterday. He needed to do something because the silence somehow enhanced the stupidity of his situation. Running his hand over his head and glad his hair was growing back out from the haircut it took him all of twenty minutes to regret, he went outside to feed the chickens. Henny had once again managed to make a hole in the fencing. Cade found all three chickens on the side of his yard and put them in the coop.

Thrilled to have something to do, he got dressed and rode to the hardware store.

As they wrapped up the final "puff piece," as Kurt the annoying publicist put it, Sistine needed a break. She walked down to the hardware store, and something in the ding of the bell and the smell of wood kept her tears at bay.

"Well, look at you, pretty lady," Mr. Graham said.

She was about to say thank you and ask him to tell her something other than the gossip about her that was all over town when Cade came around the corner.

He was speaking before he saw her. "Hey, Graham, do you have any more of that quarter-inch chicken wire? I think that will—"

He stopped. "Sistine."

"Cade."

The flecks of dust danced through the wash of light, somehow giving weight to the air between them. She fought the urge to reach out and touch something she knew was no longer there.

She cleared the emotion from her throat. "Your hair is growing in."

"It is. You did something to yours."

"It's straightened." She smoothed her hand along her hair and pretended not to care whether he liked it or not. How absurd that she would expect something so juvenile from a man she'd socked with a huge adult-sized punch.

The whole situation was such a waste. At the time she'd accepted Melissa's offer, her past had seemed miniscule compared to everything she had in Petaluma, but now she was barely breathing under the weight of how big it turned out to be.

"Are you in the market for some supplies?" she asked, cringing at the discomfort of the conversation. Talking with Cade used to be effortless and fun, but she no longer allowed those thoughts in. They were too painful.

Mr. Graham backed up behind his counter. Sistine knew that everyone had heard the news by this point and while she was happy to no longer be in hiding, the embarrassment of not having told anyone, especially the supremely pissed man in front of her, still stung.

"Tiny. The crew is packed up, but they need your—" Melissa burst through yet another door unannounced.

Sistine closed her eyes, but Cade stepped forward.

"Mrs. Dunn." Cade extended his hand. "Nice to finally meet the keeper of Sistine's strings."

"My mother-in-law is Mrs. Dunn, hot stuff. And no one's worked Sistine's strings in a long time. She's the shit these days."

"I stand corrected." His glare was chilled and painful.

Sistine shook her head. "You are married to a United States senator, Mel. You cannot be calling anyone hot stuff."

She scrunched her face, eyes still on Cade's body. "The media is three doors down, and like anyone in this village is going to know or care. You said you were taking a walk. I had no idea the action went down at the hardware store. What is your name?"

"Cade." Sistine faced her. "His name is Cade. Stop. Let's go back to my shop in front of the media so you'll behave."

"Cade. Sistine has told me absolutely nothing about you. Why do you think that is?"

"Because she's been telling *Cosmo* readers about me?"

Melissa laughed and Sistine wanted to pick up a two-by-four and slap her. She'd managed Melissa for most of her life, but it was time for her to leave now and stay away from the people Sistine wasn't ready to lose.

"Mel, doesn't Kurt want to wrap things up?"

"Oh, he'll wait. I am paying him after all." Her gaze snuck back to Cade.

Melissa drew her bottom lip between her teeth and Sistine lost it.

"Good grief. You're married. Can you shut off your sex face for a second?"

"I'm telling you that no one in this village cares."

"Town, city even," Sistine said.

"Again, no one cares." Melissa batted her fake eyelashes at Cade, who crossed his arms.

Did the man not understand the power of his fricking arms? Not helping.

"We like it that way," he said, a hint of his usual charm returning. "Keeps people away."

For a minute, Sistine thought he might smile, and her world could go back to the way it was, but he stared right through her.

Melissa's eyes went wide as she looked between them.

"Wait, are you two?" She leaned into Sistine. "Are you screwing him? Please tell me you are all over that man because if so, well done, my friend. I have taught you well."

Sistine's stomach turned. She didn't bother apologizing to Cade. What was the point anymore? She walked out. Melissa trailed after her, heels clicking.

After the crew and the she-devil had left her shop and gone back to the hotel for one last night, Sistine touched the dimmer switch that brought light to her shop. What if she'd been some woman who'd moved to Petaluma or gone to school with the McNaughton boys? What if she'd never left Bodega or hadn't been born into a family of entrepreneurs?

Tired of what-ifs, she lowered the lights and went to her apartment. When Melissa left tomorrow, Sistine would finally be able to put this behind her and get back to running her business. She had not yet figured out how to move on with the rest of her life, made clear by the recent urge to jump into Cade's arms right there in the hardware store. That part would get easier, she told herself as she crawled under the covers. At least she didn't have to answer any more sex questions. Grateful for small favors, Sistine fell asleep.

Cade went into the Tap House to help close. After Tina and Max left for the night, he texted Lauren and regretted it almost immediately. Bumping into Sistine at the hardware store had stirred up all kinds of crap he was trying to forget. That raw pain was the inspiration for the Lauren text. He thought maybe he could have a genuine relationship with any woman. Easy and playful conversation that had nothing to do with sex was not a Sistine exclusive.

Was it unfair to use Lauren for his own benefit? Probably, but he was working on not caring. Something else he was no longer good at thanks to falling hard for Sistine.

Lauren had hinted—okay, she practically begged—a few times to have sex on the bar. He might have hinted that tonight could be that stupid cliché moment to get her to come to the Tap House at eleven o'clock.

She walked behind the bar and ran her hands over his ass. Cade closed his eyes and tried to focus on the physical pleasure of a woman touching him. He knew Lauren, knew her body. Being with her should have been easy, mindless. But he clearly only wanted one touch these days because his throat felt like it was squeezing closed. Gently removing Lauren's hands from his body, he stepped away. Maybe food and conversation would work. At this point, he was grasping.

"Do you want some nachos?"

"Excuse me?"

"Food. Javier revamped the nachos. Do you want to eat? Talk about your day?"

She looked at him like he'd grown another head, and then she flashed him a perfect smile and patted him on the cheek.

"You always were a sucker, Cade. Sweet, but a sucker. Women don't eat nachos. Well, not the women you've spent the past few years entertaining."

She shook her head and walked toward the door. "You lured me out in the middle of the night. I did a touch-up shave and everything because I thought you were finally going to fuck me on this bar of yours." She put her hands on her hips. "Instead you want nachos." She giggled in that same jingly way. "Sort of how my week has been going."

"Wait, didn't you post a picture eating nachos a couple of weeks ago? Javier follows you and lost his mind over that picture. I think you may have actually inspired his revamp."

Lauren ran a hand through her hair as if she couldn't be bothered with men finding her sexy. Cade was clearly boring her now too. "Those were a prop."

"A prop? Meaning you didn't eat them?"

She scrunched her face. "No. I don't even like nachos. It was a throwback picture to Cinco de Mayo."

Cade had no words.

"No one is what they appear to be, babe. It's an illusion, you know. Whoever has the best illusion wins."

"Maybe in your world, but I don't think everyone is an illusion."

She leaned forward like he was a puppy dog she wanted to share her boobs with. "Aw, look how cute you are now. Call me if you ever want to... service me on your bar."

"Wait, you're leaving?"

She spun on her heels. "Look, actually, don't call me. You're not my Cade anymore."

He was certain he'd never been "her Cade" but wasn't going to argue.

"We had great sex. That's what you were good at, and now you're a mushy ball of love for that yarn woman." She sighed. "Such a waste. I better get an invite to the wedding. Cordial exes are trending, and I want pictures." She waved overhead and left.

Cade locked the door behind her. "You always were a sucker" looped through his mind as he loaded the remaining glasses and set the dishwasher. He walked back from the kitchen, blew out the two remaining candles, and thought of Sistine.

He'd managed a few hours of not thinking about her, but then he saw her at the hardware store and all that effort went down the drain. There were so many memories now and odd places that reminded him of her. Reminded him of who he was when he believed with every breath that she loved him. He'd never once created tangible memories with a woman that didn't involve a bed and the occasional dinner at a nondescript restaurant, and now he remembered why. When things didn't work out, he was haunted by what was and worse, what could have been.

Maybe Lauren was right. Maybe he was a sucker. As much as he wanted to believe that Sistine had played him, gotten close so she had material for Ask Amy, he also knew she wasn't Lauren. She wasn't an illusion.

And he was always going to love her. Like the music at his bar, there may be times when he'd be able to turn it down, but the buzz of her and the love he still felt no matter how hard he tried to stop would be there until his sucker heart stopped beating.

Cade hit the lights and grabbed his helmet. There was no way a woman like Sistine ever set out to hurt anyone. She had a sweater with a narwhal on it for fuck's sake. No one went to that much trouble to deceive, not even Lauren. Well, maybe Lauren.

Chapter Twenty-Six

Sistine met for a "quick bite to eat" before Melissa left and flew back to DC. Relieved and still reeling from everything that had happened, she tried to be generous as she sat across from the woman who had screwed her over more times than she could count.

"I was a bitch." Melissa slathered on her lip gloss and put the tube back into her giant leather bag.

"Yeah, you were."

"I still am. It's permanent. Probably why I'm doing so well in Washington. I don't deserve your friendship."

"We are not friends, Mel."

"Yeah, that's fair. I was talking with Kurt and we're not getting the traction from the sexy senator's wife that we'd hoped. So, we're going to take my image in a different direction."

Was this some sort of nightmare loop Sistine was trapped in?

"I don't want Amy. You can't give her back. I don't care about your contract or your threats. I don't want any part of it."

Melissa laughed. "It sounds like we are arguing over who takes the puppy after our toxic relationship."

Sistine raised her eyebrows and didn't think that description was that far off.

"I have let you push and pull me on your whim for far too long. The money was helpful, but I'm done."

"I know. So, Kurt and my other people approached *Cosmo* and they bought Amy."

Sistine let out a breath and tried not to hate Melissa, or at least hate how easy everything seemed to be for her. Hate was not good for anyone, she reminded herself.

"Some people walk in the light. Congratulations. You always win, Mel. Good for you."

Melissa slid an envelope across the table, and there went Sistine's nightmare loop again.

"You don't have to worry about me. I'm not going to say anything. I want you all on that plane and out of my village." She pushed back the envelope.

"Do you think we're products of our upbringing?" Melissa asked, seemingly off on another one of her tangents. The woman rarely spent more than five minutes on any thought, no matter how important.

"Isn't everyone?" Sistine kept it short. When they were younger, she used to give Mel all her thoughts. She told her everything back then, but she'd grown up a long time ago.

"I guess, but you've always been so normal. The most normal person in my life. Ever. Also, the most insane dresser I've ever met, but you were my normal, Tiny. I miss that."

"No, you don't. You like your crazy."

"You used to be crazy with me. Can't you keep a little of our fun? It's like you're a nun. Although a nun tapping that bartender, which is admirable." She pumped her hands like she was at a sporting event.

"You know women don't usually say they're tapping a man, right?"

"Oh, why not. We can tap too. He's hot."

"He's more than hot. He's a great guy. More than a great guy, he's… forget it."

"I wouldn't understand the gentleness of love? Why, because I have a pair of handcuffs in my nightstand?"

Sistine waited and allowed her to answer her own question.

"Fine, a couple of pairs. But, that's not the point. You're doing what we always said was shitty about women, but you're doing it to yourself. Why can't you have some of what we were? Why is it one way or the other? Missionary or tied up? You don't have to retire all your skills."

"All of that got me nowhere."

"Not true. Look at you. Business owner banging a hot bartender and running a successful column. You didn't get those fierce skills playing crabs and lobsters with your family. Fierce is learned."

Sistine laughed—she couldn't help it. Something buried deep in the back of her heart missed the insanity of the woman she once swore was her best friend.

"So is responsibility. Taking care of the people you love. Telling the truth," she said.

"True." Melissa nodded. "Not my strengths, but you've got all of that. You can have it all. I'm only saying, let's make peace. You, me, *and* Amy. She's been good to you, even when I wasn't."

Sistine had rarely thought of Ask Amy as anything more than a means to an end. When they were in college, she often felt inhibited, but Mel was right. There was something powerful about what Amy represented at that time in her life.

"I'd never thought of it like that."

"That's my point, you should. You've learned a lot from Amy and from me." She scrunched her face like she knew she was pushing it now. "Fine. Did you learn who not to be?"

"Mostly." Feelings Sistine had buried back in college surfaced. The pain of being left behind was right there and raw. Maybe Mel was right, and it was time to deal with those instead of running as fast as she could.

Melissa pushed the envelope back to Sistine. "Open it."

"I don't want to read one more lousy document."

"You want to open it."

Sistine opened the envelope and found a check made out to her for eight hundred thousand dollars. She quickly counted the zeros to confirm.

"Is this a joke?"

Melissa shook her head.

"You are giving me half the money you made from selling Amy?"

"Don't be ridiculous. I sold Amy for a few million. You don't need that kind of money in this village."

Sistine laughed, deep and sincere in a way she hadn't since breaking her own heart.

"Something like sixty thousand people live in Petaluma."

"Aw, that's cute." Melissa sat up in the chair, shoulders back as she flipped her dark silk hair over her shoulder. After all these years, Sistine still wasn't sure what fueled a woman like Melissa. All people were complicated, but even in a world of variations, Mel seemed a rare species.

"It seems like you and the villagers have a nice life. You have good friends now?"

"I do."

"Good. And you're still banging the bartender?"

"His name is Cade, and we are no longer seeing each other."

"Oh, you need to fix that."

"Too late. He thought I was someone else."

"Then he's an idiot because all of your versions are perfect, Tiny. You deserve good people and that man. I mean the body on him."

"Mel." She took her hand and fought off the visual of Cade's body. "Thank you."

"You're welcome. Stop trying to make me cry." She took back her hand. "I'm glad you've let your friends in."

"What does that mean?"

"I know I did a number on you. You've probably spent a few years whipping around like you can do all of this shit on your own. I'm glad you're better."

"So, you knew you were screwing me over."

"I'm not proud of myself, but yes, I knew there would be damage."

"Huh. That is surprisingly insightful."

"Yeah, well, enough of this introspection. I'm already paying my therapist a fortune. So, what do you think *Cosmo* will do with Amy?"

"They'll probably use a staff writer."

"Amy will never be as good as she was with us. Although under your watch, she's become way too philosophical. You've mellowed her."

"Maybe she's mellowed."

"Nah, she's still saucy. I was a better trashy slut than you were."

Sistine's eyes watered. "That's slut-shaming, Mrs. Dunn." Sistine wiped her face and was surprised when a tear slipped down Melissa's perfectly made-up face.

"Damn it." She sniffed. "Well, whatever. I'm a proud slut. When did slut become such a bad word? I miss saying "You slut.'"

"It is no longer PC, and since you are married to one of our great senators, you need to say goodbye to slut."

"I did marry a fucking senator. How did that happen?"

"He gives you everything you want?"

"Oh, honey, that is so true. And he is incredible in bed. I mean the man has an epic mouth."

Sistine shook her head. "I'm happy for you."

"You should be."

They laughed, and Melissa took her hand.

"Have you missed me?"

"No."

Melissa snorted.

"Have you missed me?" Sistine asked.

"Not really. I miss who we used to be, sometimes. You?"

"No."

"Brutal."

"I was trained by the best."

"That you were, my tiny dancer." Melissa downed the last of her wine and slipped her shoes back on. "I am off to the pool of sharks we like to call Washington."

"Don't pretend you don't love it."

"I do. We should try to keep in touch."

"No, we shouldn't. We have nothing in common anymore, Mel." Sistine shrugged. "Especially since I moved to this village. I don't think we ever had much in common."

"Sure we did. We liked to party."

"I never liked to party."

"We studied together... sometimes."

Sistine raised her eyebrows.

"Okay, fine, we were thrust together in the fishbowl that is college and we made the best of it. We were the bomb, Tiny. Look around at your little place. The money from selling Amy will keep you in string for a long time."

"Yarn."

"Whatever. And maybe my half will fund my own run for senate."

"You'll definitely have to retire slut then."

Melissa shrugged and Sistine met her gaze. "No hard feelings."

"I can't believe I'm going to say this, but no. No hard feelings, Mel."

"It's kind of symbolic, right? The three of us going our separate ways."

Sistine nodded. "I suppose it is."

Melissa left for the airport in another shiny black town car. As Sistine watched her drive away, she felt a calming sense of closure. Finally.

Cade saw Sistine go into her shop the following weekend. He'd met his parents for breakfast at Sift, and while he'd told himself he didn't want to see her, watching her flip her sign at the front door, he now knew he'd lied to himself.

After his parents left for the farmers market, Cade crossed the street and told himself if he walked into her store and felt nothing, then he'd leave and finally let go. At the tinkle of the bell on her door, the same lavender surrounding him, and the expression on Sistine's face when she noticed him, Cade knew that probably for the first time in her life, Lauren had been right. He was a complete sucker. A sucker for the woman standing a few feet from him in a knit tank top he was positive she'd made. Moving closer, he glanced at the yarn wall and remembered Trick's question. When I'm with Sistine, she is...

"Hello." She was rolling yarn on some big machine behind her register.

He nodded, not sure what to say yet.

"I'm sorry about Melissa the other day," she said.

"You don't need to be sorry."

"Okay." She focused on the yarn and Cade approached the counter.

"For anything. You don't need to be sorry anymore."

She looked up. "I'm trying to be my authentic self." She swallowed. "That's not what I meant to say. I mean, it was, but—"

"Aspen?"

Sistine nodded. "Yes, Deepak is big into the authentic self. She gave me a book."

The edges of his mouth hinted a smile and his breath caught once again at the joy of being in the same room with her. He didn't want to be civil or let anything go. He wanted her in his arms, in his bed, and playing backgammon.

"I didn't mean most of what I said."

"I know. I'm learning to embrace the Ask Amy part of me, so it's okay if you don't approve. Do you ever notice when it comes to sex, men don't seem to have the same rules?"

"I never said I didn't approve and men have plenty of rules. I can't remember the last time a woman wanted to... talk in bed."

"I did. We talked."

Her expression was both pleading and determined. Cade knew he was bound to her in a way he would never be able to shake. He cleared his throat and tried to remember his point.

"Old Man Graham is wearing that leather vest because he doesn't want Mrs. Graham to think he's old. Men fall victim to stereotypes, too. Was it my personality that first drew you in, Sistine? I doubt it."

"Oh, stop. Please don't do the sad plight of men with me. That's like those people who say 'all lives matter' anytime a person of color stands up and says 'Hey, how about us, assholes?'"

His eyes widened. "So, I'm a racist now?"

"No. You're male. Suits and hand jobs are interchangeable. You don't have to apologize for your urges—they're celebrated. Sowing your wild oats. What's that song about a woman in public but a freak in the bedroom?

"Usher?"

"No, it's the other guy in that song."

"Do you want me to look it up?"

"No, I don't want you to look it up. I'm trying to prove a point here."

"You have."

"I have?"

He nodded. "I see what you're saying, but I have been squashed by my share of female urges. We all have pressures. Maybe women put most of that crap on themselves."

She stared at him for a few beats. "This was nice."

"Yeah, I guess it was." He needed to leave or she was going to bring him to his knees. "I'll see you around, Sistine."

He walked toward the door, telling himself they could back everything up and still be friends.

"I am still going to love you if you don't mind."

Cade turned around and tried to breathe.

"At least for a while. I can't unlove you that fast and... I don't want to."

He nodded and when her eyes welled up, he held the door to keep from going down.

How did everything get so twisted?

"Okay." She quickly wiped a tear. "Good. I wanted you to know that." She stepped from behind the counter and he opened the door.

She was handing over a piece of herself. He knew that wasn't easy and despite what they'd been through, he wanted to give her something in return.

"Backgammon on Wednesday?" he barely managed to say.

Their gaze held and in a moment much like the last slow song of a great night, she shook her head. "That's not a good idea for me right now. I'm still... I guess I already said what I have to say. We'll work our way back to backgammon."

He shrugged again. Christ, his entire system was shutting down and shrugging was all he had left. "Sounds good. It's no fun now that you're beating me anyway."

She crossed her arms and uncrossed them. "One more time, I am sorry, Cade. Truly sorry that things didn't work out the way you... envisioned them."

"Me too."

Her expression softened. "Take care." She moved to her lesson table.

With his hand on the door, Cade tried to ignore the swing of her skirt and the drift of flowers and soap he knew would be at the curve of her neck.

Christ, he missed her.

"Hey," he said.

She faced him again and there he was grasping for a rope that was no doubt tied to thin air.

"It was Ludacris."

Her brow creased. "The rapper?"

He wanted to convince himself they would be fine, that he could trust what they had. He wanted that more than he wanted his next shallow breath.

"He's the one who says the line about getting crazy in bed. The song is 'Yeah,' by Usher, but Ludacris is the other guy."

She nodded. "Did you look that up?"

"No. I remembered it was playing at the farmers market last weekend."

"What's wrong with your garden? Did the kale not make it?"

"No. It's still good, going strong, but I wanted some fruit."

And I needed to get out of my house because you're everywhere and I don't know how to let you go, but I can't ask you to stay. So instead of rolling one or two women around in my bed to get you out of my system, I thought... farmers market.

She nodded, eyes glossy again. "Good. Well, I'm glad that we figured out the song and that your kale good." She looked away and then quickly back at him. "I have to get ready for my class."

"Right. I'll go."

Neither of them moved for a moment and it should have been one of those times when, standing alone in her shop, they both realized their love was worth the risk. He should have scooped her up in his arms and twirled her around while some one-hit wonder played and the movie credits rolled.

That's how it should have gone because Sistine was that woman. She was the once-in-a-man's-lifetime combination of magic and real. She was everything Jack wanted when he climbed that beanstalk and the painful reality when he fell back to the ground.

"See you around," Cade said, rubbing his arm.

She didn't look up and began sorting papers on her table.

All he had to do was extend his hand and she would take it. She said she was sorry and that should have been enough. Why wasn't it enough?

Getting on his bike, Cade wiped his eyes and pulled on his helmet. He wasn't crying because Sistine had hurt him; he was crying at the realization that he might not believe in magic anymore.

Chapter Twenty-Seven

By the time the Chop and Knit finished their debate about whether Chris Hemsworth or Chris Pine was hotter, they'd each finished a pot holder, complete with picot edging. Sistine decided that was a success.

She'd thought about closing the shop and going home for the weekend, but she needed to work, needed the rhythm of knitting more than ever. She'd called her godmother and arranged for her to come up for the Stitches Expo next year. They talked and while Sistine didn't share all the details before Auntie N hung up, she said, "Be patient. Things have a way of working themselves out. And if not, knit it out."

Sistine had locked up her shop and sat cross-legged on the floor to watch the sun set. It was possible there was more than one person for everyone. Cade had felt like her one, but there could be some other fantastic man out there who'd be willing to take on all of her, not only the tidy knitting side. Some other man who would lie next to her on the floor, no questions asked.

Or she would go back to being satisfied alone. Her shop and her friends would fill her up eventually as they had before Cade decided he wanted a mature relationship. As darkness filled her shop, Sistine grabbed a bag of barbecue chips from her apartment and hit the wall switch on her way back to the floor of her shop.

With her branches glowing above, she lay back and decided she was done crying. She apologized, told him she would love him awhile longer and that she missed him. There was nothing left to do, so she looked up at her lights, ate her dinner, and knew she would be fine. Someday.

"I'm slowly losing my mind, that's how I am." Cade tapped beers with Boyd as they stood on the back patio of their parents' house two weeks later. Being at their house normally grounded Cade, gave him a sense that all was right with the world. Not this time.

"Isn't every day supposed to get easier? I think I'm going backward. It's harder. Every fucking day without her feels worse than the one before it," he said.

Boyd was holding back a laugh, Cade could tell, but before he had a chance to call him out, their mother stood between them.

"Watch your mouth, young man."

"And that's my cue to leave." Boyd was gone before Cade had a chance to argue.

"Sorry, Mom." They stood shoulder to shoulder looking out over the rolling lawn of his childhood. "Do you want a beer?" he asked.

"When have you ever known me to drink a beer?" She took out a flask of what Cade knew was Irish whiskey, took a swig, and put it back in her sweater.

He smiled and they stood in silence, nothing but the sound of Mason telling a driving story that had everyone in the house laughing.

"How's Sistine?" his mother said as if she were discussing the weather or a new book recommendation.

"I don't know."

"I do. She's moving on."

Cade kept his eyes on the horizon and told himself he was moving on too.

"But you're not."

So much for positive thinking.

"I'm good. Things are getting better."

"No, they're not. You just ranted to your brother. You need to fix this, sweetheart, before it's too late. She messed up and she's sorry. Since when is an apology not enough for you?"

"It is, we're friendly."

"Oh, hogwash. You know what I think?"

"I bet you're going to tell me."

"You're right, I am. I think you were drawn to Sistine because you thought she was safe. You thought your heart would be safe. Why? Because she knits?"

"Mom, I don't want to—"

"Love is tough work whether she's a knitter or a bartender. She's going to screw up and so are you. Why aren't you over this by now?"

"I don't know."

"Do you remember the box of chocolates, sweetheart?"

"Holy hell, what is it with everyone bringing up the box of chocolates? Yes, I remember. Little chubby Cade gave Marnie Gomez, who was way out of his league, a box of chocolates and she threw them in the trash. I'm a big boy now, Ma. I'm over it. Women throw my stuff in the trash now."

"You were not chubby and that's beside the point. Don't have a tone with me."

Cade shook his head. He didn't need a heart-to-heart right now. What he needed was to stop standing on the sidelines watching his brothers and their wives and children. He needed to go home. Or maybe get drunk. Clearly he wasn't cut out for love, so maybe he'd become a drunk instead.

"Do you remember what I told you when you came home and said she broke your heart?"

"I don't," he lied.

"I told you to keep your heart safe and only give your love away when you knew it would be returned."

Cade's eyes burned, but he stared straight ahead. Boyd and Trick could sense a tear a mile away.

His mom took his arm, and Cade quickly wiped his eye.

"She wasn't truthful. She used some of the things we talked about in a national column," he said.

"She was up against a wall and trying to make a go of things."

"I thought she was different."

"She is, but she's not whatever this image is that you have in your mind. She's a human being, and as complicated as you are, sweetheart. You're not a kid anymore, Cade. It's not all or nothing, right or wrong. Life is more than your show behind that bar. She loves you and you love her."

He wiped his eye again. "I tried to be, to show her... Shit. Mom, can we not do this?"

She faced him, all five foot something, and yanked on his shirt until he was eye level.

"You are not one-sided. You are all of those sparks and swagger behind the bar. You are every woman you've ever taken on a great date and every silly joke you play on your brothers. You are the only man who still dances our raw turkey around the kitchen on Thanksgiving. You are my sweet boy, my big guy, and the handsome man I am proud of every day. None of us are only our outside, Cade. Boy, things would be easier if we knew what we were getting from the cover, right?" She wiped his eyes and Cade hugged her like he was a kid.

"You could give Deepak a run for his money, ya know?"

She smacked his arm.

Patrick had Hattie strapped to his chest and was showing her the flowers in their mom's planters. Cade's heart throbbed, but at least he'd stopped blubbering. Watching his brother, it was again as if they all knew a secret he'd yet to discover.

"Pretty picture, isn't it?"

Cade was startled for a second at the extra company. "Hey, Aspen. Yes, it's a great picture."

"Yeah, Hattie shot diarrhea up her back and out of her diaper about twenty minutes ago. Soaked through the carrier and your brother's shirt. It's a good thing he keeps a change of clothes in the car or we would have had to go home."

"That's weird."

"The diarrhea?"

"No, that he keeps a change of clothes in the car."

She laughed and bumped his shoulder.

"Mason is failing algebra and Boyd swears he smelled smoke on his clothes last week." Ella stood next to his mom as they watched Trick, who was now joined by their dad, Boyd, and West.

"When we first got married, your dad wasn't ready to stop partying," his mom said. "We only had Boyd back then. There were so many times I wanted to leave him those first two years, but I hung on."

"West and I can barely take care of ourselves and now we're having a baby and I'm still puking." Meg joined them. "Between our schedules, we hardly have time for..."

"Okay, that's enough. What is going on?" Cade faced all three of his sisters-in-law and his mom.

"Life isn't flowers all the time, Cade." Aspen grinned.

"And it's not the snapshot images you see of your brothers' lives any more than Lauren's tactless Instagram picture was your whole story," Ella said.

"Your brothers aren't perfect. Neither is your dad." His mom's eyes were suddenly heavy with the years she'd lived.

"Making anything work is tough. It's not about the right kind of woman or a specific time in your life. It's finding *the* woman, that person who will be elbow deep in crap if you need her," Aspen said.

"The one who will walk the floors with you. Who will give up partying or her sexy second life working for *Cosmo*," Ella added.

"We are all complicated." Meg touched his arm. "You are and so is she. But at the end of the day, when you drop to the couch, the love is all that matters, right?"

Cade was crying. It wasn't a quick wipe of a tear or anything he could hide by widening his eyes. He was tears-down-his-face crying.

"What the hell?"

They all laughed as he wiped his eyes.

"You are a wonderful man and she is your match. No one can spot a match better than you, but it's up to us McNaughton women to tell you that you're dicking it up." His mom turned to the others. "Dicking it up, that's the term, right?"

Cade once again knew he was a lucky man. He looked over at the McNaughton men, surprisingly missing from this little power talk. His brothers and their dad nodded as if to say, "Get your shit together."

He thanked the women in his life for setting him straight, and then he asked them for help.

Chapter Twenty-Eight

Sistine still wasn't sleeping well. Melissa had been out of her life for a full month and it had been two weeks since what she was now referring to as Ludacris Day. She had apologized for the last time that day and told Cade she was going to love him for a while longer. He had offered her backgammon and Ludacris and nothing more. It was time to move on, but she couldn't seem to find her way past Cade, past the "we" he offered with a willing and open heart so many months ago.

She was no longer awakened in the middle of the night by raccoons, a random shop expense, or an Ask Amy deadline. All of that was gone, but she was left with these nightmares featuring Cade lying next to her, his laugh, his face, the details so vivid she would have sworn the moment she opened her eyes he would be right there, but then she'd reach for him and he would disappear. It figured that the thong-wearing raccoons would abandon her in her time of need.

She had still not shown up for backgammon. There was no real way back to being friends with Cade, she decided, pulling on her socks and shuffling her way to her minifridge. Her stomach turned in that not-enough-sleep way as she stared at another withering head of lettuce and two sad little carrots. Checking her phone, she fell back into bed. It was only four thirty on a Sunday morning. Her shop didn't open until eleven.

No food and no sleep. How long was the universe going to punish her for squashing one man's heart? She was reaching for a pillow to put over her head when she heard the knock on her shop door. She sat up in the center of her bed.

If June forgot to wind that 1960s clock again and she was at the door for Blue Hairs at four thirty in the morning, Sistine was going to send her back to bed and buy her a new clock on Monday. Grabbing the purple cardigan she'd worn the day before, she walked out to the shop and stopped when she saw Patrick's truck through the front window and Cade standing at the door.

Heart on the verge of bursting, she opened the door and realized it wasn't a dream. There he stood, holding a huge basket of wool. Seeming to ignore her quizzical expression and hopefully her tossing-and-turning hairstyle, he set the basket inside her shop and closed the door without a word. She stepped back when something under the hanks of yarn began moving. A little lamb poked its head up and Sistine felt the tears.

Cade, his laugh full and wonderfully real, crouched down and took the lamb from the basket.

"Did you kidnap him?"

"No. He's our... well, he's mine. He'll keep Henny and Penny company and then I'll have wool. Did you know that lambs are a symbol of renewal and compassion?" he asked.

"I think I did read that somewhere." Sistine wiped her eyes and pet the downy fur she remembered so well from their first date. "He's going to be work though. Up in the morning hard work," she said.

"I love early mornings." Cade scratched the lamb's ear.

"Me too."

"Something else we have in common." He set the lamb back in the basket and when he faced Sistine, she was afraid to touch him, convinced if she reached one last time, he would disappear.

Cade shoved his hands in his pockets to keep from grabbing her in total desperation. Because he'd now decided to stop "dicking" things up didn't mean she still wanted him.

"I'm sorry," she said, her eyes glassy.

Cade struggled with why he couldn't have swallowed the whole Ask Amy reveal like a damn man and spared them both all the pain. But he supposed like Aspen said, messy life didn't work that way. Maybe they both needed time to sort things out, but he was done waiting.

"I know. Me too," he said.

"What are you sorry for?"

"For judging you based on your sweater."

She laughed, and Cade felt the pieces of his heart move closer together.

"It was stupid of me to think you were only one-sided and I'm glad you're not. I want all of you, Sistine. The good, the bad, and the kinky."

Tears spilled down her cheeks and he stepped closer to wipe them away. Her hands circled his wrists.

"I didn't mean to lie."

"You mean withhold information?"

She shook her head. "No. I mean lie. I wanted to be Sistine from the knit shop, which was naïve too. I am all my pieces. It's not like you get to rewind in life, you know?"

"I do. Believe me, there are a few moments I would like to erase, but you're right. We can't."

"All we can do is move forward. Do you know what I tell my Knitting 101 class?"

"Is it naughty?"

She smacked his shoulder. "No. Once you cast on, you're committing to the project. If you make a mistake, drop a stitch, whatever, move on and keep going. Someday you will look back on your collection of mistakes and know they gave you the skills to make your most beautiful project."

"You tell that to your knitting class?"

She nodded.

"Wow, no wonder people show up in droves. That's like crafts and couch time all in one."

"Droves. *Sherlock*?"

He nodded. "Binge watching these days."

She put her arms around his neck and the last pieces of his heart melted into place.

"I love you."

"And I you, gorgeous and wonderfully brilliant man."

"Oh, yeah. I like the sound of that. Do you think you could say that again with a British accent?" He turned, her arms still around him, and relocked the door. After finally kissing her, he moved to the front window and closed both shutters.

"What are you doing?"

"Remember the first time we lay on the floor under your branches?"

"I do."

"And you agreed to go out with me?" He flipped on the switch and the lights around the branches illuminated the dim store.

"I did. You won me over that morning."

He took her hand and sat in the same spot. "I was thinking I would like to try to win you over again."

"What about the lamb?"

"He's sleeping."

"Does this have something to do with you 'liking to play'?"

"Maybe." He drew her under him, smoothing the hair off her face. "Yes, yes it does." And then he kissed her, gentle at first, deeper in the middle, and desperate right before they collapsed on their backs. How could he have ever wanted only one part of this woman when she was everything?

Sistine woke up in Cade's arms with no sense of time or place. Warm under the flower explosion of her quilt, she smiled at the memory of him practically pulling her bed off the wall when they stumbled their way into her apartment. She ran her hand along the beauty of him and had to remind her heart to take a beat when she leaned over to see his sleeping, stubbled face dappled in sunlight, his lashes making him look younger than his years. His breath was steady and right. As she thought she could stay wrapped in him forever, she heard a distant knock. Eyes wide, her brain kicked in. What day was it? What time? "Oh my God." She scrambled for her phone and jumped out of bed.

Cade rolled on his back, one arm over his eyes to block the sun and a smile creeping to his lips. "Oh my God is right. Morning."

Sistine danced into her pants and caught sight of her crazy hair and raw lips in the mirror. Patting everything in place, she turned to him still in her bed and closed her eyes.

He sat up, somehow more beautiful with bed head, which was not helping. "What's wrong?"

"The Blue Hairs are here. I... damn, damn. I have to open my store. I should have set an alarm."

"I'm not clear on how setting an alarm would have factored into the last few hours."

She smiled like an idiot and almost climbed back into bed when she heard June.

"Sistine! Honey, are you okay or should we call the firemen?"

"Happy to call them," Gracie added.

Cade laughed.

"I need to go before they make a scene."

Cade stood and found his clothes as she reached the door that separated her from every kiss and moan of last night and her reality, her shop.

She turned back to him as he was buttoning his jeans. "Hey."

He looked up.

"I love you."

He glowed, she hadn't thought that possible for a man, but there he was with every feeling right there for her to touch. Sistine knew she would love him for the rest of her life. Like he'd said, it was never going away. No matter how complicated things got. Knit store or not, with or without electricity, his abs or a brownie belly. She would love the man until she took her last breath.

He stood in front of her now, warm palms holding her face. "I love you too." He kissed her softly and turned her back toward her door. "Better get out there before they find a way in."

She laughed and left him standing in her tiny place. It wasn't until she'd had the ladies all settled around the lesson table that she remembered the lamb.

As if on cue, she heard the baa baa and the door to her apartment open. Cade stood in bare feet, holding the lamb, and every needle clinked to the table in shock.

"Morning, ladies."

He handed the animal to Sistine and walked toward the front of the store and put on his shoes. Grin mischievous, he walked back to her and the three gaping and pin-drop-silent senior women.

"Must have left those there. Sorry." He scooped his wallet and keys from the counter and pushed them into his back pocket. Sistine could not stop staring. It was like one of those tableaus from a movie. She loved that word.

Cade took back the lamb, who needed a name, and leaned in. He stopped right before a kiss, his eyes practically reaching out to touch hers while he asked if it was all right for him to kiss her in front of the world, well, three of the biggest gossips in all the land.

Sistine's face flooded with joy that grabbed him right through his chest. Her hand caressed the side of his neck and touched his face before she tugged him down for a kiss that not only received a howl of applause from the Blue Hairs, but three or four more baa baas from their as yet unnamed baby lamb.

"Right. Well." He turned to the table and winked. "Remember, ladies, practice makes perfect."

"I'll say," June bellowed. "Kiss her again, Cade."

He wiggled his brow.

"Since when are you so comfortable with such blatant objectification?" Sistine said, pushing him toward the front door.

Cade turned one last time. "I'd kiss you anywhere with anyone watching."

She closed her eyes. "Get out of here before those three nice little ladies go up in flames."

He kissed her one last time and was gone.

Sistine schooled her love and lust expression before turning to face a table of hooting and clapping women. Things were a bit more strip club than picot-edge demonstration, but there was no stopping the overflowing happiness. She let Gracie raid the chocolate drawer, made coffee, and told three of her favorite women how she fell in love, sans the "steamy parts" they were hoping to hear.

Chapter Twenty-Nine

*C*ade settled their new addition into his own pen next to Henny and Penny. He decided Chocolate was the perfect name for the lamb and then took a much-needed shower.

He stopped by Sift to grab some of those vegan cookies Tina loved as a thank-you for dealing with his crap lately. She'd worked the lunch crowd and happy hour two days ago while Cade was busy convincing Windrush Farms that he and Sistine would make great lamb parents.

Even with the stop at Sift and the time it took him to tease Thad and Vienna about their long engagement, Cade walked into the Tap House a full fifteen minutes early for their final planning meeting for Fall Festival. Less than twenty-four hours ago, he'd been dreading the annual Main Street event, but now he could not stop smiling. He'd owned his mistake, truly forgiven Sistine for what now seemed ridiculous, given her a lamb, and had a good laugh with the Blue Hairs all before noon.

"Holy shit. Who died?" Cade stopped when he found all three of his brothers sitting at the bar sharing a plate of nachos. He kept his distance in case they charged.

Boyd patted the stool next to him. West jumped behind the bar and produced another plate of Javier's revamped nachos and set it on the bar. Reluctantly, Cade took the stool offered, setting Tina's cookies on the bar next to him. No one had said a word, which was unheard of anywhere near his family. It was strange being on the customer side of his bar, a little less powerful.

The four of them ate in silence for several crunches.

"Don't we need to get on with the meeting? We open in less than an hour."

"We'll be fine. Were you nice to my truck?" Patrick asked.

Cade nodded while he chewed, reached into his pocket, and slid the keys down the bar. "Thank you."

"Welcome."

More eating.

"What are you doing here?" Cade asked West.

"We figured since you were the last of us to dive in, we'd have a— What'd we call it again?" He looked at Patrick.

"Chat."

"What the hell? We did not settle on chat. That sounds like something your pencil-protector friends and ass wax over there would come up with." Boyd wiped his hands and put his arm around Cade, pulling him close. "Since you were so damn sinister when we fell into the deep endless pool of love, we wanted to be here for you. Give you a sort of consult for finally making things right with Sistine."

"Yeah, consult sounds official," West said.

"I know. Because I'm male, balls and all." Boyd grabbed West's nachos.

"How do you know things worked out?" Cade folded his arms.

When Patrick produced his phone, Cade would admit his pulse jumped, but it quickly settled. Regardless of what they'd been through, he knew Sistine. Trick held up his phone and Cade saw a picture of his back walking out of Knitterly, Chocolate in hand. He smiled.

"Compliments of June's Instagram," Patrick said.

"You brought the woman you love a lamb?" Boyd asked.

Cade nodded as his chest pulsed again at the thought of her face when she found him at the door. "You told me to find her chocolate and then you sicced Mom and your women on me. I had to do something. I took her to Windrush on our first date and she loved the lambs. I named our lamb Chocolate."

His brothers usually lined up to beat him over the head, but when Cade looked down the bar, they were three puppies. Three big, capable of biting at any minute puppies, but for a moment, they all seemed united in the paralysis that was being in love.

"Yeah, well enough of that shit. Did you seal the deal or are you planning one of those obnoxious movie-star proposals like West's that made ours look like a fumbling mess?" Boyd said.

"Hello. Speak for yourself. I got on a freaking plane! I had Grand's ring. I totally out-proposed West."

"And then you puked in a bag." Boyd feigned gagging.

"So? He didn't even have a ring." Patrick pointed to West.

"Hey, easy." West laughed.

"And what the hell was yours, Boyd?" Trick was so easy to put on the defensive.

Their oldest brother's eyes flew open, wide and dramatic. "I've got a kid."

"So do I," Patrick said.

"One on the way. That counts." West raised his hand like he was at an auction.

Cade was laughing so hard he had to hold his stomach. The three of them realized they were grown men fighting like boys and collapsed in laughter too.

Happy to abandon the scheduled meeting and talk about Sistine instead, Cade filled his brothers in on his plans. There were a few manly sighs and some great suggestions, including where he needed to go for the ring after he drew the ring design out on a napkin for them. In two weeks, everyone they loved and cared about would be at Fall into Petaluma. Foghorn would have their usual tent and Cade would hopefully surprise the hell out of Sistine.

He had watched all of his brothers find and propose to three fantastic women. He'd seen Bri at the bar making mushy eyes at Joe and Joe returning that same look. Cade was looking forward to the wedding that would surely follow the epic love story of Thad and Vienna, and now it was his turn to show Sistine he believed in their magic.

Pulling up his bike in front of the antique jewelry shop, Cade looked around at the streets he'd grown up on and felt this sense of belonging. That he and Sistine would stand on the foundation of their families. Holy shit, her family. He needed to talk to her dad before... did he? Did people still do that?

Remembering he didn't follow rules, Cade took a deep breath, called the Branch house, and hoped to all things holy that Jules didn't answer.

The first Saturday in September, Sistine was watching the sun set at a picnic table with her friends. Cade and his brothers were working the Foghorn tent. Boyd and Patrick handed out samples while Cade entertained the crowd.

"Look at the women. Holy hell, could they at least pretend not to drool?" Bri said, taking Hattie from Aspen and kissing her chubby cheek.

"Does it bother you?" Ella asked.

Sistine glanced over at Cade, who was in his zone, and she shook her head. "Nothing about him bothers me."

After a collective "aww," they learned that Mason now had a new car.

"Well, not new-new, but new for me. Now I have to get a job." He groaned and they all laughed. The band hit a drumroll and Sistine turned at the thunderous applause. Cade was standing on one of the other picnic tables.

"Happy fall, everyone," he said, and the crowd cheered louder. "Can someone give me a word?"

"Forever," Bri called out and squeezed Sistine's hand.

"Excellent word, Bri. Thank you. Forever is a noun meaning for all time."

"Use it in a sentence," Ella yelled.

Cade's expression grew serious and he extended his hand toward Sistine. "I will love Sistine Branch forever."

Sistine touched her chest and blew him a kiss. After so many months of hiding and angst, there was something so simple in showing everyone their feelings.

"Hey, Cade. Take your shirt off for us," some woman yelled from the crowd.

Sistine's jaw tightened and she stood to defend him. Not that he needed it. There was no way Cade was taking his shirt off. Silly in love or not, he was not that guy.

"Sure, why not," he said, unbuttoning his flannel while the crowd egged him on and the band played a thumping beat.

Sistine's eyes flew to her friends, who were all joining in. "What are you doing? He is not some piece of—"

She stopped speaking when she realized Cade's mom was crying at the next table.

Sistine turned back in time to watch Cade ball up his shirt and toss it at his brothers. Her eyes went right to his chest, and she let out a breath when she realized he had a T-shirt on.

Cade stood, arms splayed to the crowd as the cheering grew even louder, and he bowed.

"Hey, bring some of that over here," Vienna said.

Sistine had no idea what had gotten into everyone or why Cade was suddenly happy to take his clothes off. She'd almost taken her seat again when someone tugged at her sweater.

Sistine looked up to find Cade inches from her and the crowd had grown completely silent. Puzzled by his labored breath and distracted by his brilliant smile, she was going to ask what was going on when he opened his arms and she took in his T-shirt.

Will you marry me?
And by marry, I mean spend your forever with me and kiss me all the time.

She read it twice and scanned the crowd. There wasn't a dry eye as Sistine realized what was happening. Her head whipped back toward Cade in a moment of panic that he might be gone again.

He wasn't gone. He was on one knee, a ring in his hand. A thin gold woven band that looked like yarn with a brilliant blue stone in the center.

The tears were trailing to her neck at this point. "It looks like yarn." Those were, of course, the first words out of her mouth and Cade smiled up at her.

"That was the idea. Sistine Branch, thank you for not only teaching me about myself, but also showing me the infinite colors of all women. You are my match forever. You can trust that because I am the match expert."

She laughed and wiped her eyes.

"Will you marry me, Sistine?"

She nodded with the enthusiasm of a child on the Fourth of July. "Yes, yes, I will definitely marry you, Cade McNaughton." Pulling him to his feet, which was no small effort, she wiped her eyes again as he slid the ring onto her finger and the crowd around them went nuts.

He kissed her hand and then with love electric in his gorgeous eyes, he asked, "Can I kiss you?"

She drew him closer by the neck of his Marry Me T-shirt and like the first time she'd kissed him, her world changed for the better.

Epilogue

ade and Sistine Branch McNaughton promised to love one
another forever in front of their family and friends at the end
of the pier on Bodega Bay. Sistine wore a white silk skirt and a
multicolored cardigan knit from Oasis 5222. She made it known that
as their wedding day turned to the day-to-day, she would always want
to wear a piece of their magical moment.

Chocolate was their ring bearer, but Mason kept him on a leash as
he stood at Cade's side with the rest of the McNaughton men. Jules
was Sistine's Maid of Honor, leaving her boots at home in favor of a
dress. The Bitches were all at her side, as was Meg, their newly
designated long-distance Bitch.

Hattie sat with Aspen's mom and clapped through the entire cer-
emony, while Towner McNaughton, West and Meg's new baby boy
was sound asleep in his grandfather's arms.

Sistine's dad walked her down the pier while a string quartet
played "Yeah," by Usher, making the Ludacris part a bit more wedding appropriate.

For the first time since it opened when Sistine was a little girl,
the Crab Shack was closed on a Saturday for the wedding reception.
Cade and Sistine danced their first dance on the deck of the Salty

Siren, her parents' first fishing boat.

With starlight twinkling in the branches above, Cade and Sistine lay on a blanket in their wedding clothes and kissed until the first early morning of the rest of their lives.

Thank you for reading *Tap – A Love Story*! I hope Cade and Sistine's story was worth the wait. I loved writing these two and their quirky romance. If you enjoyed the book, please consider leaving a review at the book retailer of your choice, as well as Goodreads, to help other readers find this story.

Please make sure you're on my newsletter mailing list at: tracyewens.com to keep up with the latest news about my books.

Thank you, wonderful readers, for making this amazing journey possible. I appreciate each and every one of you! Keep reading for a look at *Brew – A Love Story*, which is the first McNaughton brother's story.

All the best,
Tracy

Chapter One

B oyd McNaughton was losing a lot of blood. At least it seemed like a lot. He wondered how much blood a man could spare before he passed out. Staring down at his hand, fascination quickly flipped to anxiety when he realized he didn't want to find out.

"Boyd," his pain-in-the-ass brother said, reminding Boyd why he was bleeding and pissed in the first place.

"I'm fine," he said, grabbing rags off the stack he kept clean by the tanks below the old Foghorn Brewery sign. He covered his hand, not ready to catch a glimpse at how not fine things really were. Boyd boasted a decent tolerance for pain, but this was pushing the limit.

"Come on, man, let's not do this. You're bleeding."

"As always, little brother, you get a gold star. Now get out of my way before I drop dead right here on the brewery floor. Imagine that insurance claim." He managed to raise his eyebrows in sarcasm as he pushed past Patrick.

"At least let me drive you. The color is draining from your face. Maybe we should call—"

Boyd was in his truck before he heard the rest of Patrick's assessment. He'd cut his hand. He wasn't having a heart attack. Sure, it throbbed and a drop of blood escaped his makeshift bandage and hit his jeans as he turned onto Washington, but he was fine, damn it.

The look of shock on Patrick's face was classic. One minute they were in a full-heat argument over quality vs. quantity, and the next, his brother's expression fell. Boyd noticed the blood and was more upset that he'd contaminated his work space than anything else. Then the pain kicked in and every petty concern slipped away. He became singularly focused on breathing and staying upright. Pain was powerful that way.

Had he not been the one presently staining his favorite pair of jeans, he would have found the whole scene funny. Stopping at a red light, he replayed the argument.

"You promised we'd be ready for bottles and kegs last week," Patrick said, doing that pacing thing that drove Boyd nuts.

"I don't recall promising. Did I pinkie swear?" he'd asked, focusing on adding more yeast to what he hoped would be his last batch. "I know I'm behind."

Patrick's hands slapped his sides and Boyd didn't need to look to know his brother was in the middle of a pseudo temper tantrum. Yeah, Trick was frustrated, but there was nothing Boyd could do about it.

The recipe wasn't right yet and if his time-obsessed brother didn't leave him alone, Foghorn Brewery would be pushing lemonade as their anniversary brew.

"Don't do this to me." Trick sounded defeated.

Boyd glanced up to find the also-predictable hand running through his brother's expensive haircut.

"I've got people lined up, distributors willing for the first time to carry us on a trial basis. I need to deliver when I said I'd deliver. I gave you a cushion because I know how you can be, but next week that cushion is up and you're still..."

Boyd had raised his brow, wondering if Patrick was going to go with "contemplating your navel," or—

"Messing around in your sandbox."

Of course, it was the "sandbox" today.

"You do realize that I'm three whole years older than you, right? That I taught you everything you know about the sandbox. I'm not responsible for your uptight attitude, but I'll say it again. I. Am. Older. Step back."

Boyd took in the aroma of the batch as it cooked. Lemon, still with the lemon. What was it going to take to rein that in?

"Boyd."

"Trick."

"You're acting like an asshole."

"Back at you, little man."

"How much longer?"

Boyd glanced up again. "How the hell can I make this any clearer? Are you thinking that I have a killer recipe waiting to brew but instead, I'm screwing with you? Do you think I enjoy having you flying around me like one of the witch's monkeys in that movie Mom makes us watch every year? I don't. I'm nearly there. I'll spell this one out for you too. There. Is. Too. Much. Lemon. I'm racking my brain, and you're not helping. It could be fixed and ready to brew by this afternoon. It could take me a few more days."

"We don't have a few more days."

Boyd had had it. "Fine. Then I'll piss in a bottle and we can sell that. So long as we make your precious deadline, right?"

"The beer has got to be good by now. You're obsessing."

"Good is not enough. Goddamn—" Boyd pulled his hand from the keggle and blood ran warm down his arm like something that should have been pleasant but turned sinister. Everything went slow motion and it took his brain a few seconds to catch up.

As the argument that now had him trying to remember if the ER entrance was off McDowell or Maria Drive faded into reality, Boyd grazed the edge of his wrapped hand as he turned the steering wheel and flinched.

Petaluma was a small city, so there was one ER with an urgent care in the same cluster of buildings. Boyd had considered going to urgent care, but he was still bleeding, and truth be told, he was a little nervous. He needed both hands in proper working order and that lemon balanced yesterday. Was it his turn to carpool to baseball? Was he on the schedule for Friday or was it Colton's mom picking up his son today? He'd completely forgotten about Mason. His brain must be scrambled.

If it was his turn to drive the guys, he'd need to be stitched up and on his way by two. Boyd glanced at the clock on the dash. He had five hours. Was that enough time? He'd only been to the emergency room one other time, and that had taken at least three or four hours in the middle of the night. All he remembered were connected chairs, televisions whispering infomercials, and of course, the moment one-year-old Mason's fever finally broke and he fell asleep among the colorful giraffes of his car seat.

That ER visit had turned out well, and there was no reason to think this one wouldn't be the same, he told himself. As soon as the woman in the Prius figured out which parking spot she was taking, he'd park and let the professionals do their thing. The rag was almost soaked through and the duct tape he'd found under the seat of his truck was barely hanging on. Boyd's stomach turned at the stained material and what he imagined was beneath. It was likely a lot less gruesome than he pictured, but he wasn't taking any chances by looking now.

Maybe Trick was right, and he was obsessing about the recipe. It was the anniversary brew after all, and Boyd had to admit there was pressure there. Although, he could never figure out if the pressure to create something exceptional was self-inflicted or if doing it better was why they were still in business. All Boyd knew was every morning, his first thought was some version of "knock on wood." Mason had turned thirteen a few weeks ago and Boyd made a living, a good living, making beer. He wanted to hit pause, keep everything right where it was, but he knew better. Things had a way of changing right from under him.

Shaking his head as he turned off his truck, Boyd pulled his keys free with his left hand.

First things first, his hand was priority. He slid out of his truck and bumped the door closed with his shoulder. The rest of it, including baseball practice, the lemon, and whose fault all of this was, would sort itself out once the bleeding stopped.

Ella Walters was about to hit a wall. She'd been awake for nearly twenty-four hours and hoped to God the eye drops she was fishing from the pocket of her scrubs would help to ease her scratchy eyes. Somewhere after the twenty-eight-year-old male with a kidney stone but before the seventeen-year-old female, who presented with three of her friends a little after four in the morning bawling that she was "dying," Ella had taken out her contacts and put on her glasses. When she worked at San Francisco General, she never wore her glasses. She hated having anything on her face in the frenzy of a trauma center.

Petaluma Valley was a slower pace, which she was beginning to enjoy. She was glad she'd switched to glasses because it wouldn't look good to be bumping into things when Julie Blake's parents arrived in the ER at seven thirty to claim their daughter. Julie's friends had all been picked up a couple of hours ago, which cut down on the drama significantly. Ella notified Julie's parents that their daughter was not, in fact, dying. She'd had far too many shots of Firewater, but she was now hydrated and resting.

"This time," the father said as he and his wife helped an almost sober and mortified Julie off the hospital bed. "This time, you're okay, but kids die from alcohol all the time. Do you hear me, Julie?"

The young girl nodded, pushing her matted hair from her mascara-streaked eyes as they passed the nurses' station and the ER doors closed behind them. The white walls and speckled flooring of a sterile space Ella knew better than any other was quiet again, except for the intermittent bump of the air conditioner and the rhythmic beeping monitors. Ella patted the shoulder of the unit secretary and told her she would be in the on-call room if they needed her.

The small room off the hallway and across from the vending machines was more like a large closet than on-call quarters, but Ella could have fallen asleep standing up by that point. The clean air of the small city and the easy life was making her soft, she thought as she opted for the timeworn chair over the wobbly cot in the corner. Easing onto the cool green vinyl, she rested her head back.

Before her eyes had a chance to slide blissfully closed, Bri burst through the door eating a bag of Sour Patch Kids and exclaimed she had important news. Ella, resolved that there were only forty-five minutes left on her shift, extended her hand. At the offered bag, she put a piece of candy in her mouth.

"God." She chewed enough to swallow without choking. "How do you eat those things?"

"Best candy in the world."

"That's not a candy. That's toxic waste. Look, your tongue is blue," Ella said, leaning up in the chair now.

Bri propped herself against the wall, crossed one flowery clog over the other, and stuck out her blue tongue. "My news." She chewed. "Baker, Dr. Baker, Dr. Where Does a Man Get Shoulders Like That—"

"Yes, Bri, I know who Dr. Baker is," Ella said. She would have laughed, but she didn't have the energy.

"He's getting divorced," Bri said, licking the sugar off her finger and putting the bag back in the pocket of her scrubs. Ella took off her glasses, pinched the bridge of her nose, and closed her eyes. When she opened them, Bri was waiting for a response.

Brianna Cramer, or Nurse B as most of the doctors called her, was the first person Ella met when she transferred to Petaluma Valley Hospital almost two years ago. She had wanted nothing more than a job and some solitude. She wasn't looking for a friend, but Bri was, and Ella soon learned that Nurse B often got what she wanted.

"You need coffee," she'd told Ella after their first shift. "I'm off now too, so I'll show you the best coffee."

"Actually, I'm going to go home and—"

"Coffee doesn't take that long," Bri had said with that defiant honesty Ella now loved.

They'd had coffee and Bri turned out to be a steady, this-is-how-it-is beacon in the storm that was Ella's life back then. She consistently wore some shade of pink nail polish and her hair was a dozen shades of brown. She had large, warm set-apart eyes and full lips Ella envied. Most importantly, Bri was a great nurse. She was technically proficient and cared about every patient who walked through the doors. Ella often questioned when her friend would run out of compassion.

Ella had believed she owed patients her skills and her focused attention. As a doctor, she was there to ensure nothing slipped by her and that patients left her better than they were when they arrived. Until Bri, she'd worked among likeminded colleagues, but that was her old life. She normally left the warm and fuzzy to Bri, but working in a smaller hospital called on parts of Ella that were untapped in the whirl of a big trauma center. Patients presented with less than life-threatening injuries and wanted to talk, know about what book she was reading or if she thought acupuncture really worked. Ella didn't know how to move through that kind of contact, but she was trying.

Bri and Ella became friends shortly after that first day over coffee and had never turned back even though Ella was surely hard to love during her first couple of months in Petaluma.

"Maybe I'm getting old," she said now, still trying to get the pucker of the candy out of her mouth. "I used to be the queen of the double shift. Two shifts, shower, and out with friends." Thirty-six was closer to forty than thirty. Maybe it had nothing to do with fresh air. Maybe this was her downhill shift, Ella thought.

"Wait, you had friends in the big city? Were they paratroopers or super doctors?"

Ella closed her eyes again.

"Ninja surgeons?"

She shook her head, eyes still closed.

"You're really no fun when you're tired, you know that?" Bri sat on the arm of the chair and mocked a whisper. "Back to my news. Can you believe that Shoulders and Perfect Teeth are getting divorced?"

Ella opened one eye. "Are we surprised by this? Baker is not exactly the model of monogamy."

"Oh, come on. Those are rumors."

Ella held her gaze and waited.

"You know something." She pointed at Ella and stood. "Who told you he was cheating on his wife? Why don't I know?"

"No one told me anything. It's obvious, don't you think? Does anyone really need that many extra blankets from clean linens? And why is the good doctor so helpful? Quickies among the water pitchers, my dear friend. No need for Sherlock on this one."

"Oh. My. God. That is... well, that's kind of hot. I want to be ravaged in a closet."

"Do you? By a married man?" Ella knew her friend and there was no way, but Bri hesitated and appeared to be entertaining the idea.

"With twin daughters and one more on the way?" Ella helped her along. *Christ!*

Bri finally shook her head. "Okay, yeah, that's gross."

"Took you that long, huh?"

"Those shoulders are so—"

"Bri," Ella barked, moving past her to the vending machines in the hall. Sleep was not happening and it was time for liquid assistance.

"You're right. He's a pig. Good for her, right?" Bri followed.

"There you go. There's the woman I love." Ella slid a dollar into the machine and pressed the button for Coke. She could be a commercial, she thought. Exhausted ER doctor invigorated by the fizz of caffeine finds the strength to—

"Dr. Walters, they need you," Bri said, now closer to the nurses' station.

Breaking free of her advertising dream, Ella popped open the Coke and drank half of it in one gulp. Setting her ice-cold goodness on the counter, she tightened her ponytail and waited for the twin tingle of sugar and caffeine.

"Two things," Bri said. "Campbell is running thirty minutes late." She paused, allowing Ella the expected curse under her breath.

She did not disappoint. "Son of a bitch," she said, barely above a whisper.

Campbell was coming off a three-day vacation, she thought but did not say. Bri could practically read her mind anyway.

"And... you have a hand laceration in four. Male, thirty-seven, with acute signs of a bad attitude."

"Perfect. Chart?" Her eyes cut to Bri, who scrunched her face and handed her a single piece of paper. She took a couple of steps back.

"Trina is still helping Dr. Briggs in Exam One. The guy who kicked through his sliding glass door. She said she'd be in as soon as she was free."

"Where's Wilma?"

"Sick."

Ella finished the last bit of her soda and threw the can in the recycle. "Looks like you and I get this one. Let me know when he's ready for—" She stopped. "Where are you going?"

Bri already had her keys dangling from one finger, her purse up on her shoulder as she threw another bag on top of that. "I'd stay to help, but if I don't leave now, I'll miss my flight."

"To?"

"Los Angeles. Hello. My brother's wife had the baby. Remember? I told you I was going down there for the weekend."

Somewhere Ella did remember, but all the hours and days were dancing around in her memory. Sort of like how Bri was dancing while she waited to confirm that outside of their friendship, it was all right for her to leave a doctor without an attending nurse and with a patient waiting to be seen. Bri mouthed sorry, still dancing in place. Ella laughed and shook her head, now fueled by caffeine.

"Go."

Her friend, who suddenly morphed from Nurse B to Baby Annie's excited aunt, leaned forward and hugged her. Ella wasn't a hugger, but the give-and-take of friendship won out and she allowed her arms to be pinned to her sides as Bri got it out of her system.

"When I get back, we're getting you some hugging lessons."

"Really? Is that something they're now offering at the community college?"

"It should be."

Ella pointed to the clock. "The airport, Bri. Fly safe. You can resume Operation Cuddle after you've seen your niece."

Bri hefted her bags one more time and was gone.

After a few brisk pats to her cheeks that Ella hoped restored some color, she pushed the cold metal handle of Exam 4. The caffeine humming through her bloodstream, followed closely by a serious longing for the egg-and-cheese bagel she was going to pick up on the way home as soon as she took care of Mr. — she glanced at the piece of paper, a sad substitute for a chart.

"Mr. Boyd McNaughton," she said and glanced up to find a bear of a man. He was tall, broad, and scarcely teetering on the edge of the narrow bed. Dark jeans and a flannel rolled to his elbows, he presented in what was pretty much the standard uniform for March in Petaluma. When she'd first arrived in town, she'd wondered how long anyone could live in a place so consistent, but it had grown on her and now, despite the occasional craving for superior sushi or an opera, she found she didn't miss Dr. Ella Walters, Head of Trauma, or all the drama that went along with that life. She was settling into being one of four full-time ER docs, plain old Dr. Walters. Ella had been raised to never accept being one of many and while she wasn't ready to say it out loud, she was content in the clean air of smaller.

"Yeah." Her patient shifted farther onto the metal frame as if he were sitting up taller in class, then flinched and cursed under his breath.

Full beard, but his brow was damp and what she could see of his face was pale. The guy was in pain.

Is that duct tape?

"Great. We at least have your name right. I'm Dr. Walters." For an instant, Ella moved to shake his hand, which was her usual rehearsed greeting. That was not happening with his injury, so she defaulted to what she knew. She washed up and snapped on gloves.

"Tell me what happened," she said, grabbing a folded blanket and gently lifting his forearm. She needed to get what seemed like an entire rag collection off his hand before she could tell what she was dealing with. Quite a bit of blood and yes, it was duct tape. Wonderful. She began carefully unwrapping his hand.

"Okay, well I tried to tell one of the nurses out there, but she ran off and stuck me in this room. Does anyone work here?"

Ella raised her hand, met his eyes.

"Right." He huffed and instead of releasing a breath, some of the tension, it all seemed to rattle around in his lungs. "I cut my hand."

"I can see that. On what?" She opened the rags to find a nice-sized laceration, about 53 millimeters from the side of his hand into the palm. After asking him to carefully test range of motion, Ella was confident she was dealing with a cut. A nasty one, but there were no particles embedded in the tissue, no broken bones or damaged tendons. She grabbed the saline and four-by-fours.

"A keggle."

Ella met his eyes. Dark green, thick lashes, and pupils normal. All good signs.

His expression indicated she should know exactly what a keggle was. Ella's stomach groaned. Bagel time was well over an hour out now.

She inhaled. "What is a keggle, Mr. McNaughton?"

He was seething, presumably at someone or something that had nothing to do with her. His attitude did not improve while she manipulated his hand, but suddenly the reluctant patient had an answer. Amazing what a little cold saline could inspire.

"I make beer." He winced but didn't pull away. "I was working on a small batch, trying to get the lemon under control because I'm using Sorachi Ace, which I haven't tackled since 2010."

Right when Ella thought he might be delirious and speaking gibberish, he huffed again.

"You don't need to know any of that. Point is, my candy-ass brother barged into my happy space with his 'we need this yesterday' bullshit. A keggle is a metal vat. You've seen a keg, like at a party or something?"

Ella nodded, tossing the soiled rags and holding fresh dressing to his hand now. She'd seen a keg in some movie she could no longer remember. He cut his hand on metal. That was all she needed.

"It's that thing, a keg. But mine is cut out on top. It's not finished off because it doesn't need to be. I like to get in there when I'm working. It's a huge pot. I don't cut myself on the edge. Ever."

"Until today," Ella said, meeting his eyes again.

"Until today." Frustration finally spilled off his shoulders.

He exhaled as she peeled back the compress. Things were looking better already, Ella thought. Jagged, but clean. He'd need stitches, sixteen or seventeen from the looks of it. She was approaching that glorious moment, in most emergency rooms, when the all-important doctor wished her patient well with a smile before handing him off to a nurse for stitching and after-care instructions. Any other ER and there would be no need to chitchat or put the patient at ease. She'd be less than fifteen minutes away from fluffy egg whites and melted Swiss on a toasted bagel, easy red onion, and avocado. But Trina had not even poked her head in, so to the disappointment of Ella's stomach, she was on her own. Which could be productive, she told herself. It had been awhile since she'd stitched anyone up. "Practice and patience are the keys to good medicine" was her first-year professor's motto. Right now, that certainly rang true.

OTHER LOVE STORIES BY TRACY EWENS

Premiere
Candidate
Taste
Reserved
Stirred
Vacancy
Playbook
Exposure
Brew
Smooth

Acknowledgements

I would like to thank:

Erin Tolbert for being a constant support, a lovely person, and for making me laugh.

Katie McCoach for her tremendous patience and encouragement, especially when I am late and lost.

Nikki Busch for slashing through my filler-word jungle and making sure I don't carelessly offend.

Women who show up, speak up, and lift up other women. We are mighty when we are united.

The City of Petaluma for honoring its past and making excellent beer.

My family for reminding me what is real.

Every. Single. Reader.

Tracy Ewens is a recovered theatre major who writes smart contemporary romance from a beautiful piece of Arizona desert. When not working on her next book, she drinks copious amounts of tea, prefers an exit row seat, and reads well past her bedtime.

www.tracyewens.com

www.ingramcontent.com/pod-product-compliance
Lightning Source LLC
Chambersburg PA
CBHW020416260626
47156CB00007B/2418